Amor
and
Summer Secrets

Amor and Summer Secrets

DIANA RODRIGUEZ WALLACH

KENSINGTON BOOKS
http://www.kensingtonbooks.com

KENSINGTON BOOKS are published by

Kensington Publishing Corp.
850 Third Avenue
New York, NY 10022

All Kensington titles, imprints and distributed lines are available at special quantity discounts for bulk purchases for sales promotion, premiums, fund-raising, educational or institutional use.

Special book excerpts or customized printings can also be created to fit specific needs. For details, write or phone the office of the Kensington Special Sales Manager: Kensington Publishing Corp., 850 Third Avenue, New York, NY 10022. Attn. Special Sales Department. Phone: 1-800-221-2647.

Kensington and the K logo Reg. U.S. Pat. & TM Off.

ISBN-13: 978-0-7582-2553-5
ISBN-10: 0-7582-2553-9

First Kensington Trade Paperback Printing: September 2008

10 9 8 7 6 5 4 3 2 1

Printed in the United States of America

To my parents and grandparents, for their inspiration.

Acknowledgments

Many people contributed to this story and to me becoming an author. First, I would like to thank my agent, Jenoyne Adams, who encouraged the creation of this book and who stuck with me even when I was losing faith in myself. Jenoyne promised she was "in it for the long haul," and I hope she knows how much those words meant to me. I'd like to thank my editor, Kate Duffy, for showing such enthusiasm for this project. Kate championed this book from the moment it touched her desk and that support kept me driven to live up to her excitement.

I'd also like to thank Candice Smith for her speedy and thoughtful edits.

If not for the influence of countless teachers, this book would not exist. I'd like to thank those in Ridley High School's English Department and BU's College of Communication for helping me hone my craft. Also, there are many magazine editors who kept me writing every day for years, and those experiences greatly contributed to the ease with which I write now. In addition, I have many lifelong friends who volunteered to read my novels, and I thank you all for your encouragement and wit. I'll try not to include too many of your quotes in my next book. And I'd especially like to thank Jackie Baskin for double-checking all of my Spanish phrases.

VIII ACKNOWLEDGMENTS

I want to thank my family, not one of whom laughed when I told them I was going to write a novel. I greatly appreciate the Wallachs who restrained themselves from asking "how the book was going" no matter how badly I know they wanted to—I couldn't have joined a better family. And I'd particularly like to thank Paula for taking so much time to carefully edit this manuscript. I'd like to thank my brother, Lou, for giving me work to pay the bills while I pursued this goal. I'd like to thank my sister, Natalie, for being the first person to read my first book and for telling me that she knew it was going to happen. I'm indebted to all my relatives in Puerto Rico, especially Ventura, for showing me my roots. And above all, I'd like to thank my parents, Lou and Chris Rodriguez, who instilled me with a belief that I should find a career I love. Writing truly doesn't feel like work and their support helped me to dream big.

I'd like to acknowledge my grandparents who are no longer with me, Marcello, Antonia, Raymond and Stella, for the inspiration that led to the creation of this story. Lastly, I want to thank my husband, Jordan, for reminding me of that fated psychic, for being my first reader and biggest fan, for telling me to quit my day job to pursue this passion, and for making me very, very happy. We did this together.

Chapter 1

An argument was about to erupt between Vince and my father. I could already sense it. I hated being around when they fought—like just my presence made things worse. It wasn't that I didn't get along with Vince; it was more that I got along with our parents, which irritated him to no end. I hung up my dish rag and walked to the door. The last thing he needed was to see his fifteen-year-old sister drying the pots and pans like a good little girl.

Vince tossed his dinner plate into the sink with a thud so hard it was obviously intentional. I knew he was looking for a reaction. And my father was not one to disappoint.

"Vincent Ruíz! Do you *not* have any respect for your family's things?" my father yelled from his seat at the kitchen table.

For a man who lost his Spanish accent as soon as he got off the plane from Puerto Rico, Lorenzo Ruíz surprisingly had the "Latin temper-thing" down. It seemed his voice had only one setting—loud—and if you really provoked him you could make the vein in his forehead turn purple and pulse. Not that I ever set him off, that was purely my brother's territory.

"Oh, please! 'Our family's things,' "Vince mimicked. "That's all you care about. 'Don't break the china!' 'Don't scratch the convertible!' You don't buy that stuff for us. You buy it to impress the neighbors."

He ran his chewed nails through his greasy black hair and let it fall back on his forehead. His dark eyes narrowed and his mouth curled to the left, a face I knew would only tick off Dad more.

"Oh, you think you know so much? Well, what would you do if we took this 'stuff' away? I'm sure there are other teenagers who would be much more appreciative of a new BMW. Maybe I should go ask 'these neighbors' of yours if they'd like your car, if that's who I'm *really* buying it for. I guess you wouldn't mind?" My father cocked his head to the side, smoothed his ebony mustache, and returned his gaze to the magazine he was reading.

At this point I didn't know who was being more immature, my forty-five-year-old father or my eighteen-year-old brother. I leaned my shoulder against the oak doorjamb to our gourmet kitchen, yanked my white T shirt over the top of my cargos and remained silent. Sometimes their arguments fizzled out on their own, and I was desperately hoping this was one of those times.

Vince grabbed another plate from the granite-top island and slammed it into the sink. Any harder and it would have shattered, but I knew he wasn't trying to break it. He just wanted our father to realize that he could.

"Fine. But you know what? You aren't going to be able to run my life forever! I'm eighteen! I'm an adult!" he yelled.

"Yeah, well, adults pay their own bills. So unless you want to pay your tuition to Cornell next year, I suggest you close your mouth."

"God, you just love being able to hang that over my head, don't you?"

"Do you have any idea how good you have it? I had to work full-time to pay my way through school. And you are so ungrateful!" shouted my father, smacking his hand against the glass-topped kitchen table.

My grandparents had moved their entire family—which included my dad, aged ten, and his two older brothers, my uncles Roberto and Diego—to the U.S. from Puerto Rico decades ago in the hope of finding better opportunities. They settled in a housing project in Camden, New Jersey, where my grandfather worked as a short-order cook and my grandmother raised their three sons in a city titled, "The Most Dangerous in the Nation." None of them spoke English, and my father still tells stories of running home from school during recess frustrated that he couldn't understand a word his classmates were saying.

By sixteen he had completely lost his accent, by eighteen he had graduated third in his class, and by twenty-six he had paid his way through Temple's undergraduate program (took him eight years of night classes while working full-time as the manager at a department store—a fact he never let us forget). Five years after that, and two children later, he successfully completed Temple's MBA program (also at night). He got a job in the marketing department of a start-up corporation manufacturing light fixtures. When their art-deco lighting treatments were featured on a popular television show three years later, the company quadrupled in size, my father was named partner and my entire family moved to the Main Line—an affluent collection of picturesque suburbs outside of Philadelphia. I was five at the time. I don't remember being poor, but my brother (who was seven when we moved) still talks about eating generic cereal brands like it was a tragic hardship worthy of a movie of the week.

"I'm not ungrateful! I'm just sick of you telling me what to do. All of my friends are going to Europe this summer. All of them! I can't *believe* you won't let me! I'm the only one who's gonna be stuck *here*."

Vince slammed his hands on the counter to answer any lingering questions about where, exactly, he did not want to be stuck.

I groaned and tilted my head toward the ceiling. I should've realized that was what they were *really* fighting about. Vince had been harping about this backpacking-through-Europe subject for weeks now. Even *I* was sick of hearing about it, so I knew my dad was about to launch the atomic bomb in his direction once the sentence left my brother's lips.

"Enough! We have been over this!" he hollered, rising from his chair, screeching its legs across the recently refinished oak floors. "I don't care how many of your 'friends' are going to Europe. *You* are not! And that is the end of it. Maybe if you were more responsible, you wouldn't be in this situation."

"Oh, God! Not this again! It was *one* arrest two years ago!"

"One arrest, no big deal, huh? You were sixteen years old caught drunk at an unchaperoned party that the police had to break up. Do you have any idea how much that could have ruined your life?"

I grabbed my auburn hair in my fists and debated whether or not to break up the argument before it got any worse. My mom was working at the art gallery and it was typically her responsibility to cool the tempers of the men in the household. My father and my brother were so alike—a fact they both vehemently denied—that when the two of them were in the same room for more than an hour, the energy in the house escalated. Strangers couldn't sense it; it was like our private Ruíz-family dog whistle. When Vince and my dad were about to go at it, the muscles in my neck would tense from two floors away.

My mother, Irina, who had a level of patience that could've made Ghandi look impulsive, could defuse it just by breezing into the room, her wavy blond locks swishing and her blue eyes smiling. She'd place her palm gently on my father's shoulder, make a cheerful joke, and immediately everyone would relax. I liked to think that I take after her, that my Polish side won out against my Puerto Rican side in the gene pool, but I knew she possessed a level of grace that I could never match.

"You always have to bring that up, don't you?" Vince yelled, taking a few steps toward our father to close the gap between them.

"Well, if I hadn't gotten it expunged from your record, you could've kissed Cornell good-bye."

"Yeah, because that's the only reason I got into Cornell. It has nothing to do with the grades I've been busting my butt for. But you always seem to forget that, don't you?"

"Yes, I forget. And that car you drive is just a symbol of my ignorance."

By this point, Vince and my dad were standing within two feet of each other. The tension was gripping my lungs.

"All right, that's it!" I shouted, stepping from the doorway and charging into the kitchen. "Break it up! Separate corners you two, *now!*"

I stepped in between them, put a manicured hand on each of their chests, and shoved them in opposite directions.

"Great, get involved now, Mariana," my brother huffed.

"Look, I am *not* taking sides here," I defended, shooting my brother a snotty scrunch-nosed look I'd perfected over the past fifteen years. "I just don't want you guys to kill each other before Mom comes home. Plus, she'll be pissed if you get blood on her newly refinished hardwood floors. And I'm so *not* explaining that."

My brother rolled his eyes and my dad half chuckled. But the result was what I wanted. The mood was lightened. At least for now.

Chapter 2

Lying on my white, shabby chic four-poster bed, I grabbed the buzzing cell phone beside me and glanced at the screen. "Madison," it read. Not that I was surprised, she called at least twice a day.

"Hey," I said, as I flipped the phone to my ear.

"What up, *girrl*?" she asked, in a hardcore rap voice.

Madison Fox was platinum blonde with ice-blue eyes and about as white and Protestant as they come. Her only exposure to rap was the runway show for Sean John.

I rolled my eyes and giggled.

"Well," I answered, "Vince and my father had another blowout. He's still harping about this whole Europe thing."

I lifted my hand to eye level and inspected the fuchsia polish on my nails. It was already chipping.

"Whatever, it sucks he can't go. But it's not the end of the world. There's gonna be plenty to do here this summer, like my party."

"Sure, you wanna come over and explain that to Vince? 'Cause, seriously, I'm about ready to shove him in a suitcase and ship him off to Europe myself," I stated as I flopped onto the throw pillows covering my bed.

"So Gayle called again today," Madison said, revolving the conversation back to her party once again. "Can you believe she can't find a single baker who will make a six-tier cake in the shape of Louis Vuitton purses? They're all worried about some copyright crap. Like, *whatever*."

Madison's Sweet Sixteen was only a few weeks away. For the past six months she'd done nothing but obsess over details with Gayle, an event planner to the stars (or at least to the Philadelphia elite). Madison would be the first in our entire grade to turn sixteen, so she felt it her obligation to kick the monumental year off with a bang worthy of the cover of *Philadelphia* magazine. Her parents had reserved the ballroom at the Rittenhouse Hotel, a posh hotel in Center City so glamorous and expensive it would make any bride choke with envy. She even bought a silver Vera Wang gown with matching Manolo Blahniks to catch the glint in the room's chandeliers.

"Well, Mad, maybe the cake can just be purses. Do they have to have the LV logo?"

"Uh, yeah. That's the whole point. What, do I want a bunch of knockoffs at my party?"

"It's a cake!"

"So? My parents are paying this woman a truckload! She should be able to find a baker who will do what I want. Heck, can't she just call Louis Vuitton's people and get permission?"

"I'm sure it's not that easy." I sighed.

"Anyway," Madison said, "I can't wait for my party to get here. It's the only thing happening this summer. We're gonna have, like, nothing to do afterward."

"Well, sort of. I was actually thinking of getting a job. Maybe as a camp counselor at the elementary school," I stated, as I stared at the skylight on my ceiling.

"Oh, my God! You're getting a job? Why? You're fifteen!"

"So? Most of the counselors are fifteen."

"Yeah, and they're losers."

"Madison, my dad's always up my brother's butt because he's such a mooch. At least if I have my own money I can prevent ever having the same arguments they're having right now."

"So, what? You're gonna save your money so when you graduate from high school you can pay your own way through a drunken European vacation?"

"I don't know, maybe. But at least I'll have the option. And my own bank account."

"You're such a freak."

"Am not! Anyway, I gotta go. My mom'll be home soon."

"Fine, fine. I'll see you in Spanish class tomorrow, *señorita!*" Madison teased.

"Whatever, *chica*. Only two weeks of school left!"

"You know it!"

I hung up my cell phone, rolled off the bed and walked toward my bedroom door, which held a full-length mirror. I thought once I got into high school, I'd be different. But my reflection still had the same pasty skin, wavy red hair and geeky freckles that I always had. I pressed on my nonexistent chest. I was barely a B-cup (I had too much pride to ever buy an A cup), but at least I could finally see a hint of cleavage through the top of my scoop neck tee—meaning I could see it if I squished my boobs together with my triceps as hard as I could. My legs still looked too long for my body, which while an asset in ballet class, were not really an asset amongst my peers. Even my best friends made fun of the giraffe legs that consumed my entire appearance and forced me to avoid skirts of any kind.

Truthfully, I didn't look like a single member of my entire family. My mom is stereotypical Polish—round face, blond curls, pale eyes, full figure. My dad and brother could practically pass for twins—another fact my brother refused to admit—

with dark, almost black, hair, light skin and a five-o'clock shadow that grew two hours after they shaved (my brother had a mustache before most boys his age could tie their shoes). If it weren't for our shared brown eyes, we wouldn't have a single physical feature in common.

But at least Vince's appearance hinted at the ethnicity that fit with the name "Ruíz." I, on the other hand, was often mistaken for being Irish, which really didn't bother me. Because usually when people find out I'm a "Puerto Rican Polack" they either laugh or don't believe me. Personally, I preferred disbelief, mostly because I also doubted I was a genetic member of this family. Seriously, sometimes I felt *this close* to ordering a blood test.

Chapter 3

When the top of the convertible was down, I felt like I got an entirely new perspective on the world. From the passenger seat in my brother's BMW convertible, our high school looked like a castle in a fairy tale. Tall stone buildings nestled on perfectly landscaped fields surrounded by every species of tree found in the Northeast. Spring Mills was the most affluent public school district in Pennsylvania, and nicer than most of the local college campuses.

"Dude, the parking here sucks," Vince complained as he pulled out of the gated lot and drove to the back of the administration building to look for an available space. We were running late, as usual.

"Hey, a few more days and you'll never have to park here again," I reminded him, as I stared at my classmates rushing off to first period.

"Thank God. I can't get out of here fast enough."

"You know, it's really not that bad."

"Easy for you to say. Mom and Dad practically bow down and worship you."

"That's because I don't get arrested."

"Don't start, Mariana," he droned, pulling the parking

brake on the car and pressing the button to raise the convertible top back into place.

"I'm just saying. It's your own fault Dad's always on your case. You shouldn't have gotten caught."

I unclicked my seat belt and applied a fresh layer of Chapstick while I waited for the top of the car to secure before opening my door.

"Well, it's easy not to get caught when you don't go out in the first place," Vince snapped as he slammed his door shut and hiked up his dark designer jeans, which were professionally ripped at the knees.

"I go out!"

"Dance recitals don't count."

"Vince, I have friends."

"What? The ballet crew? A bunch of wild and crazy anorexics."

"I am *not* anorexic!"

"No, but your friends are. Madison doesn't put more than a lettuce leaf in her mouth in a given day."

That was partly true. Madison did have a few issues with her weight. She was the only one of my friends who, after twelve years of practice, had never scored a solo in a dance performance and she was convinced it was because of her weight. She was a size six when we'd entered high school and now, two years later, she claimed she wore a size two but I was pretty certain there were more zeros floating in her closet than anything else.

But her lack of recognition in ballet really had nothing to do with her weight. Sadly, the girl just wasn't talented, but no one had the heart to tell her. Her father was a vice president at the Campbell Soup Company and Madam Colbert, our instructor, was not about to tell him that his daughter was a sucky dancer (Madam Colbert's husband was a Campbell's product manager). So my friends and I were left with the responsibility of trying to convince Madison that she could afford to put a little more dressing on her salad—actually, a lot more dressing.

"She eats. She just doesn't like to eat in public," I mumbled, feeling a flush of embarrassment for my friend.

"And what's your excuse? It's not like anyone can tell what you look like in those clothes." Vince looked me up and down and smirked.

"What? What's wrong with my clothes?" I shrieked, looking down at my faded boy-cut jeans and solid green T shirt layered over a yellow tank.

"Nothing, I'm sure there's an actual girl under there somewhere."

"Just because I don't wear micro-stretch hoochie-momma jeans like the girls *you* go out with doesn't mean there's anything wrong with the way *I* dress."

"Whatever, forget it," he said, turning his head away from me to end our conversation.

"Yeah, you really think you can brush me off that easily? Nice try." I pushed his shoulder, which was covered in an intentionally wrinkled button-down shirt. "Seriously, you need to let this whole Europe thing go. It's not gonna happen and the fights with Dad are getting a little ridiculous."

We walked through the stone columned entrance into the school.

"Well, if he would just freakin' let me go . . ."

"Give it up! You *are not* going. Move on. Plan a different vacation, or here's a thought: get a job."

"Mariana, I am eighteen years old. I've got the rest of my stinkin' life to get a job. If you want to spend your summer wiping snotty noses with a bunch of losers, fine. But that is *not* my idea of a good time."

"Yeah, well, Dad's not gonna pay your way forever," I stated as we walked down the hallway to our lockers.

"You're right, he's not. So why not enjoy it while it lasts?"

Vince veered off in the direction of the senior wing—located on the second floor of the main building with a view of the tennis courts and soccer fields. Freshmen were herded into the ground-level hall with classrooms that overlooked the parking lot.

I stood in front of my locker and dropped my floral cotton bag on the floor, a gift my mother purchased in Provence last year during my dad's "business trip" to the south of France. It was the first time our parents had left Vince and me home alone, and we came pretty close to making them seriously regret it.

As expected, my brother planned a party. I knew he would and I didn't want to make a federal case out of it, but I also didn't want to get involved. Drinking and puking was not my idea of a good time. So I let my older brother, who was sixteen at the time, invite some friends over, trusting that he wouldn't let things get too out of control. I was wrong.

I had gone to a movie with Madison and afterward we met her parents for dinner at this trendy Japanese restaurant on Main Street. By the time I got home, which was still fifteen minutes before my curfew despite the fact that my parents were out of town, the neighbors were screaming at my brother and threatening to call the cops on the hordes of drunken teenagers parked on their lawns. I spent more than an hour kicking everyone out of our house, then I had the pleasure of going door to door to convince all of our neighbors that the party was over and an incident like this would never, ever happen again. It was a four-hour party but it took nearly two days to clean up. My brother helped by vomiting the entire next morning and by exerting himself just enough to take out a few bags of garbage—which my friends and I spent half a day collecting. Thankfully, when our parents came back, not one neighbor blew our cover.

"Hey, Bobby," I greeted, as I swung the metal dial on my locker.

Bobby McNabb and I had been locker neighbors for the past year. We didn't share any classes or after school activities— he was more of the future-NYU-film-student type. Our locker chats were our only form of contact.

"*Hola,* Mariana," he replied, as he dug through his long skinny locker, his shaggy mop of blond curls falling onto his black-framed glasses.

"Oh, yes, let me whip out my Spanish accent for you," I joked as my locker door swung open. "So, Bobby boy, what are your plans for the summer? Ya gonna write some poetry in a coffeehouse or make a documentary on the war-torn Middle East?"

"Both, hopefully." He smiled.

"Seriously? 'Cause I was kidding."

"So was I, sort of. My parents signed me up for some summer film program in Dublin."

"Like, Ireland?"

"Well, that's where Dublin is," he teased. "It's some NYU thing."

I laughed.

"What?" he asked, his eyebrows raised.

"Bobby boy, you are destined for New York's Lower East Side. NYU might as well admit you now."

"Yeah, I guess I'm the last remaining starving artist."

"I don't know how much you can really starve in Spring Mills."

"True. But I think I can still starve in Dublin."

"Ah, something to look forward to."

Just then I felt a familiar tap on my shoulder.

"What up, Spic!" yelled Emily Montgomery as she pushed me slightly with her sculptured nails. My forehead clenched slightly.

My friends had been calling me Spic since sixth grade. They thought it was hilarious that I was half Puerto Rican, and even funnier that my teachers expected me to have some sort of natural aptitude for the Spanish language, like, just because my father was born there I must be fluent. Unfortunately, languages are not passed down in the DNA and my father never spoke a word of Spanish in our home, except when my grandparents visited. But they passed away five years ago.

My father had spent hours standing next to my grandfather's coffin (he died suddenly of a stroke), speaking in a language I couldn't understand, to relatives I barely knew. I felt almost offended. My grandfather was a part of *our* family; he and my grandmother ate dinner at our house every Sunday; they watched our dog when we went on vacation; and they bought us unfashionable clothes for Christmas. I didn't like having to share their funerals—my grandmother died a few months after my grandfather of heart disease—with strangers who couldn't even speak my language. I felt that if I hadn't met these relatives before, then obviously they didn't love my grandparents as much as I did. They didn't have a right to be there acting like they were so distraught. They should have cared about them when they were alive.

"Uh, Mariana, the bell's gonna ring any second. You ready?" Emily asked, snapping me out of my daze.

"Oh, yeah," I replied, shaking my head. "Madison was freaking about her party again last night."

"What else is new? Did you hear the hotel won't allow dogs, so she can't walk in with Tweetie?"

"Oh, my God! What is she gonna do with that silver gown she had made for her?"

"You think Madison's giving up on this? Please! She'll get that Chihuahua in if she has to smuggle the thing in her purse."

"No way. She'd wrinkle Tweetie's dress."

We both laughed. Madison's idea of a grand entrance with her two-pound dog in matching couture was a little too "Paris Hilton" for us. But we wouldn't tell her that. She was determined to upstage any *Super Sweet 16* ever aired on MTV. Somehow she watched that show and saw inspiration where I saw humiliation. At least other cultures had birthday celebrations with some religious or social significance, like Bar Mitzvahs or *Quinceañeras*, but we just flaunted our wealth for the heck of it.

"Anyway, thank God, school's almost over," Emily stated, pushing her long, chestnut locks over her shoulder. I could hear her cell phone buzz from her tiny black wristlet.

She yanked out the hot pink phone and read a text message off the screen. "It's Madison. She says she heard Friday's skip day. Everyone's goin' into Philly. You want in?"

Every year, in the last few weeks of school, the entire student body skipped class (the seniors usually determined when) and the faculty looked the other way—they used the time as an "in-service" day to get all their grades in order before the year closed.

"Where in Philly?" I asked as Emily was busy texting Madison back.

She paused and adjusted the top of her black sleeveless shirt. "We'll find out soon."

Her phone buzzed again seconds later.

"There's a free concert at Penn's Landing. Some hippie-fest

thing, but it should be fun. Madison wants us to go shoe shopping while we're there," she said, reading the screen of the phone.

"Shoe shopping? I don't even have a dress for her party yet! Whatever. Fine, let's do it."

"Very cool. Spic is in," Emily replied as her fingers flew over her phone's keypad.

I smirked and headed off to class.

Chapter 4

The lawn was damp and the music was lame. I sat on a soggy picnic blanket surrounded by girlfriends I'd known since grade school, listening to some artist I'd never heard of perform on the waterfront stage. I lifted my butt to feel the seat of my jeans. Just as I thought, wet. Now it was going to look like I peed myself. I yanked on my navy blue T shirt, even though I knew it wasn't long enough to cover the water mark. Not that many people here would notice. Aside from my classmates, everyone else at the concert was wearing at least one article of clothing made entirely of hemp.

Emily and Madison were sprawled out next to me in their bare feet, our flip-flops stacked on the grass beside us. Emily was reading some article about Uganda in the latest *Marie Claire* while Madison was busy texting her event planner.

"Yes! Gayle found the pink, rhinestone-studded cell phone holders I wanted to give as favors!" Madison shrieked.

"That's awesome, Mad," I said, half listening as I scanned the crowd.

I knew Vince was here somewhere. He'd dropped us off in the parking lot and then darted to meet with a group of jocks I didn't realize he knew. He rotated friends more often than his underwear. It was easy for him. He was universally liked by rockers, nerds, stoners, everyone. He had a knack for making any situation more fun. At church when we were little, he used to make shadow puppets on the pew in front of us as we kneeled, silently praying. I'd spend the entire hour guessing the animals he was contorting his hands into—dogs, butterflies, alligators. It made the never-ending Catholic mass move surprisingly quickly, especially since half the time was spent trying to suppress our giggles.

"Yo, Spic, is there any more water in the cooler?" Madison asked, not looking up from the screen of her phone.

"Yeah, I think so," I answered through clenched teeth. I opened the red and white cooler. I pulled out a bottle of dripping wet Evian and handed it to her.

"Uh, hello! Don't get my phone wet or I'll never hear if Gayle found my tiara!"

"You're wearing a tiara?" I asked, my eyes narrowed.

"Uh, obviously. But Gayle's trying to pawn off some tacky thing that doesn't even have real crystals. Like I would ever wear that! I swear I don't know what we're paying her for."

I did. The poor woman probably needed a team of assistants just to keep up with Madison's requests.

"Hey, Mad, this band is pretty good. Why don't you hire them?" I joked as the dreadlocked chick on stage began to yodel.

"Very funny. Besides, we already booked the same band that played at my cousin's wedding."

"Wasn't your cousin's wedding in Los Angeles?"

"Yeah, so? They're flying in."

"Oh, okay. Um, that's cool," I remarked, shaking my head.

"I don't get why they have concerts on the Philly waterfront," Emily stated, changing the subject. "It's ugly. You have a gross view of Camden. Who wants to stare at that?"

She pointed across the Delaware River to the fog of black smoke emanating from the refineries in New Jersey.

"I know. Camden literally smells like crap," Madison stated. "My dad complains about it all the time. I don't get why they just don't move his office."

The Campbell Soup Company is headquartered in Camden, New Jersey, and it is one of the few redeeming qualities about the city. I had only stepped foot in it twice in my life—for my grandparents' funerals. They wanted to be buried in the place they'd raised their family, which drove my father nuts. He worked hard to brush away his poverty-stricken past and hated any association with his former lifestyle. That's why he moved our family (and my grandparents) to Spring Mills, quite possibly the whitest town in the tri-state area.

We were so conspicuous that once when my mom's Polish relatives sent a Christmas package addressed only to "Irina Ruíz, Spring Mills, Pennsylvania," it still arrived the day after it entered the States—even without the street address. It was easy for the mail carrier to determine its destination; we were the only family with an Hispanic last name within a ten-mile radius. A fact that didn't go unnoticed by my grandfather. He never ceased to mention it and every time he did, my father's fists clenched until his knuckles whitened.

"Hello! Mariana! Earth to Mariana!" Emily yelled. "Madison wants to go look for shoes."

"I want you guys to both wear black, so you'll complement my silver dress," Madison said as she dropped her phone in her purse. "I'm thinking black strappy sandals."

"Oh, yeah, sure," I answered.

We all climbed to our feet and I neatly folded the blanket we'd been sitting on for the past two hours.

"Hey, can we get something to eat first? I'm starving," Emily said. "There's this Mexican place in Old City that's supposed to be awesome. My parents went there a couple weeks ago."

"Hey, Mariana—*Mexican.* We can visit your people," Madison joked.

"I'm Puerto Rican, *chica,* not Mexican. Get it right," I said, rolling my eyes.

"*¡Ay Dios mío!* So sorry *señorita!*" she replied with a laugh.

"Oh, you know we love you! Our little ethnic friend," Emily teased.

"For the last time, I am *not* Hispanic. My name is."

I shoved the plush blanket in my backpack and followed my friends off the field and away from the concert.

Chapter 5

South Street was mobbed. Not much of a shocker—it was June and a warm seventy-five degrees. But who would expect this many people to have nothing better to do on a workday. Don't these people have jobs?

After we had finished our Mexican meal and Madison had deemed not a single pair of shoes in Old City worthy of her party, we decided to walk over to South Street's funkier shops—which sell everything from crotchless underwear to cashmere sweaters.

"Hey, guys. I think I want to get a henna tattoo. What do you think?" Emily asked, as we strolled past a Goth clothing store.

"As long as you get it somewhere that won't show during my party," Madison said, as her cell phone buzzed for the millionth time.

"It's a temporary tattoo. Your party's not for weeks," Emily pointed out.

"Uh, sure. I saw a news special on how some of those tattoos never really go away. You can totally screw yourself up."

"That's not true!"

"Believe what you want."

"Well, I still want one. What about this place? Tony's?" Emily pointed to a sketchy parlor ahead with a tacky neon sign.

"Yeah, I think those are real tattoos," I noted, as I stopped in front and pulled my plastic tortoise-shell sunglasses down my nose to peer inside the window.

The shop's white walls were decorated with brightly colored cartoon images. I assumed a customer just picked a design for their skin straight off the wall, like I do when selecting iron-on T shirt patterns from the cheap souvenir shops at the Jersey shore.

"You know what? Forget it," Emily said, looking at Madison. "I don't want to risk ruining your party."

"You won't. But this freakin' event planner might if she doesn't find the cake I want," Madison huffed as her fingers flew over the keys on her phone. "I mean, it's her job. Just find the cake!"

"Maybe you could just stick a real Louis Vuitton bag on top of the cake as decoration?" I suggested.

"No, I want the entire thing to look like 'LV' purses, and I'm paying this idiot to do what I want!"

Emily shook her head at me as if to imply I shouldn't press this any further.

"Fine," I muttered.

We crossed the pothole-filled street in our flip-flops, our ankles twisting on the uneven surface. The air smelled of cooked beef from the cheesesteak stand on the corner. For a sandwich that tasted so addictively good, it suddenly struck me that it smelled a lot like my giant poodle Tootsie's gourmet dog food. Cheesesteaks were definitely one of those foods that smelled better when you were eating them than when you were just catching a whiff—probably because the saliva-inducing taste outweighed the funky smell.

"Hey, Mad, if I can't get a henna tattoo, how about a belly

ring?" Emily smirked. "I'm sure no one will see that under my dress."

"Are you kidding? The stud will protrude through the fabric!" Madison shrieked.

"I'm kidding, I'm kidding. . . ."

We stopped and stared through the dirty front window of a piercing shop, which looked like it hadn't been cleaned in years. At first all I could see was the reflection of my stringy hair and baggy-jeaned silhouette, but as soon as my eyes adjusted to the dim light inside, the air sucked from my lungs.

"You've gotta freakin' be kidding me," I grunted, charging toward the entrance.

I swung open the glass door, triggering the sound of tinkling bells above. My brother immediately flung his head around. I swear he knew it was me before he even caught a glimpse of my figure.

"Vincent Ruíz, what the hell are you doing here?" I whispered in my sternest voice, pushing my sunglasses onto the crown of my head.

"Dude, you sound like Dad," he responded, lifting his bushy eyebrows.

"No, I'm fairly certain that if you stick a hole anywhere in your body, Dad's reaction will be a lot louder than mine."

"Relax, I'm just getting a tongue ring," he said, shrugging his shoulders in his store-bought rock-and-roll T shirt like his plans were no big deal.

"A tongue ring! Are you crazy? What the heck is wrong with you?"

I could see his friends glaring at me like I was the field trip supervisor who had just busted them smoking in the boys' bathroom.

"Mariana, loosen up. You gotta stop acting like you're 80." His muddy brown eyes glared at me with fake sympathy.

"If being eighty means knowing better than to let some stranger dig a piece of cheap metal through my tongue, then yes, call me Grandma."

"Well, if it's just the tongue ring you have a problem with, he could get a Prince Albert," his friend chimed in with a chuckle.

All his buddies instantly laughed and threw up high-fives in every direction. I had no idea what he was talking about, but from the way he was grabbing the crotch of his filthy jeans I didn't even want to begin to imagine where he was suggesting that the spike go.

"Luke, shut up. You're not helping," Vince huffed, shooting his friend a look before turning his gaze back in my direction.

"Look, Vince, I know you're pissed at Dad . . . but piercing your tongue is stupid. You don't want to go off to Cornell being 'that guy with the stud in his tongue.' The guys in your dorm will think you're gay and girls won't hook up with you." I tilted my head to the side and swished my red hair over my shoulder.

Vince slowly stared toward the halogen lights on the ceiling. I could tell he was contemplating my last statement by the way he was chewing his lip.

"Fine, whatever. I won't do it," he conceded.

His friends instantly booed at him like angry football fans.

"God, you're so annoying. You always gotta ruin the fun."

"It's a gift," I joked.

"Little Miss Responsible," he snipped.

"Whatever."

My brother could grow up to be a corporate raider with a beautiful wife and five kids and he'd still be immature. It was a permanent character flaw and despite my best efforts to lessen the damage it caused, he still often found a way to drive our family crazy—like when he got arrested.

He had told our parents he was sleeping at a friend's house and they were getting up early the next day to go fishing somewhere in Delaware. It was two years ago and I hadn't yet learned to distrust my brother. Unfortunately, neither had our parents.

Around one-thirty in the morning the phone rang. My eyes instantly flicked open. I heard my father run to the phone, briefly speak, then hang up. He thumped down the steps and peeled out of the driveway before I could even get my slippers on. By the time I opened my bedroom door, my mom was standing in the hallway in her nightgown; she always wore a robe on top of it in front of us, so the sight of her barely dressed and without it freaked me out more than the phone call. She told me that Vince was at the police station.

They didn't get home for another two hours, and my father was still yelling when he opened the front door. I hid at the top of the stairs and watched him scorn my barely conscious brother—his eyes were lifeless, his hair was matted, his shirt was wet and his head was flopped on the back of the couch like he hadn't the energy to hold it up. Dad paced back and forth hollering about how disappointed he was, and I remember thinking that there wasn't a worse thing in the world he could have said. But Vince didn't react.

He told me later that if I ever got myself into trouble that bad I should just shut my mouth and let Dad yell. It was easier than fighting back because eventually Dad would tire and think he'd won—problem solved. Only I never wanted to see my father look at me the way he looked at my brother that night. And he never has.

"When I come home tonight, I'm inspecting your tongue,"

I warned, before turning back toward my girlfriends to leave the piercing shop.

"Don't worry, Mariana, we'll look after him," one of his buddies called after me.

"Yeah, 'cause you guys are such great influences."

"I sure hope not," he responded.

I pulled my sunglasses back down onto my nose and gave my brother one last look. He peered into my brown eyes and shook his head knowingly. I knew he wouldn't go through with it.

Chapter 6

As soon as I opened the heavy red door to our house, I was struck with an eerie vibe. There were no strange noises or items out of place—the knickknacks were where they were supposed to be, the furniture was dusted and fluffed—but something felt off, like that moment right before the guest of honor realizes there's a houseful of people waiting to yell "surprise!"

"Mom? Dad!" I shouted as I walked into the marble foyer.

I wiped my sandals on the doormat, walked toward the spiral staircase and yelled up. "Vince, you here?"

No one responded.

I walked through the living room and glimpsed the spotless kitchen ahead. There were no dishes in the sink or seasoning scents in the air. It didn't make sense. It was six o'clock, my mom should be cooking dinner. She cooked every night at this time. She loved to cook.

I continued toward the back porch and gazed into our freshly landscaped yard. There sat my brother, my mother and my father on the wrought iron patio furniture drinking iced tea like a cheesy commercial. I tilted my head as I slid the glass door open.

"What's going on?" I asked as their heads swiveled to face me.

"Mariana, sit down," my dad said, patting the navy blue cushion on the chair beside him.

My brother was smiling—not a happy smile, more like a sneaky "I know something you don't know" grin.

"Okay, what's up?" I asked, my eyes darting from side to side.

"Iced tea?" my mom asked, grabbing the crystal pitcher and a tall glass from the bamboo tray beside her.

"Um, okay. Uh, will someone please tell me what the heck is going on?"

"Dad and I came to an arrangement," Vince said as he stared at his designer sneakers.

"You're going to Europe!" I squeaked, my hand shooting toward my mouth.

"Not exactly. But I *am* traveling."

"Okay, then what? Where are you going?"

I grabbed the glass of iced tea from my mother.

"Lemon? Sugar?" she asked in her sweetest voice.

"Sure."

My mom was smiling so wide that it almost looked robotic, like her face was programmed to stay in that position. It wasn't a good sign.

"All right, why are you all being so weird?"

"We're not being weird," my mom said in a flat, peaceful tone. She was bracing herself for an argument. I could tell. She was setting a mood.

"Look, Mariana. Your brother and I talked," my dad started. "I knew he was serious about wanting to travel. But I didn't think it was safe for him to be so far away unchaperoned. So I came up with a compromise."

"I'm spending the summer in Puerto Rico," Vince interjected, glowing.

"That's awesome! Good for you!"

My mom and dad exchanged a look.

"I still have family there," my dad added slowly. "And an
aunt and uncle of mine have agreed to be hosts for Vince . . .
and you."

"And *me!* What do you mean, *and me?*" I coughed as I
choked on a gulp of sweetened tea.

"I thought it would be a good learning experience for
both of you," he stated as he stared at the recently manicured
bushes rather than my horrified eyes.

"What? What are you talking about? I don't want to go
anywhere."

"Mariana . . ." my father continued sternly.

"Don't *'Mariana'* me. Didn't it occur to you to ask me
first? This is ridiculous. *Mom!*"

"Honey, look, it'll be fun," she offered. "You'll get to go to
the beach. You'll meet your relatives, be in a different country."

"But I have friends *here!* I have Madison's party! I can't
miss that. I *won't* miss that!"

"Your friends will still be here when you get back," my dad
added gruffly.

"Dad, are you nuts? I can't do this to Madison. She's counting on me!"

"She has an entire staff to count on," he huffed.

"That's not what I meant and you know it! It's her six-
teenth birthday! That's a once in a lifetime thing. I have to be
there for her. She's my best friend!"

"Mariana, I realize you're upset now," my mother cooed.
"But once you get to Puerto Rico, you'll forget all about this
and have fun. Really, you will."

"You honestly think I want to *forget* all about my best friend? Are you mental? Have you ever had a friend in your life?"

"Oh, come on, Mariana! You're missing some stuck-up, superficial party for a spoiled little rich girl. Who cares? You're better off." Vince pumped his eyebrows.

"I don't care what you think of her. Like you have room to talk. Trust me, I could say a lot worse about *your* friends," I snipped, my eyes frozen. "Madison's a good person. And she's my best friend. This party is the most important thing in her life. I'm not going to miss it. Why the heck am I even being dragged into *your* mess?"

I jumped up from my chair and swung around to face my parents.

"I am *not* going."

"Mariana, you have plenty of summers and birthdays to spend with your friends. It's not the end of the world," my dad said, unsympathetically.

For the first time, I understood just how Vince felt when he fought with our father; Dad didn't hear a word we said, nor did he care what we thought. His mind was made up before our mouths even opened. We were in two totally different realities.

"You really think this is just a birthday? No big deal? God, you really have no idea what goes on in my life! What type of parents are you? I've done nothing wrong!"

My dad blew a puff of air from his cheeks and glared at my mother, the vein pulsing on his forehead. She immediately stood up and rested her hand gently on my shoulder—a move I've seen her do a thousand times.

"Mari, it'll be fun. Trust me. A tropical island. Your parents nowhere in sight. You can hang out with Vince. You'll do all kinds of stuff, *together* . . ."

A spotlight suddenly lit up in my brain. I finally understood what was happening here. I *had* to go with Vince, but not as his traveling buddy. I was his fifteen-year-old watchdog.

"Oh, this is great! You act like an irresponsible idiot and now I have to go babysit you from across the ocean! Thanks for ruining my life, Vince!" I screamed.

"You are *not* babysitting me!" Vince jumped to his feet.

"Like hell I'm not!"

"Mariana, listen to me!" my father shouted, slamming his hand on the iron armrest as he stood. "You are going to Puerto Rico with your brother. It'll be safer if the two of you are there together. Plus, your Spanish is better."

"Says who? I got a 'B' in Spanish last quarter." Tears filled my eyes. "And you never even talk about Puerto Rico. You don't speak to anyone from there. Since when do you care about any of those people? I care about my friends *here*."

My father looked into my teary eyes. He paused for several seconds, and I actually didn't think he was going to respond until he added, "You have a lot of family there you should meet. I probably should've gone back, with all of you, a long time ago. I think this'll be good for all of us. At the end of the summer, your mom and I will come visit. We'll all travel back together. Mariana, it's done. It's settled."

I swallowed a knotted lump in my throat. He already had the plans made. He probably had them made before he even told Vince. Anything I said at this point would be futile. My father had no intention of taking my feelings into account. He didn't care about my friends or Madison's party or what I wanted. I had no choice. He was sending me off to slaughter (or Puerto Rico) whether I wanted to go or not.

Chapter 7

Emily and Madison accompanied us to the Philadelphia International Airport. They cried hysterically the entire twenty-minute drive while my father shook his head and glared at them through the rearview mirror. Over the past two weeks, before school had officially let out, I begged my parents non-stop. I had never done anything to upset them before in my life. I assumed that all those years of obedience had to amount to something. I was wrong.

My father was determined to ship us off to some island he hadn't laid eyes on in thirty-five years. It was a literal "guilt trip"—his twisted way of making up for ignoring his family there—and even worse, for having been successful here. Like shipping us off to stay with them would prove he didn't think he was better than they are, that he still thought of them, and that he was still one of them. Only it wasn't true. He had left and never looked back. If he really cared about a single one of the people he and my grandparents had left behind to "seek a better life," then he'd be visiting them *with* us, not just schlepping us off first class.

"I can't *be-be-believe* you're really *go-going*. I can't believe *y-you're* really gonna miss my *p-paaarty!*" sobbed Madison, her pale skin red and blotchy. She was already on her second box of tissues and her hair was sweaty from hours of crying.

She didn't take the news well. Actually, it was safe to say that if she had access to my father and a guillotine she would have ordered "off with his head." It was a rampage worthy of an epic legend. Not to mention poor Gayle, who had to reconfigure the seating charts, the grand "best friend processional" (which was to be choreographed to some club song I'd never even heard of), redistribute the flowers dedicated to my bouquet, alert the photographer of one less "friend" for the staged Kodak moments, and of course, deal with a hysterical Madison.

At least now, Madison finally believed there was truly nothing more I could have done to change my father's mind, and that I really was an unwitting pawn in his evil plot to ruin my life. Last night, she and Emily slept over and helped me pack. They spent so much time trying to convince my father he was making a mistake (Madison tried to show him her entire three-ring binder full of Sweet Sixteen party plans, down to the colored swatch of her dress) that I almost thought he was going to kick them out. No bother, he just tuned them out the same way he tuned me out. He was mentally incapable of understanding how much I would be missing, how two months away from my two best friends, whom I had spent every day with since kindergarten, felt like a death sentence. I had no desire to miss out on the biggest and most important day in my friend's life just to visit some "Puerto Rican paradise" I had no interest in.

I didn't want to turn into some freakish JLo wannabe, eating rice and beans and speaking in some language that I couldn't even comprehend in my classes, let alone in an actual foreign environment. I wanted cheeseburgers and American top forty and people who spoke English fluently. This whole island was going to be a bizarro world. We weren't even staying in the city. We were staying in some mountain hick town where my dad grew up, and where no tourist ever ventured. Everyone was going to be old and wrinkled and . . . foreign. And back home, the world was going to go on without me; Madison's party was going to happen without me.

I snarled at the back of my brother's head as I suppressed the urge to reach over the car seat and choke him with my bare hands. All those times I watched his back, and the one time I needed him to stand up for me, he bails. Why? Because it served his own interests to keep his mouth shut. That was all he cared about—himself. I felt the heat building in my head like a time bomb.

"We're here!" my mom sang from the front passenger seat as our Lexus SUV stopped in front of the Departures drop-off.

"I still can't believe this," Madison cried.

"Two months! And the party!" Emily whined, tossing her hands in the air.

"Look, you guys, I can't even think about that. I can't even think about the party or I'm gonna lose it," I squeaked, trying to hold my voice steady. "I brought my laptop. I'm gonna e-mail you guys every day, okay? We'll set up a chat room in IM, and you'll have to tell me every single detail. Madison, I'm so sorry I won't be there."

"God, could you guys be more melodramatic?" Vince moaned, stepping out of the vehicle in his ripped jeans and Foo Fighters T shirt. With his grimy black hair and scruffy two-day-old beard, all he needed was painted black fingernails and he'd look like a member of the band.

"Hey, just because *you* don't have any friends who will miss *you* this summer doesn't mean you have take it out on *me!*"

"No, I have friends. They just have better things to do than act like a bunch of crybabies. Geez, two months on a tropical island. Woe is you," he scoffed, throwing his black carry-on duffle bag over his broad shoulder.

"Yeah, you're right. Woe *is* me. This is all your fault!" I yelled, throwing a dog toy I picked up off the floor of the car. It landed with a thud at the back of his ratty head. Vince spun around, his lips tightening as his eyes darted for ammunition.

"Kids, don't," my mother quickly warned. "Let's not make a scene."

"Sorry, Mom, if I'm embarrassing *you*," I said, cocking my head.

Ever since she took my father's side on this, I've put her in the same enemy camp. I was suddenly seeing her unending patience as pathetic passivity. The sight of her made my teeth grind.

"Mariana, don't speak to your mother like that," my father ordered as he pulled out my suitcase.

"Oh, sorry. Thanks, *Mom*! I'm so happy you planned this trip without asking me. When I get back, be sure to let me know what college you've decided I'll be attending and any new extracurriculars you've signed me up for. Hey, maybe you'll go the extra mile and arrange my marriage while you're at it."

I knew I was only making things worse, but there was something about this phony good-bye scene that made me want to add at least a smidgen of authenticity. It's not like my parents had earned any polite discretion. Sure, I knew many kids would love to spend the summer without their parents in Puerto Rico. But, frankly, I wasn't one of them. And no one, other than my friends, seemed to understand that.

"Mariana, I wish there was something more we could do. Maybe you could just hide out in an airport bathroom and we'll pick you up after your plane's left. You can stow away at my house the whole summer," Emily whispered, putting her

arm around my terry cloth–covered shoulders. I was wearing a
turquoise hoodie and matching pants. I figured if I had to en-
dure the mental torture of a four-hour plane ride, I might as
well be comfortable.

"Spic, seriously, my parents will fly you back for the party.
I could have Gayle arrange it," Madison suggested once again,
not realizing the racial slur she threw out in my dad's presence.

I quickly caught my father shoot her a disgusted look. He'd
heard them call me "Spic" before and he'd ranted about how
offensive it was, but he didn't get it. They weren't making fun
of me. They thought the nickname was cute. Besides, it's not
like I was *really* Hispanic, so why should I be insulted?

It's not half as bad as the nickname I got saddled with last
year. My European History class had just finished an entire lesson on the Spanish Armada, the fleet of ships that sailed against
England in 1588. A kid in my class, Hugh Larson, seemed to
find the name hysterical, so much so that he pinned the nickname—Spanish Armada—on me, I being the only "Latina" in
our entire grade. My brother and I officially made up Spring
Mills High School's one percent Latino population, a fact that
was hard for our classmates to overlook. So for the rest of the
school year, my entire history class called me "Spanish Armada." I didn't take offense, and actually, sometimes it was kind
of funny. But I was more than happy to see the course end in
June and the nickname die with it.

"Mariana, it's time to go," my father instructed from the
curb, where he was guarding my luggage. "Madison, I'm sorry
she's missing your party but I'm sure you'll have just as much
fun. Now, Mariana, say good-bye to your friends."

For a split second I wanted to shove him into oncoming
traffic.

I turned to Madison and Emily and tears instantly spilled
from my eyes. I'd never had to say good-bye to them before. At

least not like this. Sure, we'd all gone on vacation with our families before, but those trips lasted two weeks, tops. This felt like forever.

"I'm gonna miss you guys so much," I cried, spreading my arms wide.

"I'll miss you too," they replied in unison.

"You have the best birthday party ever! And send me all the pictures!"

I stood there for a couple of seconds hugging them, crying. A part of me was hoping, silently, that they'd really miss me at the party, that it could never be as much fun without me. That I mattered that much.

"All right, Mariana, you be careful over there," instructed my mother as she put her hand on my back to break up the group hug.

"I will," I said, wiping my nose with the back of my hand.

I looked fiercely at my father. I had nothing to say to him, and I was not going to give him the satisfaction of a "good-bye." He glared right back at me.

"Mariana, Vince, hurry up or you'll miss your plane," he ordered without an ounce of sentiment.

I sighed and turned my back to him. Vince was already standing at the automatic glass doors to the airport, waiting for me. I stormed toward him without looking back at my parents.

"Good-bye, Mariana," my father yelled after me. "And Vincent, don't get into any trouble. The neighbors over there might not be as nice as the ones here, so don't throw any parties."

I stopped in my tracks and coughed unexpectedly. My parents knew about the party Vince threw last year? Since when? My eyes shot toward my brother. His expression was flat. He didn't seem surprised.

Suddenly, it all made sense. *That* was why my brother was

not allowed to go to Europe, *that* was why he was so willing to accept this Puerto Rico alternative, and *that* was why I was being forced to babysit him. This was all because of that stupid party. If I had just been as irresponsible as him, if I had just gotten wasted like he did, I wouldn't be in this situation because then they wouldn't trust the two of us together. Now I couldn't tell if I was being punished for lying (by omission) on Vince's behalf or for being trustworthy enough to look out for him.

Chapter 8

My white iPod headphones were plugged into my ears as I sobbed silently to my most depressing playlist. I was seated in the window seat with my legs pulled up to my chest, staring at the clouds as the plane moved farther and farther from home.

The thoughts of everything I would be missing swirled in my head. What if I came back and Emily and Madison had formed this tight bond with no room left for me? What if it's the greatest party of our lifetime and they have all these inside jokes I don't understand? What if they get boyfriends and no longer want to hang out with a single loser?

Truthfully, none us of had ever had a *real* boyfriend. The last boys we dated were in fifth and sixth grades, and they didn't count. It was more like everyone in our class thought we were supposed to be dating, so we all paired up in matching couples—one girl for every boy. But we didn't hold hands, hang out or even speak to each other in person. It was too embarrassing.

Since we got to high school, we hadn't really met too many guys worth pursuing. And there were certainly no guys pursuing us. Not that we hung out with people outside the walls of Spring Mills. All of our free time was spent happily dedicated to ballet, which didn't introduce us to very many boys. It was hard to make new friends, but to be honest, I would rather have two great friends I could trust with my life than a flock of so-called "friends" to occasionally hang out with but who would stab me in the back the moment the opportunity arose.

Now I was going to Puerto Rico where I had no one but my brother. And considering this whole mess was his fault, I wasn't currently placing him on my list of allies.

"Mariana, come on. Stop crying," Vince whispered, nudging my elbow with his.

I continued staring out the window and pretended not to hear him.

"I don't get why you're acting like this is the end of the world. Do you realize how awesome this is gonna be? Trust me, it'll be a lot more fun than if you stayed in crappy old Spring Mills." He yanked my headphone cords until the earbuds fell from my lobes.

"God, that's so easy for you to say, isn't it? Vince, you're going off to college in September. Your life in Spring Mills is over. You don't care what happens there. Great," I snapped, my head jerking to face him. "But mine isn't."

"So? You miss one party. Trust me, there are going to be others. Heck, your sixteenth birthday is in October. You can have a huge blowout then and put Madison's to shame. I mean, do you think that much is gonna change in two months?" he scoffed, as he flipped through the latest *Sky Mall* magazine.

"Vince, how long did you go out with Suzy Taylor?"

"Two months," he mumbled.

"And when she slept with Sam Jenkins and the whole school found out, did it not bother you because it was *only* two months? Because nothing happened during those two months? Because those two months were no big deal?"

Vince didn't answer, not that I expected him to.

"A lot can happen. And regardless, who wants to go home feeling like an outsider in their own life?" I asked, shaking my head.

"You're never gonna be an outsider with Emily and Madison. Come on, you guys practically communicate telepathically."

It was exhausting trying to explain how I felt to a boy who was not at all empathetic. I closed my eyes and let the buzzing of the plane's wing fill my head.

"Mariana, we are *going* to have fun."

"You don't know that," I whispered as I opened my eyelids and smoothed my palms over my messy red hair. "You have no idea what it's gonna be like there. We might be the only people under eighty-five."

"So, we'll make new friends."

"*You'll* make new friends. It's easier for boys," I said, my fingers fidgeting.

"It can be easy for you, too. Maybe now that you're surgically removed from Emily and Madison you'll actually talk to . . . *other people*," he said dramatically, raising his hands and wiggling his fingers in front of his face like a low-budget magician.

"Vince, seriously, now is not the best time to be giving me attitude." I returned my gaze to the clouds outside my window.

"Dude, right here, right now. As you cry your little eyes out, I predict that you are going to have the best summer of your life—way better than any stupid party. I predict that in two months, when we're back on this plane, you're gonna be crying that you have to leave Puerto Rico," Vince said, slamming the tray table in front of him for emphasis.

"Yeah, what do you think this is? *Dirty Dancing?*" I asked. "That stuff doesn't happen in real life."

I popped my earbuds back in and tuned my brother out.

Chapter 9

When the plane's wheels landed on Puerto Rican soil my stomach swished in waves. I wasn't sure if it was from the rocky landing or the impending situation, but at that exact moment, I almost had to pull out the barf bag from the seat pocket in front of me.

I closed my eyes and breathed slowly.

"Dude, we're here," Vince cheered, grabbing my biceps with a shake—the absolute last thing I needed. He jumped up from his seat, long before the fasten seat belt sign was turned off, and was hit with an evil eye from a nearby flight attendant. To appease her, he slightly squatted in the vicinity of his seat, ready to pounce the minute the plane pulled into the gate.

I, however, was planted in my seat fending off ripples of nausea when the pilot finally triggered the overhead light. I waited until the passengers around me had retrieved their bags before tugging my pink duffle bag from the compartment above—it was embroidered with my initials MLR (my middle name's "Louise," after a great grandmother I never knew). It must have weighed at least thirty pounds and of course I had no help with it since my brother was already halfway up the aisle headed for the door. I threw my black laptop bag onto my other shoulder and followed the mad rush of passengers.

As soon as I stepped into the brightly lit Luis Muñoz Marin international airport, I was smacked with a spectacle of tan strangers rushing and pushing in every direction. The chaos reminded me of a Discovery Channel special I saw on killer bees, and an instinctive part of me felt the urge to cover my head and run.

"Vince. Vince!" I yelled to my brother who was darting ahead of the crowd like he actually had a clue where he was going.

He stopped, adjusted his black Foo Fighters T shirt under the strap of his duffle bag and turned around. "What?"

"I need to use the bathroom," I half whispered, half yelled.

"*Mariana!*" he whined. "We just got here. Couldn't you have gone on the plane?"

"Well, it's a little late for that now, isn't it?"

I turned to assess the faces of the travelers surrounding us. None of them caught my eye, and they all seemed to be in quite a hurry.

"Excuse me. Excuse me," I said to a twentysomething woman passing by. She mumbled something in Spanish and kept walking, never breaking her stride.

"Excuse me, sir," I tried again, touching the shoulder of white-haired man sifting through a carry-on bag.

"*No hablo inglés,*" he muttered, not looking up.

"Oh, okay. Um. I can do this. Uh," I said under my breath. "*¿Dónde. Está. El. Baño?*" I asked so slowly that I must have sounded mentally retarded to any native speaker within earshot.

The old man looked up at me with confusion. Clearly he did assume I was retarded, and pointed down the terminal. "*Allí,*" he stated.

I thought back to the Spanish lesson we had on "*Aquí, allí, allá.*" I was pretty sure *"allí"* meant "there." So I took a wild guess that the bathrooms were down the terminal over "there" somewhere. I walked toward my brother, who was standing with his arms crossed and his gray sneaker tapping impatiently.

"Look, I need to find the bathroom," I said, as I walked in the direction the man had pointed. "Just look for the *'baño.'* It's gotta be around here somewhere."

We walked several paces. The thick crowd of travelers engulfing us made it hard to absorb our surroundings, and the duffle bag on my shoulder felt like it weighed more than I did. My bladder was about two seconds from exploding.

"Hey, look!" Vince pointed to a sign a few feet above him. It said "Toilets" in English.

"Okay, now I feel like an idiot," I muttered.

There was a line of at least three women in front of me, and all of them were rattling off in Spanish. After five years of language classes at one of the best public schools in the nation—classes I received no less than a "B" in—I realized I could not understand one word they were saying. They might as well have been speaking Japanese.

The reality of the situation began to sink in. I was the annoying tourist—one of those foreign strangers who take up the entire sidewalk in Philadelphia mumbling in some ridiculous language with guidebooks and cameras in their hands, begging for directions in some indecipherable accent. I made a mental note to be nicer to tourists when I got home.

Chapter 10

By the time I emerged from the bathroom, Vince's eyes looked like he was on a mission from God. The minute he saw me, he rapidly lifted his duffle bag from the white tiled floor and spun around with determination.

"The baggage claim is this way." He pointed to a sign clearly translated in English. "Alonzo should be there by now. At least that's what Dad said."

Alonzo Santiago was our father's first cousin, which I'm pretty sure made him our second cousin. We actually met him once twelve years ago when he vacationed on the East Coast. My family took him to the Jersey shore, thinking that since he was from the islands, he must be a big fan of beaches. However, the minute the native Puerto Rican dipped his big toe in our ice-cold Atlantic waters, he ran screaming back to his towel. According to my mother, Alonzo spent the rest of the day asking my father, in Spanish, exactly what was appealing about soaking yourself in a murky freezing ocean and why in the world so many people were there. If the day was like any other day at the shore, I'm guessing that every inch of coastline was covered with a beach chair, towel or umbrella.

However, I barely remember him. I was only four years old at the time. Dad showed us pictures of the visit a few days ago. I still wasn't speaking to my father, so I couldn't voice my initial reaction, which was that Alonzo looked a lot more Puerto Rican than my father. Alonzo appeared young in the photos, in his twenties at most, with tan skin, black hair and black bushy eyebrows. Being as though he was the only relative currently in Puerto Rico who had actually previously met me and my brother, it was determined that he would greet us at the airport. Of course, he hadn't seen us in more than a decade, so I had no idea how the man was going to pick us out of a crowd.

I struggled to keep up with my brother as he sped through the airport. For a kid who had never left the States and had very limited exposure to airports (his only other flights were our family vacations to Disney World), he seemed to be developing a rather rapid sense of direction.

I, on the other hand, did not share his traveler's instincts. The entire airport looked like a Sudoku puzzle. Everything from the people to the shops to the vending machines to the never-ending maze of corridors seemed amazing. It just reinforced my feeling that I didn't belong. If I had traveled alone, I was pretty sure that I'd be wandering around aimlessly for hours mumbling to myself and sobbing quietly.

Once we located the baggage claim, it took another thirty minutes for our luggage to come down the belt (so glad we rushed). We headed through the exit onto the sidewalk where passengers were inevitably greeted by friends, relatives, chauffeurs or no one.

"You realize we don't even know what this 'Alonzo' person looks like, right?" I pointed out as I dragged my black rolling suitcase (which was almost as tall as I was) and lugged the bags on my throbbing shoulders. I was sweating under my terry cloth clothes and the smack of humidity from the tropical air wasn't helping.

"Well, if he hasn't changed at all in the past twelve years, then I think I know what he looks like," Vince said.

We stared at the hordes of strangers chatting in Spanish. Not a single face looked familiar.

"How the heck are we going to find him?" I asked.

"I have no idea."

Out of desperation, I scanned the names the chauffeurs had scribbled on their white cardboard signs: Rodriguez, Gonzalez, Smith. My gaze slid from sign to sign until I finally clapped eyes with my own name: Mariana and Vincent Ruíz.

"There! Over there!" I yelled, pointing at a fair-skinned man with white hair dressed in green plaid shorts and a white golf shirt.

"They sent a driver?" Vince asked as he held my arm and guided me through the crowds.

"I guess."

A few paces out, the man realized we were headed straight for him and smiled. "Mariana? Vicente?" he asked.

I barely understood the pronunciation of my own name. He called me, "MARI-AAAHNA." And my brother went from being Vince to "VICENTAY." We had been on the island for about an hour and already my sense of self was being stripped.

"We're looking for Alonzo," Vince stated cautiously, glaring sideways at the man.

"Sí. Sí. Alonzo," he said, patting his chest.

In a matter of seconds, the youthful dark-haired Latino I remembered from photos became a white-haired golfer who looked more British than he did Puerto Rican. I could only imagine how different we must look to him—we had both grown at least two feet since he last saw us.

Alonzo quickly grabbed the bags off my shoulders, giving me a sense of relief I hadn't felt since before I was ordered to take this trip, and led us toward his car. Walking behind him, pulling my gigantic suitcase, I realized just how tight his plaid shorts were. They were practically glued to his bony butt (not that I was looking, well not like *that*). I just wasn't sure if he had outgrown his clothes or if tight male shorts were in fashion in Puerto Rico. Either way, it fit with the curly gray chest hair protruding from his unbuttoned collar.

Alonzo stopped at a dark green sedan, opened the trunk, and the three of us worked together to hoist our heavy bags inside.

"We're going to Utuado, right?" I asked as I opened the rear passenger door and plopped down, exhausted.

Vince clicked his seat belt secure in the front seat (I gave him shotgun because I had no desire to be stuck entertaining this stranger for the duration of our ride), and Alonzo turned on the ignition.

"*Sí*. Utuado," he said, reversing out of his parking space.

"How . . . far . . . away . . . is . . . it?" I asked, speaking slowly and loudly like he was hearing impaired. I wasn't sure why I thought that would help.

"*¿Como?*" he asked, twisting his neck to glance back at me.

"Utuado, how far away is it?"

"*Sí*. Utuado," he said.

"Uh, Mariana, I don't think he speaks English," Vince said softly, turning to give me his wide-eyed, this-person-is-crazy look.

"Okay, then."

I thought for a few moments. I couldn't seem to remember

the word for "far" but I knew "close" was "*cerca,*" so I formu-
lated the best Spanish translation I could manage.

"*¿Dónde está* Utuado? *¿Es cerca de aquí?*"

Alonzo rapidly mumbled off a half dozen sentences in response that I couldn't even begin to understand, but I was
pretty sure I caught the phrase, "*dos horas,*" which meant two
hours. I took that to mean we had a long car ride ahead of us.

Chapter 11

I was once on a wooden roller coaster. My dad took us to Coney Island two years ago and convinced us that our trip to the famed Brooklyn amusement park would not be complete without a ride on the Cyclone. Personally, I had no desire to step foot on the splintering contraption, but I also didn't want to spend an hour alone on the boardwalk as my family waited in line to ride this "historical landmark."

I reluctantly boarded the coaster car with my brother, plopping down on a red plastic bench protected by a lap bar that, while fitting snuggly across Vince's thick thighs, landed a good six inches above my own. I tried to complain to the ride technician, but apparently the safety device was supposed to be that inadequate, because she launched the ride without bothering to respond.

After that, all I really remember is screaming uncontrollably until my throat burned, and then soaring—at around sixty miles per hour—down a hill so steep I lifted from the seat, my butt elevated in the air like a magic trick, while my freakish brother waved his arms above his head. My white knuckles clutching the bar were the only things keeping me from plummeting to my death.

Now as I sat in Alonzo's hunter green sedan, flying up a mountain road, my hands clenching the gray door handle, I was struck with a very similar sensation.

It seemed that Utuado was not just "in the mountains," it was at the tippy top of the mountains. Lush green hills filled the entire drive until we finally passed the "town." A small concrete square hosted a band playing what I assumed was salsa. A yellow church flanked one end, while the other three sides were filled with ailing shops and restaurants, a Payless shoe store and a Chinese takeout (which I found oddly comforting). Then we turned up a narrow two-way road, wide enough to fit one car, and stared down the edge of a cliff (honestly, it felt as high as the Empire State Building) with absolutely no guardrail to stop our fall. And the road didn't only go up, it curved back and forth creating a path similar to that of the orange cones in a driving test—a constant tight zigzag. And as we "zigged" we couldn't see if there was another car "zagging" from around the other side.

Of course, none of this seemed to faze our dear cousin Alonzo. He rocketed up that mountain like a NASCAR driver taking a practice spin. Since I barely knew the man and he was more than twice my age, I felt too uncomfortable to scream as freely as I wanted, but I did let an occasional "Watch out!" slip through my lips when we flew too close to the edge. Alonzo, who I'm pretty sure didn't understand a word I was shrieking, found my entire reaction to the trip absolutely hysterical. And my brother laughed right along with him. With no way to communicate, Vince and Alonzo seemed to have already become the best of friends.

I, on the other hand, was silently cursing my father for setting me up with a lunatic escort and secretly imagining how awful my parents would feel if I plunged to my death while on a trip they forced me to take. I closed my eyes and tried to focus on a happy place—my life back in Spring Mills, Madison and Emily, my dog Tootsie—but my stomach was shifting so much that I couldn't relax.

Finally, the world slowed. I felt the car straighten out, our speed decrease and the engine roar to a stop. I inhaled deeply and unclenched my eyelids. We were parked in front of a light blue cement house with a pitched roof. It was one story and had an open-air porch jutting from the side. Surrounding it were dozens of tropical trees with dangling green bananas nestled above beds of bright pink and orange flowers—and a flock of wild chickens. Alonzo muttered something in Spanish before I opened the car door. The ground felt strong and solid under my feet, calming my uneasy equilibrium. The smell of damp earth washed over me. But before I could stop to register my surroundings, the cobalt blue front door swung open and out ran a heavy-set older woman and a gray-haired man who, from where I stood, looked nearly identical to my late grandfather. They were headed straight for us.

Chapter 12

It wasn't exactly a smooth introduction. The couple, who had my brother and me locked in bear hugs, rambled endlessly in Spanish assuming we understood every word. Even if I did speak the language, I doubted I would have been able to squeak a word into their nonstop chatter. All I deciphered was that they were our hosts Carmen and Miguel Mendez, our great aunt and great uncle.

Uncle Miguel was my dad's father's (my grandfather's) brother. I had never met him before; actually, I had never even heard his name uttered before my dad brought up this trip. No one ever talked about our extended family in Puerto Rico, which was partly why I felt less connected to them than I did the casts of most reality TV shows. Frankly, I was surprised they even knew I existed; it's not like any of them cared enough to attend my grandfather's funeral. Puerto Rican relatives from up and down the East Coast paid their respects, but not a single resident of the island itself—not even his own sibling. I couldn't imagine missing my brother's funeral. Heck, I'd sell everything I owned to pay for a ticket to see him one last time—despite the fact that he was currently responsible for destroying my life.

I peered intently at my great aunt and great uncle. They

didn't seem like heartless people. Judging from the enormous grins on their faces (my uncle's dimples looked exactly like my grandfather's), they were genuinely excited to see us. Great Uncle Miguel even had tears in his eyes. And as I stared at him, standing on Utuado soil, I could almost feel my grandfather's presence. I half expected to turn around and see his spirit standing behind us, like some scene from a hokey crime drama the moment after the victim's killer has been brought to justice.

I wanted to tell my great uncle how much he resembled his brother, but I lacked the sufficient Spanish vocabulary to express the thought. It only took a few seconds to realize that neither my great aunt nor great uncle spoke any English. And for the third time since our plane touched down, I found myself wishing I had devoted more time to studying for my Spanish classes.

My great aunt Carmen, however, did not seem to notice a language barrier. She continued to babble in Spanish without pausing to catch the glazed expressions in our eyes. Her mouth was glued in a smile, revealing a set of yellowed teeth that looked as though they hadn't spent much time at the dentist. Her long black locks were in need of a touch up (her gray roots were about an inch long) and they fell just to the top of her massive cleavage. Even I couldn't help but stare at the enormity of her chest (a gene that apparently hadn't been passed down to me).

Great uncle Miguel was about half her size—at least two inches shorter and about fifty pounds thinner. His nose was long and pointy at the tip, much like my father's, and a full mane of cropped silver hair covered his head—quite impressive considering I had twentysomething male cousins who were only a few follicles shy of a cue ball. His yellow-and-blue floral button-down (I was tempted to call it a Hawaiian shirt, but being that we were in Puerto Rico I thought maybe it was a "Puerto Rican shirt") was soaked with giant round sweat stains that I pretended not to notice.

Carmen, who still hadn't let go of me, led me from the road toward her house by my biceps. I turned and saw Miguel guiding Vince in much the same manner, while Alonzo stood at the car unloading our bags from the trunk. (My big suitcase weighed more than I did and it had taken the three of us to load it into the trunk, so I had no idea how he was going to haul it out solo.) We hurried across their front lawn, and I noticed that the grass was brighter than it was back home. It matched the sea of emerald that had surrounded us on the drive.

We walked to the front door, and I could hear what sounded like a party inside. Numerous voices boomed above the sounds of salsa and clinking glasses. Aunt Carmen tugged the screen door open and dozens of eyes immediately shifted in our direction. Conversations ceased and all I could hear were the beats floating from the radio. I stepped inside, my pupils struggling to adjust to the dim light. It was early dusk, but no lights were on and I quickly guessed it was to keep the room cool. The house clearly wasn't air-conditioned, which explained Miguel's sopping shirt. The air was thick with the smell of spices and perspiration, and I could feel beads of liquid already forming on my forehead (whether I was sweating because of the temperature or my anxiety, I didn't know).

"Um, *hola*," I said meekly, flicking my hand in an embarrassed wave.

The crowd took a collective inhale before sputtering simultaneously and rushing toward me like the paparazzi to a diva. At least twenty strangers buzzed in my ear, hugging me and chatting nonstop. I twisted my neck and saw Vince engulfed in a similar spectacle. With so many different voices in such dense accents talking all at once, I couldn't make out a single Spanish word they were saying other than *"hola," "chica"* and what sounded like the name "Lilly."

Confused and uncomfortable (I was never big on people

touching me, not even ones I was related to), I tried to introduce myself.

"*Hola. Me llamo* Mariana," I shouted.

But they still kept uttering "Lilly" repeatedly while stroking my hair and patting my face. I tried to squirm away, stretching my head back and raising my shoulders. I briefly caught a glimpse of Vince laughing hysterically. He was having a much less difficult time with their up-close-and-personal introductions. His face was beaming and his arms were spread wide like a king greeting his subjects. I could tell he was loving this.

"No, you don't get it. My name's Mariana. I'm not Lilly," I stated as I tried to weasel free from the pack.

"*Soy* Mariana. *Me llamo* Mariana," I repeated slowly, thumping my chest as they continued repeating "Lilly."

"Vince, a little help here," I called, turning toward my brother, who was still laughing and enjoying himself. "Who the hell is Lilly? They think I'm Lilly."

Finally, the familiar sounds of English emerged from behind me.

"They're not saying you *are* Lilly. They're saying you *look like* Lilly," said the young, feminine voice.

Everyone instantly hushed. I spun around and was face-to-face with my own reflection. Well, *not really*. But I was staring at a girl who could pass for my sister, if not my twin.

She was about my age and roughly the same height and weight. Her hair was the same shade of brownish red, her face was round and pale, her cheeks pronounced and covered in freckles, and her eyes small, almond-shaped and brown.

"Whoa," I mumbled.

"I'm Lilly," she explained, though I had already figured that out.

Chapter 13

Before leaving for Puerto Rico, I had many expectations—most of them bad. I expected it would be miserably hot, I expected no one would speak fluent English, I expected the food to be spicy and odd, and I even expected our accommodations to be less than stellar. And while, so far, I appeared to be right-on with several of those predictions, what I never fathomed possible, was that I'd finally meet the relatives who shared my physical image. For the past fifteen years I joked to my parents, and anyone who would listen, that I was switched at birth, that there was some horrible mishap at the hospital the day I was born and my parents mistakenly brought home the wrong infant. Clearly I didn't resemble them. I was obviously Irish, Scottish or possibly Finnish. Certainly there was no way I had Puerto Rican blood flowing through my veins.

As I stood staring at Lilly, I realized I was wrong. Very, very wrong.

"Who are you?" I whispered, shaking my head.

"Lilly Sanchez," she stated matter-of-factly. She was visibly less fazed by my uncanny resemblance to her.

"Dude, you speak English," Vince said, as he trudged over.

I almost forgot we were still standing in our aunt and uncle's living room surrounded by dozens of people. Some had taken seats on metal-framed chairs and couches with pastel printed cushions, which back home would have been considered nice patio furniture, while others stood around or leaned on the hard cement walls. No one was moving and they were all staring at us like we were the main event for a show that finally got started.

"Hey, I'm Vince."

My brother stuck out his hand and shook Lilly's. I was still gawking at her openmouthed, unable to move and contemplating the reality of human cloning.

"Uh, this is Mariana. Don't mind her. We just spent four hours on a plane."

"No problem," said Lilly. "And really, don't let the relatives freak you out. They're always like this. They get excited when the mail comes."

She adjusted the low scoop on her tank top, which exposed a good three inches of cleavage—the one clear trait that offset our appearances. With her denim miniskirt and white high-heeled sandals, she could have doubled for a "mall chick" in a 1980s rock video. But considering I was still in the same terry cloth outfit I had worn on the plane, I wasn't in a position to be knocking anyone's appearance. If I didn't shower soon, I was pretty sure people would start to smell me from across the ocean.

"So, Lilly, do you live here?" Vince asked.

"Yup. So do my parents, but it's my grandparents' house."

"So Miguel and Carmen are your grandparents?"

Lilly nodded, her red ponytail bouncing. "Yeah, on my mom's side."

"So if our great aunt and uncle are your grandparents, what does that make us?" Vince asked, looking at me.

My brain finally started to unfog, and I began to mentally

outline our family tree. My father's father's brother's daughter was her mother. So Miguel (who was my grandfather's brother, and my dad's uncle, and thus my great uncle) was her grandfather.

"Hold on. I think I got it," I said, staring up toward the ceiling as I thought. "If Miguel is Dad's uncle, then his daughter—your mother—is Dad's first cousin. So you're my dad's *second* cousin, which I'm pretty sure makes you our *third* cousin."

I smiled triumphantly. Lilly and Vince glared back at me cross-eyed.

"Whatever," Vince said. "So are we related to everyone here?"

"Well, *I* pretty much am. So, I guess in some way or another you must be too. Third, fourth, fifth cousin's uncle's sister's nephews," she joked.

Vince laughed. They were already getting along.

Finally, Lilly turned and addressed the crowd of relatives who were still openly gaping at us. She jabbered off something in Spanish and when she finished, they all immediately began conversing amongst themselves.

Lilly flipped back around. "Wanna see your room?"

I noticed she said "room," not "rooms," and my heart froze. That couldn't have meant what I thought it meant. Vince and I both grabbed our carry-ons from Alonzo, who had been standing in the doorway (I noticed my jumbo suitcase wasn't with him and guessed it might take a team of engineers to hoist it from the car), and followed Lilly down the long, yellow hallway.

"What did you say to them?" Vince asked. "To your relatives. Back there."

"I told them they looked like idiots and to stop gawking at you guys."

"You know, your English is *awesome*," he added.

"Well, it should be. I go to an English-language school

about an hour from here. My mom's the secretary, that's how I got in. Practically every American-born kid on the island goes there. I speak English all day, every day surrounded by Americans."

"Is that a bad thing?" Vince asked, sensing the tone in her voice.

"I prefer to hang out with the locals," she said flatly.

"So, you're in high school?" he asked, letting her comment drop.

"Sort of. It's a kindergarten through twelfth grade school. I'm fourteen. Well, I'll be fifteen in a few weeks. There's a big party. My mom's obsessing about it."

"Hey, Mariana, a *party!* A *birthday* party! Looks like you won't be missing so much after all." Vince grinned.

I was listening to them talk but couldn't think of anything to say. It was like my mind wasn't only blank, it was no longer working. I was on shutdown. It had been a long day, and I doubted it would end anytime soon.

Chapter 14

Even though I braced myself for less than pleasant accommodations, even I didn't expect to be bunking with my eighteen-year-old brother for two months. We'd had our own rooms since birth and those bedroom doors were a necessity. The Ruízes weren't a "naked family"—one of those families where the mom walks around in her bra and the dad in his boxers, and the kids wear nothing but towels to get from the shower to their bedrooms. That wasn't us.

We wore robes over our pajamas, even in the summer. We would never open the bathroom door while someone was in the shower, despite the two opaque curtains. We didn't go into a bedroom without knocking. We had boundaries.

But now, it seemed I was expected to not only sleep in a cement room without air-conditioning on a twin bed with a rock-hard mattress and a moldy-scented sheet, but I was also expected to sleep right across from my brother's similar sub-par twin bed. I was going to have to change my clothes in front of him, every day. I was going to have to smell his rank breath and boy odor while I slept. I was going to have to let my laundry touch his. And our only bathroom was shared with the entire household—seven people, including us. I might as well have been camping.

Not that I had time to focus on this much. As soon as Lilly showed us to our room and we plunked our carry-ons onto our beds (the mattresses made a sound similar to wood when hit with the luggage), we were called back into the family room for dinner. I was exhausted and wanted to nap (or tap my heels and be transported back to Spring Mills), but I reluctantly followed my brother toward the scent of food.

"Hola." Vince smiled and waved his hand in a giant semi-circle. *"Me llamo* Vince."

The entire crowd of strangers chuckled slightly. I merely flicked my hand in their direction.

"Uh, they want you to sit at the table. To eat," Lilly explained, pointing to a long wood table covered with dishes of food from one end to the other.

I looked at Vince and he shrugged with ease. It came so naturally to him—the ability to adapt to any situation or, even better, make it more enjoyable. He could have fun at a funeral, if it were socially acceptable. At that moment, as he pulled out a chair, relaxed in his seat and shouted "Let's eat," I actually wanted to *be* him.

Everyone followed his lead and rushed to the food. There clearly wasn't enough room for each person to sit, but it seemed to have been predetermined who would get a chair. The one next to Vince was glaringly left vacant, waiting for me. I stared past it and out the front window and saw Alonzo standing behind the trunk of his car, with another man, yanking on my suitcase. He had a foot on the bumper to brace himself as he pulled, and I felt mildly guilty for causing such a problem. I would have gone out to help if I thought I could do some good, but I was lucky I was even able to wheel it through the airport. Unless they wanted me to do pirouettes around the vehicle, I didn't think I'd be much use.

"Aren't you gonna eat anything?" asked Lilly, as she heaped some rice on her plate.

I looked at the spread and didn't recognize a single edible item aside from the yellow rice with meat that my grandmother used to make, though I had never eaten it before. I wasn't big on rice that wasn't white. Not Spanish rice, not Chinese fried rice, not even whole grain rice. And now, that same rice I'd snubbed hundreds of times before was looking like the most appealing food on the table.

"Mariana, sit down and eat," Vince said, widening his eyes for emphasis.

I could tell he knew what I was thinking. I came out of the womb a picky eater. My mom still told stories of me refusing to drink a bottle as a baby. She was so concerned that I was allergic to the formula that she rushed me to the hospital for emergency tests. According to the physicians, I had no physical reaction to the formula at all. I apparently just didn't want to drink it. And when I got to solid food, my mother ended up pureeing her own peas, carrots and apples because I spit out anything that came in a jar. I, of course, don't remember any of this, but it sure sounded like something I would do.

I pulled out a chair that clearly didn't match the one Vince was sitting on. Mine was light maple and had a blue-patterned cushion and a low back, and his was a dark mahogany wood with a white cushion and a high back. I realized all the chairs were different and wondered if it was an intentional design element, or if they just couldn't afford a set of matching chairs. I sat down and glared at my empty yellow plate.

"Just eat something. It's good," he whispered, covering his mouth so Lilly wouldn't overhear.

"What is all this?" I asked, staring at the heaping piles of food.

"This is like grandma's rice, only it has sausage *and* chicken," he explained, pointing to a large mound on his dish before moving on to the rest. "This is some sort of fried fish, but be careful, it has bones. I think that's ham. These are fried bananas. You'll like these. They're sweet. This is some sort of soup with meat in it."

"*Asopao,*" Lilly corrected. "It's chicken with mashed plantains. It's *huge* here."

I forced a smile before turning back to my brother with wide-eyed concern. I hated anything mashed. In all my life I hadn't eaten even a teaspoon of garlic mashed potatoes or sweet potato puff. I also refused to eat any meat still attached to a bone—I felt like a cavewoman picking up and gnawing hunks of flesh. I didn't even eat ribs or chicken wings back home. So that ruled out the assorted pig parts and fish. Fish bones were the worst—small, sneaky and deadly. I always felt like it was the fish's way of getting back at us for the hook in its mouth. It was only fair.

I surveyed my options and decided on a small pile of Spanish rice with a tiny bit of yellow-colored chicken and a large mound of fried bananas. Vince was right, the bananas were my favorite thing on the table.

"Do *not* make a face while you're eating," Vince whispered sternly.

He sounded like Dad, though I would never tell him that. It would only make him angry.

I pushed my food around the plate, spreading it out in the hopes of making it look like I ate more than I did.

"You don't like it?" Lilly asked suddenly from across the table.

I looked up from my plate and caught her staring at my uneaten meal.

"No, no. It's great." Dozens of eyes snapped toward me, including my Aunt Carmen's. "Really, it's good."

I smiled for effect and took another bite of my bananas. Thankfully, the crowd was satisfied and looked away.

"Well, you're not eating much," Lilly stated.

She seemed a bit offended, and I wondered if she helped cook the meal. The last thing I wanted was to make the one person who actually spoke English dislike me, or worse, think that I was rude. I had never been accused of being rude in my life.

"No, it's all great. I'm just not that hungry. From the plane and all. I'm exhausted."

It was only a half lie. I really was tired. And I was also willing to ignore the rumbling in my belly if it meant I didn't have to consume any more strange foods.

"You know, I think I'm gonna go to bed. That's okay, right?" I asked Lilly.

She looked back at me with one eyebrow raised. "Um, it's like eight-thirty. But if you want to go to bed, go for it. I won't stop you."

I took that as a green light and stood up from the table. My Aunt Carmen's head swiveled toward me the minute I rose and her eyes instantly landed on my mostly untouched plate.

"Um, *gracias. Gracias. Fue muy buena,*" I stated, before quickly turning away.

I darted to my room and shut the door without glancing back. I was alone.

I peeled back my stale sheet, pulled down the dirty white shade covering the lone window (apparently, plastic shades were considered a window treatment in Puerto Rico), and fell on the hard mattress. Tears immediately spilled from my eyes. I wasn't sure if I was crying because I was homesick, lonely or just drained. I guessed it was a combination of all three.

I stayed in bed, quietly sobbing for almost an hour. I couldn't remember the last time I cried like that, but it almost felt good, like it needed to come out. Eventually I got up and changed into a pair of gray cotton shorts and an old Eagles T shirt that smelled like home. I collapsed into the bed and by the time I drifted off to sleep, I could hear everyone had moved onto the outside porch. From the echoes of clanking bottles, it sounded like a party. Vince and Lilly were laughing.

Chapter 15

I woke up disoriented, covered in sweat. Everything in the room was powder blue: the walls, the ceiling, even the cement floor. A bookcase held three rows of paperbacks, along with stuffed animals, silk flower arrangements, dusty candles and statues of Jesus and Mary. The air was unbearably humid and held a pungent, yet familiar, smell. A loud snore broke through the stench, which I finally recognized as my brother's sour morning breath. It wasn't a dream. We were really in Puerto Rico.

The light creeping through the shade was so soft I knew it was early morning. Part of me wanted to stay in bed and not dare venture through the house alone, but I guessed Vince would be out cold for quite a while and my bladder was ready to pop. I unglued the damp cotton sheet from my skin and retied my sticky red hair in a high knot. The cement floor felt soothingly cool under my feet and I knew this must be why there were no rugs in the house.

I opened the door to the hallway. It was silent. My chest loosened as I realized that everyone was still asleep. I padded into the bathroom and was hit with the smell of cleaning fluid. Clearly it had been recently scrubbed, not that it helped the appearance much. The whole room looked straight out of the 1970s—minus the disco ball.

The toilet was olive green with a cracked faux-wood seat and a fuzzy orange cover on the lid (with a matching fuzzy orange tissue box holder). The tub, in a matching shade of olive, had a mosaic of black scratches and permanent mildew circling the drain. The brown-and-white striped shower curtain hung from rusted hooks with a thick layer of mold along the bottom. The tiles on the walls were tan and the grout in between them was spotted black. I flushed the toilet and headed to the kitchen.

The clock on the wall read a quarter after six in the morning. I didn't even get up that early for school.

Immediately my eyes shifted to the dinette set, which looked like a holdover from *Happy Days*—chrome-framed chairs with yellow vinyl seats and a chrome table with a white Formica top. The retro look was actually back in fashion— Emily's parents had just purchased a similar dinette for their Jersey shore house. My great aunt and great uncle probably had no idea they could sell it for good money on eBay. They probably didn't know what eBay was.

But that wasn't what caught my eye. On top of the table sat stacks of magazines, dozens of torn glossy pages, and a big three-ring binder. I lifted the pink plastic book from the table and read the cursive penmanship elegantly scrolled on a sheet of paper slipped into the cover's clear plastic sleeve. It read: *Mis Quince Años,* Lilly Sanchez.

I flipped it open; about fifty more plastic sleeves were filled with magazine cutouts of ball gowns, dolls, champagne flutes, pillows, jewelry, and tiaras. It was like a low-budget version of Madison's party planner. All the details were there, and then some, just without the bling.

I thought back to the blur of last night, and Lilly making a comment about her upcoming birthday. Apparently, it wasn't just a party she was having, it was a *Quinceañera*. I had only been to one in my life. I was eight years old.

My father had lugged us to the Bronx to attend a party for a bunch of relatives I didn't see again until my grandfather's funeral. The girl, *la Quinceañera,* whom I haven't seen since, wore a white dress poofier than most wedding gowns and sat on a throne holding a jeweled scepter. She was caked in so much makeup that I couldn't believe she was only fifteen; her hair was frozen a foot above her head in an elaborate up-do, and she was adorned head-to-toe in chunky sparkling jewelry. She had two tiaras (one for the church service and one for the party) and two sets of shoes (again, she changed at the reception). It was a spectacle so elaborate that a stranger would have thought she was a visiting queen being doted on by her royal subjects. More than a hundred people had packed this family's backyard, including a live ten-piece band.

The whole ordeal seemed outrageous to an unaccustomed eight-year-old, and for a moment I wondered if that's exactly how Madison's party would seem if a stranger happened upon it.

I returned the book to exactly where I'd found it, knowing it was an invasion of privacy just to have opened it.

My throat was dry, but I didn't want to get caught rummaging through the refrigerator (I had already rummaged through their party plans). I stared at the fridge; it looked oddly familiar with its rounded sides and single white door. My grandparents had a similar "ice box" in their house in Camden and it reminded me of stolen sodas. My parents never let us have caffeinated drinks when we were little, so my grandfather used to tiptoe to the fridge, hide two cool cans under his shirt and slip them to us when my mom wasn't looking. She'd pretend not to notice. Only I didn't feel comfortable stealing sodas today, not from a bunch of relatives I still considered strangers. So I grabbed a clean glass from the plastic drying rack and filled it with tap water.

Outside on the porch, dozens of empty beer cans and half-drunk bottles of rum littered the floor. I had never been drunk in my life, yet my middle-aged relatives seemed to have no problem knocking them back. Vince probably had a blast with them last night. I couldn't believe I was less fun than a bunch of old fogies. I mean, really, how sad is that?

I rested my shoulder against a white porch post and tried to spy the nearest house. It had to be at least a football field away, but I could barely see it through the mesh of exotic trees and plants, which looked nothing like the oaks, evergreens and manicured lawns we had back home.

Suddenly, a giant brush of leaves swished. Wood snapped and I quickly stepped back, clutching the handle of the screen door. I was halfway inside when Uncle Miguel emerged with a machete in one hand and bunch of bananas in the other. He was hacking at the vines so wildly that I couldn't tell if he was pruning purposefully or just getting plants out of his way. But as soon as he caught a glimpse of me, he halted.

"*Hola,*" he shouted.

"*Hola.*"

He flung the machete over his shoulder, wiped the sweat off his wrinkled brow and walked toward me.

"*¿Quieres comer?*"

It was the offer for food I was waiting for. I quickly nodded.

"*Sí. Gracias.*"

I followed him into the kitchen and sat at the dinette set, pushing some of the magazines and torn pages aside.

"*Una fiesta. Quinceañera,*" Uncle Miguel stated, pointing to the stacks of party plans.

He opened the refrigerator, which was filled with aluminum foil–covered leftover containers.

"*¿Huevos?*"

He lifted a brown egg from the door and held it out for me. I had never eaten a brown egg before, my mom always bought the white ones, but I had seen them at the grocery store. I was pretty sure they came from chickens.

"*Sí. Gracias,*" I said again, nodding my head.

He cracked a half dozen eggs into the black pan on the stove, pulled a fork out of a drawer and gestured to me with his spinning wrist. I assumed he was asking if I wanted the eggs scrambled, so I nodded.

A few minutes later he set two plates of scrambled eggs on the table and pulled some sliced ham out of the fridge, as well as a large glass bottle of orange juice and a bowl of tropical fruit. I spooned a forkful of eggs into my mouth, and made a mental note that scrambled eggs in Puerto Rico tasted just like they did in Spring Mills.

Chapter 16

My brother and Lilly arose about three hours later. By that time the entire family had stirred and my uncle had left for his job at a hotel, which I was only able to deduce because the word "hotel" was the same in Spanish and in English.

His departure left me with a lot of quiet time. I don't think I'd ever before spent so much time alone and unstimulated. At home, I was always preoccupied by a television or a computer or a cell phone or all of the above. Currently, I had none of those things. The TV was in Spanish, my computer had no Internet access, and the phone didn't have long distance.

I wanted to leaf back through Lilly's *Quinceañera* book, but I knew how annoyed I would be if some stranger snooped through my personal property, passing judgment on my taste and style. So I kept the book closed; instead I thumbed through the stacks of magazines (they were public property, I could buy them at newsstands, so I thought they were fair game).

First, I couldn't get over how tacky everything was—even the magazine layouts. There was an entire section on pillows, apparently used to kneel on during the ceremony. Don't their churches have kneelers? They weren't even elegant pillows crafted of raw silk or satin; they were white frilly pillows covered in lace fringe and pink ribbons. They were shaped as hearts (hello, she's fifteen not five!) and all embroidered with that cheesy "Hallmark font."

Next, came the tiaras. Yes, Madison was planning to wear a tiara, but I could guarantee anyone that her specially ordered headpiece from Swarovski was strikingly different from the white, flower-embroidered ones in these magazines. Last time I saw hair ornamentation like that was at my first Holy Communion, and most of those pieces were crocheted by girls' grandmothers.

The dresses—wow, the dresses. I'm no fashion expert, but every single one looked like a cross between a wedding gown and a tutu (and I had plenty of experience with tutus). I couldn't understand why any girl would want to wear a pseudo wedding dress before her wedding day—talk about stripping away the magic. At least Madison was wearing a silver slip gown that was "sultry," not "sweet."

By eight o'clock, I had scoured all the pages and I couldn't wait for the household to wake up and entertain me. I was running out of snarky opinions.

My Aunt Carmen appeared in the kitchen first, utterly shocked that there were two sets of dishes resting on the drying rack. I tried my best to explain to her that I was quite satisfied with the meal I had already eaten, but she insisted that I eat at least another piece of fruit (she sliced up a mango and shoved it at me) just to prove I wasn't starving. I did. It was easier than trying to search my Spanish vocabulary for enough words to protest. Lilly's father, whom I still called *Señor* Sanchez despite his objections, came barreling in next. He didn't eat anything. He merely kissed Aunt Carmen on the cheek and rushed out the door. Finally, Lilly emerged—her auburn hair matted at the nape of her neck and her mascara smeared around her bleary brown eyes.

"Uh," she grunted at me as she opened the refrigerator and took out what smelled like pineapple juice. "Want any?"

"Nah, I already ate."

"Seriously? How long have you been up?" she asked, scratching her butt.

"A while."

"Figures, you went to bed before the sun went down."

"Yeah, I guess. I see you're planning quite a party." I nodded at the stacks of clippings and magazines I had carefully returned to their original positions.

"Oh, yeah. It's my *Quinceañera*. It's like the most important thing in my mom's world," she groaned as she took a sip from her glass.

"Oh, so these are all your mom's plans?" I asked.

"Yup. She's pretty much running the show. I just told her to tell me when to show up."

Now that at least made a little more sense. I could imagine a mother choosing all of the items I had scanned earlier. But I still couldn't imagine a teenage girl not being concerned with her own birthday party.

"Don't you care? About all the details? I mean, this is a pretty big deal, isn't it?"

"Oh, yeah. It's huge! There's gonna be, like, a hundred people here."

"Wait, you mean 'here'? Like, in this house?"

"Not exactly, but yeah. We're having it in the yard. My mom's renting a tent."

I thought back to Uncle Miguel swatting at the stray vines with his machete. It made more sense now.

"That's a lot of people."

"Oh, it's the Who's Who event of Utuado." Lilly chuckled. "Seriously, I'm so over *Quinceañeras*. I've been to, like, twenty this year alone. There're only so many times you can watch a girl do the same waltz and pretend to be interested."

"But it's your birthday party! It's your big day!"

"Oh, yes. It's the day I become 'a woman.' " She placed her hand sweetly on her heart and laughed, rolling her eyes. "The whole frills and lace thing just isn't my scene."

Before I could protest and point out the importance of such an event, Vince emerged in the doorway looking like the walking dead. His muddy brown locks were shooting straight in the air, his face still had creases on it from his pillow, and the corners of his eyes were crusty.

"Have a good time last night?" I asked, sounding more like Mom than I intended.

"Totally," he groaned between yawns. I could still smell the beer on his breath.

He walked straight over to the fridge, opened it, took out the orange juice, grabbed a glass from the drying rack and poured. He didn't once pause to consider whether it was rude to go into someone else's refrigerator without an invitation. That thought would never cross my brother's mind.

"Hey, so do you guys know we have to work today?"

"What?" my brother and I shrieked in unison. Vince almost dropped his glass.

"Work. Today. At my grandfather's hotel," she said, like it was the most obvious thing in the world.

My first thought was confusion that my Uncle Miguel *owned* the hotel. I thought he just worked there. My second thought was who exactly signed us up for child labor? Sure, I was fifteen and sure, I had been hoping to work this summer back in Spring Mills, but it seemed a little presumptuous that these distant relatives would just assume we would work at their family business without even asking. What, were we expected to pay off our rent like indentured servants?

"Um, what the hell are you talking about?" Vince asked bluntly.

"Your dad arranged for you to work at the Villa del Mar this summer. At least that's what my parents told me. Don't worry, it doesn't suck that much. Plus, my grandfather is the biggest pushover. We won't have to spend that much time actually *working*," she stated with a smirk, as she pumped her eyebrows.

"What do you mean? You think we can get out of it?"

"Vince! We are not 'getting out of this!' " I yelled. "These people are hosting us for two months, and if Dad told them we'd work then we'll work. It's not like we've got anything else to do."

"Speak for yourself," he huffed.

"Seriously, it's not a big deal. I ditch work all the time. And there's even a bar on the first floor where my family hangs out."

The idea of working and having something to occupy my time while I was here actually sounded rather pleasant. But it was clear I was the only one who felt that way. With every word Lilly said it was becoming more conspicuous that the only thing we had in common was our appearance. And the more she and Vince agreed, the more alone I felt.

Just then, the telephone on the kitchen wall let out a loud ring. Lilly yelled something toward her grandmother's bedroom, which I assumed was the equivalent of "I got it!" in English, and picked up the bright blue receiver.

"*Dígame,*" she stated, before her eyes quickly flicked toward me. "Hold on. She's right here."

"It's for you," she whispered, holding out the receiver.

I grabbed the phone out of Lilly's hand, harder than I should have, and flung it to my ear. "Hello?"

The minute I heard my mother's voice, tears welled in my eyes. It was an involuntary reflex. I didn't want to cry, and I definitely didn't want Lilly to see me cry, I just couldn't help it. It was like the wind got sucked out of my gut the minute my mother spoke.

"Mom?" I squeaked, tears rolling down my cheeks.

I glanced at my brother, who looked annoyed at my slobbering reaction.

"No, Mom. Ev-everything's fine," I stuttered between cries. "I just, I just miss home."

Vince forcefully ripped the phone out of my hand and whipped it toward his mouth.

"We're working at some stupid hotel! What the heck, Mom? When were you going to tell us *that*? Or should I ask what else you've got planned, huh?" he screamed into the receiver.

I wrestled the phone away from him and softly returned it to my ear. My mom was talking at warp speed on the other end. It sounded like she was apologizing, but it really didn't matter what she was saying. I just wanted to hear her voice.

Chapter 17

It was more of an expanded bed-and-breakfast than a hotel. The small building was located near the University of Puerto Rico Utuado campus and catered mostly to traveling locals or visiting relatives. There were twelve clean, but not very fancy guest rooms (a couple shared the same bathroom) and, as Lilly promised, there was a bar on the first floor. In Philly it would be considered a rather seedy dive bar, but in Utuado it seemed fairly standard with its wood-paneled walls and smell of stale beer. The entire establishment consisted of about a dozen tables, a pool table and a porch used solely for playing dominos. They served one type of beer, an island favorite called Medalla Light, a couple flavors of the locally distilled rum, and some light snacks cooked by my Aunt Carmen.

But none of this prepared me for the bar's *baño*, which made most highway rest stops look like the Four Seasons. First off, there was no toilet. Second, there was no sink. There was a waist-high wooden shelf with a drain in the center. The occupant was simply expected to pee in the drain. It didn't flush, because it didn't need to. It was like urinating in a gutter. Next to the shelf was a metal spigot (that back home would normally be connected to a gardening hose), and using the water from it you could rinse your hands. The water, of course, was swallowed by the same drain in which you just peed. So, mentally, you either just peed in the sink or washed your hands in the toilet.

Lilly laughed hysterically when I ran out screaming and holding my nose.

"Sorry, I couldn't resist! You should see your face." She giggled. "Only the old guys use that bathroom. There's another one, I swear!"

She took us on a brief tour of the hotel, including the bathroom in the lobby, which wasn't luxurious but it at least had a toilet—that flushed. Then she informed me that I would be working at the front desk. I immediately deemed myself important and assumed the title of "concierge." I set up my post behind the desk, alphabetized a list of local menus and memorized a few catch phrases: *"¿Hace mucho calor, verdad?"* I doubted I would need to know many other weather statements (it's a tropical island; it's always hot). Vince was a bellhop. Being that there were only twelve guest rooms and the hotel was never filled to capacity, it didn't seem as though either of us would have much to do. This fact left Vince sulking on a wooden stool in the corner of the lobby watching Spanish soap operas (of which he could not understand a single word). One hour into our four-hour shift and he was already trying to talk me into ditching.

"Seriously, Mariana, you're getting on my nerves. We have nothing to do! I say we just leave. Uncle Miguel probably won't even notice."

"Vince, it's a job! He's expecting us to be here," I huffed. "Man, you really don't have a single responsible bone in your body. What the heck are you going to do at Cornell next year?"

"I'm going to pledge a fraternity and drink a lot."

"Yeah, that'll go over big with Dad. I dare you to fail out. Really, I do. I would love to see what happens. Truthfully, I think it would be justifiable homicide on Dad's part."

"I'm not gonna fail out. Not everyone has to obsess about things the way you do."

"I don't obsess."

"Oh, my God!" Vince shouted, rising from his stool and crossing the room to the desk I was standing behind. "You are the queen of obsessive. Seriously, how long did you whine about missing Madison's party? And have you stopped thinking about home once since we got here?"

"That doesn't mean I'm obsessed. That means I have a life at home worth missing. Sorry if you can't say the same!"

"Oh, please! I've got a life. I just don't mope around crying about it all day. . . ."

"You know, Vince, shut up!" I yelled, cutting him off and slamming my hands on the front desk.

"It's the truth!"

"You're such a jerk!"

"Brat!"

"What are you two screaming about? I can hear you from upstairs," Lilly said, as she bounded down the steps carrying a white plastic laundry basket brimming with sheets.

Apparently she'd been working at the hotel since she was twelve, which I found rather odd since there are laws against that sort of thing. Regardless, I got the distinct impression that she used to work the front desk, but since she lives in Utuado, and thus is not treated with the same polite "visitor" gloves that we were, she was tasked with laundry duty for the duration of the summer. Part of me felt guilty that she was now stripping beds, but I also had no desire to take on that responsibility . . . so, given the situation, I thought I could deal with the guilt.

"Sorry," I mumbled, still glaring at my brother.

"Lilly, when can we get out of here?" Vince asked.

The boy truly had no tact.

"Actually, I'm pretty much done," she said, dropping the basket on the white tiled floor. "Lemme just throw this stuff in the washer and we can head out."

"What? How? Who's gonna watch the place if we go?" I insisted.

It was my first real day of employment and it didn't feel right to walk out before the end of my shift.

"I'll just tell my grandfather we're getting lunch. Trust me, he won't expect us back and he really won't care," she said, as she lifted the laundry basket off the floor and rested it on her hip. "I'll be right back."

I frowned at Vince the moment she disappeared from sight.

"I can't believe you're doing this."

"Doing what?"

"Ditching work on the first day. We've been here for what, thirty-six hours? And you're already causing trouble."

"I'm not causing trouble. Lilly said it was okay." His eyes contorted like he was incapable of comprehending my point of view. "Mariana, this may come as a shock, but in this situation, on this island, with *her* relatives, Lilly may know a little more about 'right' and 'appropriate' than you do."

I dropped my head to stare at the black Formica-topped desk. He had a point, though I refused to admit it. I scanned the registry; there were only three rooms occupied and I had already watched all three guests exit the hotel for the day. If we stayed, we'd just be babysitting an empty lobby and my Uncle Miguel probably knew that, which could be why he was so lenient about Lilly ditching.

"Fine," I muttered.

"All right, you guys ready to go?" Lilly cheered as she hopped back up the steps from the basement laundry room.

"Absolutely!" Vince replied. "So what do you wanna do? I was hoping we could go into Old San Juan, or maybe go to the beach? But really I'm up for anything you feel like. Do you have a car?"

"Well, I can't drive. But you can, right?" she asked Vince, who nodded. "Because we can take my grandmom's car. One of my friends is having her *Quinceañera* tonight. The reception is at this place in San Juan. I already spoke to her and she said it's cool if I bring you guys. There are already gonna be, like, two hundred people there. And I figured we could go into San Juan now and just hang out for a bit."

"Awesome!"

"You guys have something nice to wear?"

"Totally," Vince responded. "Mariana, how long will it take you to get ready? You're not gonna shower again, are you?"

That was the last thing I wanted to do. I sorely missed my white marble tub back home with the white fluffy towels and gardenia-scented candles. It radiated spa-like peace—unlike my current accommodations, which made me want to sprint to the nearest hotel (not my uncle's hotel, of course). When *Señora* Sanchez walked in without knocking this morning and peed midway through my shower, I almost lost it. She didn't even flush the toilet.

But that wasn't what was holding me back from Lilly's proposed plans.

"I'm not going," I mumbled, while staring at my feet.

"What? You are *so* not staying here," Vince ordered.

"Well, I'm not crashing some stranger's party."

"Mariana, really it's not like that. I already spoke to her. She invited you," Lilly insisted.

"Look, if some strangers just showed up at Madison's party, she'd be pissed. I'm not going to do that."

"Who's Madison?" Lilly asked.

"It's her stupid friend from home!" Vince shouted. "I can't believe you're going to let them dictate your plans from across the ocean."

"I'm not! It's just tacky, Vince. *Quinceañeras* are a big deal. You don't just show up the day-of uninvited."

"You *are* invited," Lilly repeated.

"The girl's a complete stranger. I'm sorry, Lilly. Thanks for trying, but no," I insisted.

"Then what the heck are you going to do all day?" Vince asked.

"I was thinking I could just hang out on my laptop for a while, write some e-mails. Do you know a place where I can get Internet access?"

I refused to look at Vince while I said this because I knew he was going to flip out. I was doing exactly what he was accusing me of—refusing to make a new life for myself here.

"You are so lame! I can't believe you're going to spend the summer on your freakin' computer whining to your friends from home. News flash, Mariana: They're not sitting at home obsessing over you. Emily and Madison—they're out right now. They're having fun," Vince harped.

He may have thought he was persuading me, but all he succeeded in doing was further emphasizing my need to connect with my girlfriends. I didn't want them to forget about me. I didn't want to be excluded from their lives. At least if I could talk to them regularly, if only on the computer, I'd still be in the loop. I wouldn't miss *everything*.

"Look, you guys do what you want to do. And I'll do what I want to do. *I* want to go to an Internet café. Lilly, is there one around here?" I asked, firmly.

Lilly looked at my brother. He shrugged his shoulders and rolled his eyes.

"Uh, yeah. There's one down the street from here, near the library. I'll take you there."

"No, I can find it myself." I grabbed my black laptop bag, which I had brought from the house, thinking that the hotel had Internet access (I seriously needed to remember I wasn't in Spring Mills anymore), and headed for the door.

"It's two blocks down on the left," Lilly instructed, her eyes darting between me and my brother.

I could tell she was waiting for him to stop me, but I knew he wouldn't. My mind was made up and Vince knew that.

"See you guys. Have fun," I stated as the glass door to the hotel swung behind me.

I looked out at the strangers on the sidewalk. It was the middle of the day, one o'clock. Madison was probably lounging by Emily's pool right now, smeared in SPF 4, complaining about how some new tragedy was threatening to ruin her Sweet Sixteen. I could visualize the entire scene down to the pitcher of overly sweetened iced tea. Only every time I did, I saw myself beside them. Where I was supposed to be. Where I wanted to be.

Chapter 18

I sat at the Internet café alone. Lilly and Vince had jetted off to San Juan together. It was clear that Lilly might look like me, but she definitely acted like my brother. The two of them were perfectly suited for each other. They were probably getting ready right now to whoop it up at this Puerto Rican fiesta, thankful that I didn't tag along and ruin it.

I logged on to Instant Messenger and almost cried when I saw Emily's screen name. A message quickly popped on my screen. They were hanging out at Emily's house, sunbathing by her pool just like I thought. They said they kept the computer running just in case I tried to contact them. They missed me.

EMBOT: Hey, Spic! It's Madison. How's island life? Ya tan yet?

(I glanced over my shoulder to make sure no one could see my screen. Somehow having the word "spic" displayed in a Spanish-speaking environment seemed wrong. I was almost embarrassed.)

MARIRUIZ: I've been here, like, a day. I'm as white as when I left.

EMBOT: And you'll be that white when you get back. You don't tan.

MARIRUIZ: No, I don't.

EMBOT: So what's it like there?

MARIRUIZ: Sux. Everyone speaks Spanish.

EMBOT: What'd ya expect?

MARIRUIZ: I dunno. Whatev. There's one girl, some cousin named Lilly, who speaks English. But it's freaky. She looks just like me.

EMBOT: Shut up! Really?

MARIRUIZ: Yeah.

EMBOT: Like you've found your twin in the world?

MARIRUIZ: Not exactly, sort of.

EMBOT: Well, it's cool you have someone to talk to.

MARIRUIZ: I guess, but aside from the red hair we're crazy different. Get this, she and Vince are crashing some girl's birthday party right now.

EMBOT: What! OMG! I would freak if someone did that to me! Hello, Gayle's been working on this seating chart for months!

MARIRUIZ: I know! I mean, the birthday girl's a friend of Lilly's. But it's not like she knows us. I'm not just gonna show up there uninvited.

EMBOT: Well, of course you wouldn't, because you have class.

MARIRUIZ: I know. So how are the Sweet Sixteen plans going?

EMBOT: It's nuts. Can you believe Gayle's trying to get me to do a cake that's shaped like shoes? She's so trying to ditch my LV purse idea. And she wouldn't even make the shoes Manolos, like whatever. I'm not having a Payless Shoe birthday cake!

MARIRUIZ: Seriously. I wish I could be there!

EMBOT: And check this out—Emily's got a date with your locker buddy Bobby!

MARIRUIZ: *My* locker buddy? I thought he was going to some film thing in Dublin.

EMBOT: Mari, it's me, Em. I can't believe Mad told you that, it's not a big deal. We're going to some indie-film downtown.

MARIRUIZ: OMG! That's a real date!

EMBOT: Don't say that! He leaves in two weeks for Dublin so I don't want to read too much into it.

It was already starting. I had only been gone a day, and already Emily was going on her first real date and I wasn't there to share it with her. They tried to downplay it for my benefit, and the two of them repeatedly told me how much they missed me. I wanted to believe them, and I might have been able to convince myself it were true if they hadn't dropped the major bombshell—Orlando Bloom was in Philadelphia shooting an action flick and Madison's dad's coworker had a connection with a casting director in town. He was getting them both roles as extras in a Hollywood feature film. They were going to spend at least three days on a movie set, in scenes *with* Orlando, and they were going to get their hair and makeup done by professional makeup artists.

It took every ounce of self-control I had not to smash my head against my laptop repeatedly. I knew that if I were a true friend, I would have put aside any feelings of jealousy and have felt nothing but joy for their good fortune. After all, it wasn't their fault. Only my brain suddenly shifted to an image of me sticking sharp pins in a Voodoo figure of my father. For fifteen years, nothing had happened in Spring Mills. The most exciting person to visit was a senator who spoke at our school, and that was only because he was the uncle of one of the students in our class. He was sixty years old and fat. He was no Orlando Bloom.

To make matters worse, after dropping the news, my bestest buds told me they had to go because their pizza had arrived and they wanted to have time to eat before they "practiced for their scenes." From the way they were typing, I almost thought they were getting their own trailers. The shoot wasn't for another couple of days, but of course they couldn't ditch me fast enough so they could focus on it and not have to worry about lonely old me—the big downer.

I clicked off my computer. It was only two o'clock. That gave me the rest of the day to do nothing but seethe at my misfortune. I trudged back to the house. When I got there, Lilly's mom and my Aunt Carmen were arguing over the clippings in the *Quinceañera* book. I couldn't understand a word they were saying, but after months of watching Madison go at it with her mom over her Sweet Sixteen, I had a pretty good idea. I stood at the doorway watching, not wanting to intrude, until my Aunt Carmen saw me, jumped up and ran to the stove.

She said something that I thought translated into "dinner in an hour," so I nodded and smiled.

There were two things I could do here: I could go into my bedroom and hide until I was called to dinner, or I could volunteer my help for the party. Lilly might not be into details, but with all the time I had spent around Madison lately, I pretty much was an expert in them.

"*Señora* Sanchez?" I asked tentatively.

"*¡Angelica! ¡Por favor!*" she corrected.

"*Sí, sí,* Angelica. *¿Um, esta es para la Quinceañera, verdad?*"

After that I understood the words "yes" and "Lilly," but then my cousin went off on a rant that I wasn't even sure I could have followed if I did speak Spanish fluently. I walked over, sat down and grabbed the magazine she was holding. She was looking at dresses. I had a feeling that this was where all those countless hours in boutique dressing rooms with Madison were about to pay off.

I grabbed the stack of magazines and after a lengthy effort on everyone's part, I was able to finally communicate that fifteen-year-old teenagers don't want to look like fairy princesses, they want to look like women. I threw out all of the lacy, tutu-like, long-sleeved, puffy-shouldered dresses that Angelica was keeping photos of in the binder. And after more than an hour of analyzing every picture available, I was able to find one that I thought would be acceptable and flattering on Lilly's rather curvaceous fourteen-year-old figure. It was pink, most were, with one-inch wide straps that went over her shoulders and crossed in the back. It had a fitted bodice that would show some cleavage, but not too much, and a dropped waist that flowed into a nice, smooth silhouette (nothing Cinderella-like). It took quite a long time for us to have this conversation, but by the end of it Angelica cried with happiness and I was rather proud of myself for having conducted an entire conversation in Spanish—no matter what the topic or how long it took.

By the time we were finished, dinner was ready and the table was set. My poor great aunt must have been so offended by my not eating her overabundance of food the night before that she went out of her way to cook me a special dinner—a plain chicken breast with fried plantains. Around the table sat Uncle Miguel, Angelica and her husband Juan, Alonzo and his friend José (who I recognized from the night before as the guy helping Alonzo with my luggage). I got the impression that Alonzo and José might be roommates because they arrived at the house in the same car and ate off each other's plates. Aside from me, everyone else dined on a mountain of yellow rice and roasted pork.

I never told Aunt Carmen I preferred plain foods. She must have studied my plate last night and figured it out, which was something I would have done if I were in her shoes.

★ ★ ★

I went to bed early, only I couldn't sleep. I never had insomnia, but tossing around endlessly was the worst form of torture I could imagine at the moment. I remained wide awake at two o'clock in the morning, thinking about Madison and Emily and Orlando Bloom, when the front door to the house crashed open. I heard Lilly and Vince barrel in, hysterically laughing and knocking over a chair in the living room. They sounded drunk, which shocked me since they were coming from a fifteen-year-old's birthday party. I couldn't imagine getting drunk at Madison's Sweet Sixteen, let alone at some quasi-religious birthday celebration in front of family members. But either Lilly didn't think her state of mind was a big deal or she was too wasted to mask her condition, because she was talking so loudly that her parents' door slammed open.

Angelica's voice boomed at her daughter like a foghorn. I couldn't make out every word. (Really, I only understood the curses and that's because back in Spring Mills, all the boys in my class made a concerted effort to learn how to curse in Spanish). My brother and Lilly instantly fell silent—their only defense. I was pretty sure breathing their alcohol-laced breath and slurring rebuttals was not going to get them anywhere, and I was rather impressed that even in their drunken state they realized that too.

After several minutes of screaming, a fit that would have made my father proud, Lilly's mom was satisfied. I heard her tiny feet charge down the hallway and her bedroom door slam shut. A few moments later, Lilly and Vince were whispering outside my door.

"So, uh, what was she so pissed about?" Vince asked. Clearly, he hadn't understood a single word Lilly's mother had shouted.

"Uh, we're drunk, stumbling in at two o'clock in the morning and we left my grandma's car in San Juan." She hiccupped. "Like your dad would be any cooler, Vince?"

"It's VICEN-TAY," he corrected with a chuckle.

"Oh, I forgot, your Puerto Rican alter ego."

(I rolled my eyes when I heard this.)

"Whatever." Vince burped. "Dude, I had a blast."

"Good, now if you can only get Mariana to hang out with us then maybe I wouldn't get in so much freakin' trouble. . . ," Lilly mumbled.

I quickly sat up when I heard my name. I had never actually overheard anyone discussing *me* before. While I assumed girls from home probably talked about me behind my back (girls talk about everyone), I had never listened to a live conversation about myself. My stomach knotted as I concentrated on their voices.

"What? Why's Mariana getting you in trouble?"

"Because my parents made this big deal out of me hanging out with her while she's here. I'm supposed to include her in my plans and, you know, be friends with her."

"Good luck with that."

My mouth hung open. My brother had sold me out. Here was this girl, a virtual stranger, telling him she was forced to put up with my presence and he just agrees with her. He didn't even defend me! I felt my temperature (which was already peaking due to the sweltering, unair-conditioned bedroom) reach a new high.

"I know, but what's her deal? She's so uptight," Lilly snipped.

"Seriously, Mariana's cool. She's just kinda stubborn. She'll come around. Eventually she'll get bored enough to hang out with us," Vince stated, not offering me very much redemption.

"Well, I hope she does soon. Otherwise, I'll be spending my summer grounded, and that's the last thing I need. I know she's your sister and all, but she needs to lighten up."

I heard Lilly's voice fade as she said good night to my brother. She was headed to her bedroom. I dropped back on the mattress, curled on my side and hastily pulled the sheet up over my head. Vince turned the doorknob and staggered into our room moments later. He called my name once, but I pretended to be asleep.

Chapter 19

For the next two weeks I didn't say more than a few words to Lilly. We'd go to work at the hotel, eat dinner at the same table, watch TV on the same couch and all the while I'd pretend not to see her.

"Mariana, want to go into Old San Juan? We can sightsee, go to El Morro," Lilly would suggest.

"Nope," I'd reply curtly.

"Want to go out to dinner tonight? I can take you to some of the cool local places."

"I'd rather not."

"Maybe we could go to the beach? I have a friend who can get us into The Ritz-Carlton's beach."

"I don't feel like it."

Every time I rejected her plans, she was forced to stay home. It was clear from the glaring looks of her mother that Lilly was not allowed to go out without me. And I had to hand it to the girl, she was trying her hardest to persuade me to leave the house. She must have suggested everything from a road trip to the El Yunque Rain Forest to bingo at the local church to get my butt in gear. But I had no intention of appeasing her. I was perfectly content to stay home and read a book from the library or sit at the Internet café chatting with my girlfriends. Lilly, however, was not so content, and I loved watching her squirm as her mother forced *Quinceañera* plans down her throat.

Last night, they actually spent an hour sifting through photos of what looked like Barbie dolls dressed in *Quinceañera* dresses. Apparently the doll was to be presented during the reception to symbolize the perfection of the day, which would have been sweet if the entire concept didn't make Lilly want to poke needles in her eyes. The party was in less than a week, and unbeknownst to Lilly, I spent almost every afternoon lately poring over party details in the kitchen with her mom while Lilly was stripping beds at the hotel.

Angelica had taken quite a liking to me and was pulling me out of work as much as Uncle Miguel would permit. We got along great with the exception of our significantly dense language barrier and our drastically different tastes in fashion. I was never into clothes or makeup, but I didn't live in a bubble. I knew what was in style. I just preferred my baggy clothes and undyed hair, but that didn't mean my jeans weren't expensive and that my shampoo wasn't from a salon. Angelica, however, was a "more is more" kind of woman. Her hair was bleached blond and shellacked into a low ponytail that looked almost painful. Her faced was covered in countless layers of colorful makeup that implied electric blue eyeliner was still all the rage in Utuado. Her tops were tight and all her pants were at least two inches too short.

So when it came to selecting matching jewelry for Lilly's *Quinceañera* dress, we crashed heads immediately. She actually wanted Lilly to wear yellow gold. It was as if the woman was trapped in a time warp. No one's worn yellow gold in at least a decade unless it was intentionally kitschy. Just the thought of clashing yellow gold against a pale pink dress would have given Madison night sweats. Of course, I couldn't actually say any of this. I couldn't really say much of anything in Spanish, except for "no, no, no."

I knew Angelica couldn't afford any high-priced bling (she was sewing Lilly's dress herself), but that didn't mean we had to sacrifice good taste. With enough care I was able to point her toward some delicate pieces that would complement the dress and not look cheap. When we finally settled on the white gold locket, I thought I was going to tear with joy.

The only *Quinceañera* aspect I didn't touch was the menu. My Aunt Carmen seemed to have that taken care of. She was actually going to cook for all one hundred and twenty-two guests herself, with no catering staff. I didn't even think that was humanly possible. And from the way she was frantically running around the house these past few days, I was wondering if it really was.

None of this changed the fact that I was still mad at Lilly for talking behind my back. I wasn't doing any of this for her. I was doing it for Madison. If I couldn't partake in her Sweet Sixteen planning extravaganza, I could at least commiserate by sharing party details of my own. Madison loved hearing all about the tiaras and the "court." Lilly had fourteen friends participating in her celebration, which was apparently typical for *Quinceañera*s, but I still found it a little excessive (even for a bridal party). Angelica assured me that the number was supposed to be symbolic with Lilly being the "fifteenth" member of the court. But still, I wouldn't want a bunch of acquaintance-friends to share in my day just to bulk up the numbers.

Regardless, neither Vince nor Lilly knew I was doing any of this. I told them I was "helping around the house" every time I left work, not that Vince would have noticed.

He quickly made his own way in the world as "*Vicente*," with no need for me or Lilly. He was going out every night (with no effect on Lilly's homebound status), hanging mostly with Lilly's dad, Juan, our cousin Alonzo, and their friends. He'd slug beers and pretend he understood what they were saying (he was *Vicente*, after all). For a kid with only two years of Spanish under his belt, he was learning the language rather quickly. At the hotel the other day, I heard him give a guest directions to a local restaurant. His grammar wasn't perfect, but he got his point across. I found it annoying.

On the fifteenth day of my Lilly boycott, Angelica was busy finishing "the dress." The party was in two days and Lilly was refusing to be fitted. She told her mom to just sew it and put it on a hanger. She'd put it on the day-of. She didn't care. This clearly sent her mother into a panic-stricken frenzy and left me stuck behind the hotel's front desk for the day. We had only four guests, and they were all out. So I snatched my dust rag and swept it over the desk for the tenth time. I refused to skip out of work early, even though I knew that's what Lilly and Vince wanted. Despite all the effort I was putting into her party, I still hadn't forgiven her for saying I was "uptight" and ruining her summer. At the very least, she should apologize.

"You know, there's a theater in San Juan that plays movies that aren't dubbed in Spanish. Wanna go? There's a listing in the paper. I could go get it if you want."

Vince, who was sitting on his usual stool watching Spanish soaps, quickly turned toward me, his eyebrows raised. My glance shot between the two of them. I blew a puff of air from my cheeks and tilted my head.

"I don't like movies," I snipped.

Vince immediately jumped from his stool, charged toward me and grabbed my arm. He dragged me by my arm from the lobby into the bar, and pushed me toward a wooden stool.

"Sit!" he ordered.

"What's with you?" I asked, rubbing my arm as I perched my butt on the ripped leather cushion.

"What's with *me*? What's with *you*?" Vince tossed his hands in the air.

"Nothing, I'm fine," I defended, still rubbing my arm and refusing to look up at him.

"You are? Then why won't you hang out with Lilly?"

"Maybe I don't want to." I looked up and cocked my head to the side.

"Mariana, you're acting like a three-year-old. This isn't like you. What the heck do you have against Lilly? She's trying to be nice to you."

"Yeah, sure she is. And exactly how nice is she behind my back?" I asked, shaking my head and tossing my auburn hair over my shoulder.

"What are you talking about?" Vince took a few steps back.

"Vince, I heard you guys come home the night of that party. I heard you talking outside the door about how I'm 'uptight' and 'stubborn' and how she *has to* be friends with me because her parents are *forcing her*. She's not being nice, she just doesn't want to be grounded." I spat out the words.

"She *is* nice and you would know that if you hung out with her. Maybe if you started acting like yourself, like a normal person, you guys could actually *be* friends."

"How can I be friends with someone who would trash me behind my back, to my own brother, after knowing me for less than a day?"

"I wasn't trashing you," Lilly stated as she walked into the bar.

Her voice was calm and her posture perfect as she glided over. Her ease shocked me. Here she was, walking into an argument, an argument about her, and she seemed completely unfazed. She even looked confident.

She stopped a few feet in front of me and sucked in a long breath.

"When my parents found out you guys were coming, of course they wanted me to be friends with you both. It makes sense, we all live in the same house, we're all close to the same age."

"Lilly, I *heard* you. This nice routine of yours is just an act so you don't end up grounded like you said."

"Well, maybe if you loosened up, maybe if *for once* you actually tried to have fun, you'd find out that Puerto Rico, Utuado, the place I live, doesn't suck all that much."

"I never said it sucked," I mumbled.

And it was true, I hadn't—but I had thought it. It suddenly struck me how offended I'd be if some stranger visited me and criticized Spring Mills after just a few days.

"You didn't have to," Lilly shot back, running her hand through her auburn hair. "It's all over your face every time you look around our house or talk about your friends from home. So my family's not rich, and my *Quinceañera* isn't going to be this big blow-out like the Sweet Sixteen you're missing 'back in Spring Mills.' But that doesn't mean we're losers."

"I don't think that. I don't."

I looked at Lilly for several moments, saying nothing.

"So, whatever, can we, like, end this? All be friends now?" Vince asked.

What a typical guy. Everything was so simple to him. Guys fought, made up, moved on. Sometimes I envied the simplicity in which they lived.

Lilly and I stood in silence.

"So, can we get out of here? Go to the beach or something?" Vince asked, looking at me with hope in his eyes.

"Fine," I said, nodding. "But I want to stop at the Internet café first."

"Mariana!" Vince cried.

"What? I want to check my e-mail. Madison's party is tomorrow. I'm sorry, but it's her birthday and it's important to me."

"Errr," he growled, rolling his eyes.

"Whatever, it's fine," Lilly stated.

I followed them out of the hotel moments later, my laptop bag on my shoulder. We weren't exactly the three musketeers, but it was the first time the three of us had ever left work together. The first time we'd ever done anything together.

Chapter 20

The Internet café was never crowded. Most of the time I was the only person in it. It was a small beige room with large desktop computer terminals against three walls, and round tables scattered throughout for laptop customers. In the corner was a coffee bar that also sold snacks and sandwiches (every sandwich included ham, don't ask me why but it was an extremely popular meat product in Puerto Rico). At night the café doubled as a bar, selling beer to local students from the University of Puerto Rico—they called it "UPR," which I liked because it sounded familiar. It reminded me of "UPenn" or "PSU."

I sat down on an orange plastic chair at a small table a few feet behind Lilly and Vince, who both logged on to desktops. I could see that Vince was checking the Phillies' stats. Vince was an all-star first baseman in Spring Mills. He was recruited to play for Cornell, though he denies that being why he got in. I logged on to my e-mail and saw one message from Madison and Emily, which was odd. They usually sent me at least two per day. The message was marked "urgent" and the subject was "We're famous!" I quickly clicked it open.

What up, Spic!

Madison here. We just finished our first day of filming with Orlando Bloom!!! It was soooo awesome! I can't even describe it in an e-mail. But let me tell you, he's so much hotter in person. And I spoke to him! I was stalking him all day and when I saw him go over to the snack tables, I pounced. We both reached for the same water bottle and for a second, our hands touched—flesh to flesh. I *felt* Orlando Bloom! I told him I thought he was doing an amazing job in his scenes and he thanked me, asked my name, and wished me luck with my acting. He thinks I'm an actress!!!! I can't believe Orlando Bloom knows I exist in the world. But that's not even the best news. It turns out he's staying at the Rittenhouse Hotel—he's going to be there when I have my Sweet Sixteen tomorrow. Gayle's sending his assistant an invitation. Orlando Bloom might be at my Sweet Sixteen!!!! I can't believe it!

Anyway, Emily's sitting next to me and she's freaking out because she wants me to tell you our other *big* news. So here it is—we're going to be interviewed live on the radio!!! Eagle 102FM was at the set today and they want to do a bit on their morning show about what it's like to be an extra. They asked Em and me to come down to the station for an interview!!! We have to be there at, like, six in the morning, but whatev, that'll give me plenty of time to get ready for my party. We're going to be on the radio! How cool is that? You have to tune in. They're going to air it live and you can listen to it on their Web site tomorrow at 6:30 A.M. You better listen!

Love ya!

The soon-to-be famous Hollywood Divas,
Mad and Em

I almost puked all over my laptop. There wasn't a single particle of my being that was happy for them. I knew that was wrong, I knew that I was a terrible friend, but that didn't stop me from wishing the set of that movie would spontaneously combust. Only that would probably make them more famous, *"We were there when Orlando almost died . . ."* I could already see it.

"This is unbelievable!" I yelled. "I'm missing everything!"

I slammed my laptop closed and shoved my fingers into my frizzy hair (the humid climate really wasn't agreeing with the curls I usually tried to suppress).

"What? What happened?" Vince asked, swiveling around in his chair.

"Emily and Madison are in a movie with Orlando Bloom. They're getting interviewed on the radio, *and* they're inviting him to her Sweet Sixteen!"

"Seriously?" he asked, his eyes popping.

"Yes!"

"Wow, that's really cool."

"Shut up!"

Lilly chuckled quietly from her seat next to Vince.

"What are you laughing at?" I yelled.

"Nothing. Sorry," Lilly mumbled. "These are your friends?"

"Yeah, my *best* friends. But it doesn't look like they're missing me much."

"I told you they weren't going to sit around crying over you," Vince said. "That's why you need to go out. And you'll have to do something *big* if you're gonna top Orlando Bloom at her birthday party."

"I can't believe this. I don't even want to think about it," I said, shaking my head. "He's not going to go. He can't go. He's a movie star. He's got better things to do. But still, they're in his movie and they're gonna be on the radio and her party's tomorrow! I'm missing everything!"

"I say we get out of here. Let's do something!" Vince suggested, jumping from his plastic chair.

"I don't want to." I sighed, closed my eyes and dropped my head back.

"What's wrong with you?" he yelled. "Do you hear yourself?"

"I just don't feel like going out. My life sucks."

"Mariana, you've been sulking for weeks now and it's getting annoying. You don't have to be depressed and miserable in order to be loyal to your friends. They're not doing that for you."

"Vince, I'm not in a good mood."

"No kiddin'. That's why you need to go out. Let's go to San Juan or something." Vince flicked a glance at Lilly.

"That'd be cool," she added.

"Come on, it'll be fun," he wheedled.

"No, I don't want to. Besides, I need to get up early tomorrow to hear their interview and send Madison an e-card before her party."

"Are you freakin' kidding me? You're scheduling your life around them? They're *not* here!"

"I know, Vince, that's the point. Being in a movie, hanging out with Orlando Bloom, that's a big deal. I *want* to hear it. I want to be a part of it somehow," I said, shrugging my shoulders.

"You're being ridiculous."

"I don't care what you think."

"You should."

"Why? Because your judgment is so great? Please! How long did you know Dad knew about that party you threw?" I asked, slapping my hands on the table.

I had debated the whole flight over whether I should bring up Dad's little surprise comment at the airport. At the time, it seemed pointless. I was going to Puerto Rico. My life was ruined. Nothing was going to change that outcome. Plus, I didn't have the energy to fight with him. But in this moment, with my brother being all self-righteous like he knew what was best for me, I couldn't help but throw it in his face. Just because we were in Puerto Rico, didn't mean our entire lives in Spring Mills were wiped clean. He wasn't any more mature or responsible now than he was then.

"I don't want to talk about that," he said.

"I know you don't. Because apparently your bright idea to throw a party last year is what kept you from Europe this summer, isn't it? And it's what's keeping me from Madison's party!"

"Shut up, Mariana."

"No, 'cause I'm right. Dad found out about the party and punished you by not letting you go to Europe with your friends. Then he punished me by forcing me to come here and babysit *you*."

"Oh, really! Now who's being forced into doing things by their parents?" Lilly shouted, rising from her chair. "You got pissed at me because you thought my parents were forcing me to hang out with you and there you were, forced to come here by *your* parents. Gee, thanks."

I looked at Vince and swallowed hard. I didn't know what to say. I sort of forgot she was there.

"Nice going, Mariana," Vince snapped.

"Oh, don't change the subject. Point is, Dad busted you for the party and that's why we're here. No offense to you, Lilly, but this whole trip wasn't exactly my idea."

"Yeah, that's a surprise," she droned.

"Oh, please! Don't you have a party to plan?" I asked Lilly, my eyebrows raised. "Your *Quinceañera* is in *two days*, your mom has been going absolutely bonkers, your grandmom has been cooking 'round the clock and you just want to go out for the evening?"

"Hey, this party wasn't exactly *my* idea. I wanted them to skip it and buy me a car. But, *noooo*. My mom insisted I couldn't 'back out on tradition.' She doesn't care what I want."

"Yeah, I know the feeling," Vince muttered.

"Exactly. You've got issues with your parents and I've got issues with mine."

"You know, this party's really important to your mom," I said.

"Yeah, and I'm sure coming to Puerto Rico was really important to your dad."

"Good point." I nodded.

"Look, let's forget all this. Are we going out or not?" Lilly shifted her brown eyes between the two of us.

"Yes."

"No."

Vince and I said in unison.

"How 'bout we just go to a movie? We won't even have to talk," Lilly noted.

Finally, I nodded and grunted, "fine."

It took another thirty minutes of arguing over action flick versus romantic comedy, but eventually we settled on a big budget thriller. We all went to the theater together and sat in silence.

Chapter 21

After the movie, I plunked down for another meal of chicken breast and plantains. I called it *"el usual."* Vince thought I was crazy for eating the same thing repeatedly, but it didn't bother me. Puerto Rican *mofongo* and *asopao* just wasn't my thing.

The fact that my aunt had time to make dinner amazed me. The house had become Ground Zero for the *Quinceañera*. Every surface in the kitchen was covered with a pot, pan, or foil-covered dish. I had never seen anyone make rice for one hundred and twenty-two people before, nor had I ever seen *"calderas"* large enough to conquer such a task. It was utter chaos. The air was so full of pepper and cilantro from the *sofrito* that I was fairly certain it would never be expunged from the fabrics in the house. Not to mention, the constant use of the oven and stove was doing nothing to help the sweltering temperatures. I couldn't stand in the kitchen for more than a minute without getting dizzy. The only one my aunt permitted to help with the cooking was Angelica—my Uncle Miguel and cousins Juan and Alonzo were busy trying to construct a tent on the recently machete-pruned lawn.

The party was in two days and the birthday girl, Lilly, was

downgraded to sleeping on the couch. Her room was now storage central. It was filled with party favors, dishes, table-cloths, folding tables and chairs, champagne flutes (plastic and glass), flatware, and centerpieces. Everything was so strategi-cally placed that if you pulled one item out, the room's entire contents would fall over. I had never been to a wedding at home, but I imagined the scene would be similar. I couldn't understand why anyone wouldn't prefer to leave all this mess up to the banquet staff at a hotel ballroom.

But despite the cooking, cleaning, sewing and landscaping, everyone still found time to sit down to dinner, together, and fight over the *pegao*. With the amount of Puerto Rican rice my aunt was cooking, there were plenty of crusty bottom rem-nants to go around. Even I ate some.

"You know, that movie was lame. I figured out the ending, like, halfway through," I noted between mouthfuls. "And I'm still surprised that it was in English."

"Puerto Rico *is* part of America," Lilly stated as she gulped down her water and dug her fork back into her plate.

"Not really," Vince mumbled.

"Yes, really," Lilly snipped.

"Anyway," I interjected. "Back in Spring Mills, you would really have to go out of your way to find a movie that wasn't in English."

"Well, this isn't Spring Mills." Lilly sighed. "So . . . what's the deal with this Sweet Sixteen you're missing?"

"It's for my best friend. It's going to be amazing. Every-one's going to be there."

"Except you."

"Pretty much."

"And you're really pissed at your dad."

"Pretty much. Are you still mad at your mom?" I whispered.

"No. How could I be? I'm not a complete brat. I realize she's been slaving away over this party. I just wish—"

"That she listened to you," I interjected.

"Exactly. So your friend's party is tomorrow; we must, like, have the same birthday," Lilly pointed out.

"No, her birthday isn't for another two weeks, but this is the only date she could get at the hotel, *and* it's a Friday. Madison freaked when she found out. It was a *huge* deal. You really don't want to hear it. But trust me when I say there's an event planner in Philadelphia who almost lost her life."

Lilly laughed. "Wow, event planners and hotels. You must think my party is pretty lame, huh?"

I didn't know how to answer that. Compared to Madison's, Lilly's party was a cheap knock-off. It would have all the glitz and glamour of my third-grade birthday party, and there certainly were not going to be any Orlando Bloom sightings. Given the choice, I would hop a plane back to Philadelphia in a heartbeat—but I didn't have a choice, that was the point.

"I'm sure your party's gonna be nice," I answered, staring at my plate.

"Uh-huh," Lilly said, with a half chuckle. "So, you dance, right?"

"That depends. Will there be ballet at your party?"

"I hope not," she quipped.

"Then I can't make any promises."

Back home, I was one of the best ballerinas in my company. But I never branched into other styles. My instructors always scorned me for lacking a dancer's "passion." The elevation of my jumps, the extension of my arms, the flexibility in my back couldn't be beat, but they said I "didn't *feel* the music." And they were probably right, given that I had no idea what "feeling" the music even meant.

Lilly paused for several seconds. It seemed like she was debating whether to ask me something.

Finally, she opened her mouth. "So you're missing a lot back home. Are you pissed that your friends are in that movie and you're not?"

"No, why would I be?" I stated a little too quickly.

"Well, because back at the café you sounded kinda of mad at them. . . ."

"I'm not mad, I just wish I could be in it too."

"So you're jealous."

"No, that's not what I'm saying."

"It's okay if you're jealous. Everyone gets jealous."

"I'm not jealous. I just miss them."

"Okay, fine. Do you think they miss you too?"

"Of course!"

The question was absurd. Of course they missed me. They'd cried at the airport. They wrote me tons of e-mails. I'm sure that they wished that I could be on the set with them, and that they were distraught that I was missing the big party. I knew they were thinking of me.

"So you're gonna listen to that radio thingy tomorrow morning?"

"Definitely."

"Can I come?" she asked, her eyes focused on her plate, which held only a few remnants of sauce from the food she'd scarfed down.

"You wanna come? But you don't even know them. And it's at six-thirty in the morning."

"It's okay if you don't want me to."

"No, no. It's fine. It'll be cool for you to hear their voices. You'll get to know them in a way."

"All right, it's a plan."

That night, Lilly and I sat on the porch staring at the big

white party tent, chatting and listening to the tiny frogs chirp. The green-and-brown coquis were only about an inch in size (I hadn't seen one, but I could hear thousands) and they sang through the darkness. I slept to the sound of the frogs every night. So far, it was my favorite thing about the island.

Chapter 22

We slid into the Internet café right as the sun was coming up. There was a twentysomething guy in a dirty red baseball hat snoring at one table and a brunette with a painfully tight ponytail behind the café bar, falling asleep on her arm. The minute we opened the door, she jumped like a gunshot had gone off.

"Sorry we scared you," I said in a hushed voice.

I didn't know why I whispered, it wasn't a library. It just felt impolite to speak loudly so early in the morning.

"We're gonna log on." I patted the laptop bag hanging from my shoulder.

The woman grunted and waved her hand, exposing the soppy sweat stain on the armpit of her T shirt. I cringed.

Lilly and I grabbed a round table near the front so we could benefit from the orangey light streaming from outside. The place only had one overhead—greenish—light illuminated, probably to keep the temperature of the room down. Like much of Utuado, the café was not air-conditioned.

We plopped into two hard, cheap, white plastic chairs and I immediately flipped my laptop open. We had five minutes until the interview. I raced to the radio station's brightly colored Web page, opened the media player on my laptop and waited until the live broadcast zoomed in with perfect clarity. I adjusted the volume.

"I didn't know you could listen to radio on the computer," Lilly whispered, her coffee breath hitting my nostrils.

Puerto Ricans were big on coffee. It was locally grown, very dark and very strong. My aunt and uncle always had a pot brewing, and Lilly had packed us a Thermos for the occasion. I had never really drunk it before (my parents didn't let me, they thought it would stunt my growth), but it wasn't too bad.

After a few minutes of the latest Top 40 hits, the DJ's voice emerged.

"All right, you're listening to Eagle 102. This is Larsky and the Crazy Crew and I'm here talking with two of the extras in the upcoming blockbuster *Full Count*."

I heard Madison and Emily's familiar giggles. I grabbed Lilly's forearm, stretched my eyes and smiled. At this hour of the day, with neither of us wearing any makeup and both of us with our auburn hair pulled into ponytails, it struck me yet again how much we resembled each other. The same freckles, the same cheekbones, the same small brown eyes. I still hadn't gotten used to it.

One of the DJ's co-hosts suddenly erupted into a booming laugh, and I shook my head and turned my attention back to the radio.

"So, girls, tell us your names, how old you are and where you're from."

"I'm Madison. I'm from Spring Mills. I'm fifteen, but my Sweet Sixteen is tonight!"

"I'm Emily. I'm also fifteen and from Spring Mills." (She laughed awkwardly as she said that. I could tell she was nervous. Her voice was shaky.)

"Now, you girls have spent three days on the set with Orlando Bloom as extras in his new movie. What was that like?"

"Omigod. It was so awesome. (It was clearly Madison
speaking.) Orlando's, like, super nice."

"Yeah, and he's really down to earth," Emily added.

"So did you girls actually meet the man himself? Did you
talk to Orlando?"

"Madison did," Emily huffed quickly.

"Yeah, Orlando came up to me at a snack table. He gave
me advice on my career and told me he thought I was doing a
great job. Orlando was really nice, like super-duper nice. We
had an instant connection. I think we, like, really hit it off."

(Wait, she didn't tell me that. First off, she said *she* stalked
him at the snack table. Second, she complimented his acting,
not the other way around. And third, since when are she and
"Orlando" on a first name basis?)

" 'Hit it off,' really? You saying there might be a little romance there?"

"Omigod. I dunno. I mean, he asked if he could come to
my Sweet Sixteen tonight. Everyone's gonna be there. But I
think he has a girlfriend. But maybe if they break up . . ." She
giggled.

Oh. My. God. My jaw swung low and I glared at Lilly. She
clearly didn't know how to react. As far as she knew, everything Madison said was true and this was an accurate represen-
tation of my best friend. Only it wasn't. Unless Madison had
turned into a pathological liar. I couldn't believe how she was
milking this.

"All right! You heard it here first. One of Philly's own
striking up a romance with a Hollywood heartthrob (I could
hear Madison and Emily laughing in that fake way they do in
front of teachers and parents).

"So girls, this is your first movie, right?"

"Yeah," they said in unison.

"Would you do it again? Would you recommend other people try their hand at being extras?"

"Absolutely! It was the best!" Emily squeaked, with a high-pitched voice.

"Totally. This has been, like, the best experience. And I can't wait for my party tonight. This break has been awesome. I wouldn't change a thing. Best summer ever!" Madison cheered.

After that, the DJ switched topics to a discussion about girls who cheated on their boyfriends and got caught. Only my mind was still reeling over Madison's last comments, "*I wouldn't change a thing. Best summer ever!*"

How could she not miss me at all? Wasn't there even a tiny part of her that thought: *Gee, I wish Mariana were here with us?* Apparently I was utterly replaceable—by some Hollywood hottie who'd probably forgotten she exists. I slammed my laptop closed, startling the guy in the baseball hat still sleeping at the table beside us.

"What's wrong?" Lilly asked.

I closed my eyes and blew out a puff of air.

"They were acting so fake. And none of that stuff was true. She totally exaggerated. I can't believe she would lie like that," I ranted.

Lilly said nothing.

"They made it all up. Like she and Orlando Bloom are seriously going to start dating? Does she really think he's gonna go to her party? She's such a liar," I continued rapidly, my hands flailing as I spoke.

"They're just trying to sound cool. It was their fifteen minutes of fame."

"Try their fifteen minutes of *fake.*"

"Dude, whatever, they suck," Lilly teased.

"But they don't," I whispered, my voice cracking.

"Look, they can make up stories all they want. But that just tells you that they're not *really* having fun, right?"

I closed my eyes, and took a few deep breaths. I wanted to believe Lilly, but I couldn't shake the feeling that I was being forgotten. Secretly (and I would never admit this), I had hoped that they would at least mention me on-air, give me a quick shout-out or something. So much for best friends.

"You know, you have *my* party tomorrow. Orlando Bloom might not be on the invite list, but it should still be fun," Lilly said.

I opened my eyes. She was right. I did have a party to go to. I had my own life.

Chapter 23

I woke up early the next morning, as usual. Only when I opened my bedroom door, I found the entire house bustling with pre-*Quinceañera* energy. Angelica was running down the hall in her nightgown, foam curlers secured to her hair. My Aunt Carmen was cursing at my uncle from behind her permanent place at the stove. Cousins Juan and Alonzo were hauling items into the outdoor tent. And Lilly was sitting at the kitchen table in a cotton robe, calmly sipping a cup of coffee.

"Wow." It was all I could think of to say.

"Exactly," she muttered. "Wow."

"I feel I should help out."

"Oh, don't even try," she said, her eyes wide. "They'll eat you for breakfast."

"Have they noticed that you're sitting here?"

"Well, my mom's yelled at me to get in the shower at least three times. The ceremony doesn't start for three hours. How long does she think it takes me to get ready?"

"For most girls, on a day like this, a while," I said, nodding. "Who's doing your hair?"

"My mother," she spat out.

I winced slightly.

"I know!" she yelled. "What am I gonna do? You know she's gonna plaster it in some three-foot-high beehive!"

"Maybe you could tell her you want to wear it down?" I suggested.

"I think she'll have a heart attack."

"Most likely." I nodded again. "So, have you seen your dress yet?"

"No, I'm saving it for last. I can't imagine what type of frothy pink nightmare my mom's sewn together. I'm just gonna smile and nod, smile and nod."

I still hadn't told Lilly that I had secretly helped plan her party, and that I had voiced an opinion on virtually every single detail. She might be flattered, or she might think I'm a total control freak psycho, especially since we weren't speaking half the time. Plus, if she didn't like the dress, I'd feel like the most worthless person ever. I'd have ruined her whole party.

Just then, Lilly's mom came barreling in screaming something in Spanish. Lilly immediately started yelling back, and then finally she groaned and stood up.

"I have to take a shower now," she choked through clenched teeth. She swallowed one last gulp of her coffee.

"Smile and nod, smile and nod," she repeated.

My Aunt Carmen was frantically stirring pots on the stove. She had every burner blazing along with the oven. Sweat poured down the back of her neck as she silently mumbled to herself incoherently. Despite being thirsty, I didn't think it safe to disturb her for a glass of water, so I strolled outside. The giant white party tent was fully constructed, draping from towering poles to the grass below. For a bunch of amateurs, the scene inside was rather impressive. Dozens of white round tables were set up with white folding chairs, a wooden dance floor was in place before a small stage, and a long head table stretched in front of two dozen chairs. People, who I assumed were relatives, were darting in every direction, hollering and pointing, and I seemed to be the only one without anything to do. My mother would be horrified if I didn't help out.

"Alonzo! Alonzo!" I yelled as I took off after him.

Alonzo was dashing between tables holding a stack of pink tablecloths. He screamed to his friend José, who was carefully arranging small bouquets of flowers in ceramic vases and ignoring his calls. Alonzo shook the tablecloths over his head, shouting *"Rosa! Rosa!"* repeatedly, which I knew either meant "pink" or "rose." José's flowers were yellow.

"Alonzo!" I shouted again.

"Hola, Mariana," he muttered, flicking a hand at me as he scurried off in the opposite direction.

Clearly he was busy, so I decided to offer my assistance to José.

"José! José!" I called as I rushed to where he was hunched over dozens of yellow and white flowers.

He didn't look up.

"José! *¿Necesitas ayuda?"*

He grunted, ignoring my offer to help, as he poured water into a vase.

"Es muy bonita," I added. I figured the compliment couldn't hurt. The scene *was* beautiful, but apparently that wasn't what he wanted to hear.

José swung his face toward me, babbling in Spanish at the top of his lungs and pointing at Alonzo.

"¡Bonita! ¡Bonita!" he hollered, wagging his finger in Alonzo's direction. He was speaking so quickly all I could catch were the words for colors, *"amarillo, rosa, blanco."* Alonzo, who was previously too preoccupied to notice my existence, caught José's rant from across the room. He charged over, waving a pink tablecloth over his head, his voice screeching.

If I didn't know better, I would have thought they were

professional event planners. They would have made Gayle proud.

"Lo siento," I mumbled, as I backed out of the way.

My Uncle Miguel rushed by me next, carrying a stack of ceramic plates close to his chest. For a man his age, I thought he probably shouldn't be given the heavy-lifting duties, so I jumped in front of him hoping to offer assistance. Instead, I succeeded in startling him. Uncle Miguel stumbled backward, the plates clanking as he adjusted his grip. He quickly caught his balance and gave me a stern, wide-eyed look. Lilly was right, they were going to eat me for breakfast.

After that, I trudged back to the house and found Vince seated at the kitchen table, slurping down a glass of juice.

"Dude, this place is nuts," I muttered.

"That's why I stay out of the way," he replied.

"Where's Aunt Carmen?" I asked, noticing the oddly vacant post beside the stove.

"No idea. She rattled off something at me in Spanish and then just ran off."

"Well, what'd she want?"

"No idea, something about the stove," Vince grumbled.

"What?" I shouted. "Vince, these burners are still on."

"So?"

"This food is still cooking! Where's Aunt Carmen?"

"I told you, I don't know."

"Vince, did she want you to do something with the food?"

"Mariana, I don't understand Spanish. She knows that, she wouldn't give me anything important to do."

"Vince, no one here is thinking clearly. José and Alonzo were ready to kill each other over the tablecloths!"

"She'll be back in a minute. Relax."

I stared at the simmering vats of soup and rice. There were

no lids and all of the pots were above a high fire. I had never cooked anything that didn't require a microwave. But even with my limited experience, I was fairly certain the soup was about to boil.

"Vince, what was Aunt Carmen doing with her hands? Do you think she was saying to turn off the burners? Like maybe when they start boiling?"

"Mariana, I have no idea," Vince grunted as he flipped through a newspaper.

"Wait, is that the shower running?" I asked, jerking my head toward my brother.

"Probably, it's been running all morning. There's gonna be a drought in Utuado tomorrow because of this stupid *Quinceañera.*"

"Vince, is *Aunt Carmen* in the shower?"

His head shot up. "No. She couldn't be."

"Everyone else has showered besides us. They've been up for hours. . . ."

"Oh, my God, the stove!" Vince yelled, jumping to his feet.

"That's what I'm saying!"

"No, Mariana!"

"What? Don't blame this on me!"

"No, turn around! The stove!"

I spun around to find soup frothing and boiling over the rim of the silver pot. It was flowing onto the stove, sizzling against the blue flames and splashing on the floor.

"What do we do?" I shouted.

"Turn it off!" Vince yelled.

"Which burner is it?"

A puddle of broth formed on the floor as more scalding liquid continued to erupt from the pot. Vince rushed over, a sneaker squeaking as it slid in the lake of yellow soup. I reached out to grab him, only the weight of his fall yanked me down with him. We both were stumbling to our feet, legs and arms flailing, soup dripping everywhere, when Aunt Carmen raced in.

"*¡Ay Dios mio!*" she screamed, her hands flicking toward her mouth. She zipped toward the food she'd been slaving away on for almost a week and swiftly spun all the burners off. She hoisted the cauldron of soup from the stove, and barked in Spanish at Vince and me. There were actual tears in her eyes.

I kept squealing, "Is it ruined? Is it ruined?"

But Aunt Carmen obviously didn't understand and just kept shrieking back in Spanish. Finally, the sounds of English emerged from the hallway.

"No, it's not ruined."

I swiveled around to see Lilly, her auburn hair teased into an up-do that would have made Marge Simpson proud. It was frizzy and curly and so high and frozen I was certain there was a fresh hole in the ozone somewhere above Puerto Rico.

"The soup'll be fine. But my hair might need to be amputated."

After combing out the mess of crunchy knots, shampooing, rinsing and repeating several times, and thirty minutes of thorough blow-drying, Lilly's hair finally resembled hair again.

"Wow, Mariana, I can't thank you enough." She sighed as I wrapped her hair around a thick round brush.

"No problem. I mean, I'm not a hairdresser or anything, but I do know how to blow dry."

"Anything's better than that formation my mother concocted. Why did I let her do that to me?"

"Because she's your mother."

Lilly's mom pounded on the bathroom door again, jiggling the handle and shrieking so loud the whole town probably heard. She was wholeheartedly against our decision to re-style Lilly's "formal do."

"I swear I'm going to kill her. I really am. We're both not going to get through this day alive."

"Oh, it won't be that bad. You'll have fun," I said as I pinned the sides of her hair in place.

"I'll have fun at the reception, once I'm with my friends."

"So, what are they like?"

"My friends? They're cool. Most of them speak some English. And my escort goes to the American school with me. You'll like him."

"Your escort? You mean your boyfriend?"

"Oh God, no. We're just friends. Alex and I have known each other forever."

I had never had a male friend in my life. Well, not really. I couldn't imagine talking to a guy like I do Madison and Emily.

"Speaking of friends, wasn't that girl's Sweet Sixteen last night?"

"Omigod! I've gotta check my e-mail!" I yelled, dropping the brush.

"Did you forget? Is that possible? You've been talking about it nonstop since you got here."

"I don't know. I guess I was just so mad about that radio show."

"Well, go. Leave! I can take it from here. By the time you get back, I'll be all sprayed and shiny."

I handed Lilly the hair dryer and sped out of the bathroom.

Chapter 24

My e-mail account showed more than twenty new messages, all from Emily and Madison. Part of me didn't even want to read them. I knew they'd just be some excited ramblings about how much they didn't miss me.

I double clicked the top item; it was a photo attachment. When the image opened on my screen, my jaw fell faster than my mood. It was a photo of Orlando Bloom and Madison smiling together in the middle of a crowd of screaming classmates.

Orlando Bloom was actually at her Sweet Sixteen party.

I almost threw up in my mouth.

I clicked the next e-mail. It was a long message from Madison.

> Spic! Oh, my God! You're not going to believe what you missed! We had the greatest time of our lives. My party was sooooo awesome! Orlando Bloom showed up! He stayed for, like, twenty minutes and talked to me the entire time. He didn't even look at another girl. He's so hot! It was amazing!
>
> And it totally made up for all the crap Gayle screwed

up. Can you believe after promising me she'd have my Louis Vuitton cake, she got one without any of the LV logos!!! It was just covered with brown and gold checkers—like she totally knew that wasn't the LV pattern I wanted. And then the salads had these huge walnuts in them—whatever, I hate nuts! My mom completely bitched her out. I mean, she was trying to ruin my party!

And you're not going to believe this, but Julie Sutter wore a silver dress the same shade as mine!! I'm so pissed. Everyone knew I was wearing silver. Plus, I won't even get into the tacky gifts people gave me (gift certificate to a bookstore and a donation to save the wildlife—hello?!). Thanks for sending that necklace, by the way. It's sooo pretty.

Anyway, I gave Orlando my number last night and I'm hoping he's going to call any minute. I would totally move to L.A. for him. I could be Mrs. Orlando Bloom!!

Love, your birthday Diva,
Madison

I closed my laptop without replying. I didn't even read the other messages she'd sent. My mind was reeling, and I didn't have time to deal with Madison's dramas. Not today. I had another party to go to.

When I got back to the house it was brimming with relatives. Lilly's court had arrived in tuxes and formal gowns covering every shade in the rainbow. Alonzo and José were tying each other's Windsor knots and Lilly's father was chugging a beer.

"¿Donde está Lilly?" I asked, peering around.

Alonzo pointed toward the bedroom and smiled. I bolted down the hall and halted in the doorway to her room.

Lilly was standing with her back to me gazing into a full-length mirror. Her red hair was flowing over her shoulders in elegant waves, perfectly complementing the lines of her gown. She looked radiant.

"Lilly, oh my God!" I gasped.

She spun around, tears in her eyes.

"You did this?" Lilly squeaked.

"No, no your mom did. It's beautiful. You're beautiful!"

"But my mom, she told me what you did. How you helped . . ."

"No, really. It was no big—"

"Seriously, I don't know what to say. . . ."

"Don't worry about it. I mean, what are distant cousins for?" I joked.

Lilly chuckled and wiped her eyes.

"You know, there's a house full of people waiting for you," I pointed out.

"Well, I'm ready," she stated with confidence.

We walked out of the bedroom together.

Chapter 25

The church was mobbed. There was no air conditioner, naturally, and a few slowly rotating ceiling fans provided the only relief. My long navy-blue dress was already sticking to me, and the thong of one of my dressy flip-flops was digging into the webbing of my big toe. Vince tugged on the collar of his shirt, poking me with his elbow.

"Can you sit still?" I whispered.

"I would if it wasn't two hundred degrees in here."

"Well, get used to it because I'm guessing this ceremony isn't going to be all that snappy."

Just then, the organist began to play and everyone stood to face the church doors. The entire spectacle was so wedding-like, I half expected them to play "Here Comes the Bride," or at the very least, Pachelbel's Canon in D Major.

The doors swung open and in walked the processional of Lilly's friends. One purple halter dress followed by a lime-green strapless gown followed by a canary-yellow v-neck so low I could almost see her belly button. Each girl held the arm of a guy in a tuxedo with sweat dripping down his brow. As the last couple sauntered in, the music began to slow. Organ chords buzzed in my ears, and my eyes locked with the final male escort. His brown eyes smiled as his dimples flexed. My breath froze in my lungs as I followed his strut down the aisle. When our eyes caught, he grinned. Before I could fully absorb the moment, the doors swung open one last time.

The organist blasted a fresh tune and Lilly strolled in on her father's arm with a doll in a matching pink gown resting in her other arm. She'd told me earlier that it was supposed to symbolize the "last doll" she'd ever own, however, Lilly had stopped playing with dolls as soon as she was old enough to speak. It was just another tradition forced on her by her mother. So was the embroidered tiara that sat on her head. But none of this affected the glowing smile she wore as she passed her guests.

When she reached the altar, her godparents, whom I had yet to officially meet, took her doll and presented her with a bouquet of pink and white lilies, which while somewhat cheesy in the name-play, were also rather sweet.

As soon as the priest opened his mouth, so did my brother.

"How the heck are we supposed to know what's going on? The whole thing's in Spanish," he whispered.

"It's a Catholic service. We've been to plenty. How different could it be?"

"Well, I really don't get the point of all this. Big deal. She's fifteen. So that means she's a woman *now*? 'Cause I'm pretty sure she was a woman when she sprouted those bombs."

"Vince! She's your cousin, don't talk about her boobs!"

"Actually, have you noticed that every girl here has huge boobs?" he continued. "Her court looks like a Latina Victoria's Secret runway."

"You're in a church," I reminded him.

"So?"

"And you're probably related to half the people whose cleavage you're checking out."

"Well, if that priest would stop rambling maybe I wouldn't have to look at boobs to pass the time."

"Shhh! I want to pay attention."

I watched as Lilly kneeled on the white satin pillow I had selected, sans the frilly trim. It was embroidered by her mother with Lilly's name, the date and the phrase, *"Mis XV Años."* Her mother strolled to the altar to replace the white embroided tiara on her head with the faux crystal one we chose together. It was her crowning moment as a "princess before God," which was amusing since Madison had worn one similar on her Sweet Sixteen just to be "princess of the world." God had nothing to do with it.

The organist launched into another rousing performance as the crowd collectively stood. Everyone sang in unison.

"This is so lame," Vince whispered. *"No hablo Español."*

"Who cares? Like you sing in church back home when the songs *are* in English?"

"What? You don't think I can sing? Because *I* can sing."

Vince shot me a sly smile, then cleared his throat. He closed his eyes, clenched a fist to his chest and softly began crooning the words to Guns N' Roses' "Sweet Child O' Mine" to the tune of the Spanish hymn.

Every word to the metal ballad was sung in tune to the organist, and as much as I wanted to tell him to stop, I couldn't help but laugh—even when the heads began to turn around us. The more inappropriate my laughter became, the harder it spewed out. It didn't help that the chubby two-year-old next to us was shrieking in tune with my brother and that when the music finally ceased, the toddler kept right on squealing.

And squealing. Then he threw a program at us.

"Okay, so do that brat's parents not see him?" Vince whispered. "Did they lose their sense of hearing when they procreated? Or do they just like being obnoxious?"

"You mean like *you* do?" I smirked.

"Hey, at least I was singing softly. He's screaming like a lunatic."

The baby wailed again.

"Shhh! They might hear you."

The toddler grabbed the black suspenders hooked on his blue trousers and let out another wailing screech.

"You mean they might hear me over the sounds of their freakish child? Doubt it. Plus, no one here speaks English."

"True." I nodded, as the toddler howled again. I pressed my finger to my ear. "God, do you think it was your Axl Rose impersonation that set him off or is he just possessed? 'Cause I think the holy water's gonna start bubbling any minute now."

"Now you're talking." Vince laughed.

Just then, Lilly's godparents approached the altar with a bible and a cross for the priest to bless. Her mom then presented Lilly's new *Quinceañera* jewelry on a pillow for the priest to sanctify as well. As soon as Lilly saw the shiny white-gold locket her eyes welled. She flicked it open and inside was a picture of her and her parents. She hugged her mom and shifted her eyes to where I was sitting. Her teeth gleamed as she smiled at me and winked. She knew I had picked it out. It was the best gift I had ever given anyone, and it wasn't even mine to give.

An hour later—after three readings, two more songs, and a communion line that could have stretched the circumference of the earth—the mass wrapped up. Lilly stood and took the arms of her parents, her dad on one side and her mom on the other. She recessed down the aisle, nodding at me as she passed. The toddler next to us acknowledged her with another high-pitched yell.

"For the love of God, someone get this little Satan out of the building," Vince whispered.

"I know. I think my ears are starting to bleed."

I stood up to exit the pew when a hand grabbed my arm. I swung around, startled, and looked straight into the eyes of the toddler's mother.

"I hope we get to spend some more time together at the reception," she quipped in perfect English before swooping her child up into her arms and leaving the church.

Chapter 26

The tent was hot. Scorching, one-hundred-degree, can't-stop-the-sweat-from-rolling-down-my-face hot. About a half dozen tall metal fans were blowing at maximum speed, but the air was too humid to cool off. Every inch of the massive tent was filled with tan bodies glistening in perspiration.

A large brass band rocked on stage, blaring its beats under flashing, colorful lights. Couples filled the floor in front of them, their hair saturated and their hips swaying to the pounding rhythms. The whole place smelled like summer: sweat mixed with coconut mixed with perfume mixed with adrenaline. I seemed to be the only female who missed the memo about the proper way to deal with the heat. The other women wore sleeveless gowns that fell no longer than their knees, and each had her hair pulled elegantly off her sticky neck.

In comparison, I looked like I was about to run errands. I'd worn the dress a thousand times back home, to church and to dinners. But the sleeveless navy frock with a hemline that brushed my ankles looked like a parka in comparison to the other partygoers. I was the only woman not in high heels, and my auburn locks were falling limp around my face. I had added a hint of mascara and pink lip gloss before entering the reception, thinking it was an "evening look," but clearly I was out of my league. I made the mistake of assuming the "brides-maids," or members of the court were the fashion victims in neon fabrics, only I was wrong. I wasn't in Spring Mills any-more. Our urban fashion rules didn't apply.

Dozens of tan, exotic teens and twentysomethings, pre-sumably Lilly's friends and relatives, crowded the tent's bar. I grabbed Vince's arm.

"Is it just me or do I look like a nun compared to the women here?"

"You didn't notice that at the church?" he asked, his eye-brows raised.

"No! Did you?"

He shrugged.

"Eh, don't feel bad. I'm the only guy here without a skintight shirt and revealing chest hair."

We both laughed.

"Wanna get a drink?" he asked.

"You know I don't drink."

"So?"

He pulled me toward the bar and past a line of watchful teenagers.

"¡Ay, Americana!" yelled a guy in a hot-pink button-down and hip-hugging pants.

"¡Ay, guapa!" called another.

"¡Americana! ¡Que bonita!"

"Hey, we're half Puerto Rican. How do all these people know we're not from the island?" I whispered to Vince. Appar-ently, we had our nationality stapled to our chests.

My brother laughed in a way that made me think he wasn't laughing with me. And if I'd felt like a plain Jane misfit a few moments ago, now I was a glowing green alien from the planet Neptune.

"Vince, I don't think I belong here."

"It's your cousin's party, of course you do."

"Yeah, that's not what I mean," I responded, as I watched a guy look me up and down and swipe his hand through his greasy black hair. "I think these guys are looking at me like I'm a turkey dinner."

"That's because you're a tourist. They assume you're easy."

"What?" I yelped, my eyes wide.

"Mariana, all tourists are easy. Everyone knows that. They're on vacation looking for a fling, a great story to tell . . ."

"So is that why you hang out on South Street?"

"Well, it's not for the cheesesteaks." He chuckled.

We slowly made our way to the bar. About two dozen bottles of Bacardi and Barrelito were stacked in plastic milk crates along with trash cans full of iced beer.

"What do you want?" Vince asked me.

"Nothing, water maybe."

"Mariana!"

"I don't like beer."

Actually, I never understood what was so appealing about the beverage. The few times I'd tried it, I thought it tasted like dishwater. My brother told me I'd get used to the aftertaste, but I didn't spend that much time trying to enjoy food items that were actually good for me, so I didn't see why I should do it for beer.

"Mariana, we're in the rum capital of the world. Try something new."

"Fine, *un* Coca-Cola, *por favor,*" I told the bartender. "No rum."

The man looked at me cross-eyed, then handed me the can and an empty glass.

"You suck," Vince muttered.

Just then, the band cut the music and the conductor made

a booming announcement into the microphone. The entire crowd turned toward the tent's entrance as the curtains draped back. The band swung into a jazzy Latin beat as Lilly's court strutted in to the music. The couples danced and shimmied as they entered, with the final girl walking in alone.

The band swiftly changed tunes and in walked Lilly, her hair pulled up in a loose, high ponytail and her tight pink dress clinging to her curves. She was arm-in-arm with the dimpled-face stranger from the church—her escort, Alex. I followed his tall frame as he led Lilly onto the floor and presented her to her father who was clutching a pair of high-heeled shoes. Her mother brought out a folding chair and Lilly gracefully sat down. Juan lifted her ballet flats from her feet and replaced them with the white strappy sandals. They were meant to be her first pair of high heels (yeah, right) and a symbol of her emergence into womanhood. (I wasn't sure why choosing to wear painful shoes meant she was grown up, but it was touching nonetheless.)

She took her father's hand as the band slowed to a waltz. In a frame that would have made a ballroom dance instructor proud, Lilly and her father floated to the music. Her mother's eyes teared and my Uncle Miguel tightly gripped my aunt's hand.

"What is this, a wedding?" Vince huffed.

"Shut up, Vince."

"It's a 'father-daughter dance!' " he snipped.

"So?"

"So, don't you think that's a bit much for a birthday party?"

"No. I think it's nice, actually. It's better than a bunch of shallow bling."

"Huh," he puffed. "Seems like someone's been out of Spring Mills too long."

★ ★ ★

Vince and I plopped down at a table alongside Alonzo and José.

"Las flores son bonitas," I said to José, commenting on the beauty of his centerpieces.

The yellow and white flowers looked rather striking against the pink tablecloths, though I knew Alonzo hadn't felt that way. My cousin looked at his friend and smiled.

"Sí, son bonitas," Alonzo agreed.

Just then, the waltz drew to a close and Juan dipped his daughter to a clatter of applause. For a girl who was anti this entire party, she certainly basked in the spotlight. All eyes were on her, especially those of her male friends. Lilly took a gracious bow and then the band ripped into a lively Latin beat. The dance floor immediately filled with dozens of twirling pairs who looked like they'd spent years on the professional ballroom circuit.

"Wow," I mumbled.

"Seriously." Vince paused before nodding to a group of Lilly's girlfriends who were swiveling their hips liberally with their partners. "And the chicks are hot."

"Is that all you think about?"

"Yes. Yes, it is."

"You realize most of 'em are jail bait."

"Whatever."

The crowd suddenly parted and Lilly cut through it, her eyes sparkling as she strolled a path through the guests.

"So you guys want to dance?" Lilly asked, grabbing both our hands and bouncing with energy.

"Um, not just yet," I stated, swallowing hard.

"Oh, come on Mariana!" Lilly cried. "You're the one with the technical dance training."

"Yeah, I don't think that's applicable here."

I blinked at the swirling people in front of me.

"Oh, loosen up. I wanna introduce you to my friends," she said, heading into the thick of the crowd.

"In a minute. I'm just gonna hang here for a bit and finish my drink."

"By yourself?" Vince asked; clearly he was planning to follow Lilly.

"Yeah, it's cool. You guys go. I'll be here."

"Okay, but don't get too comfortable. We're gonna come back and get you," Lilly insisted.

I nodded, and she and Vince disappeared into the horde of Latino strangers.

Everyone looked so effortless in their movements. Even the way they walked was in time with the music. Just how they rested against the bar looked sultry. Their voices were breathy, their skin gleamed rather than sweated. And here I was: I didn't drink, I couldn't salsa, and I wasn't the slightest bit sexy. To be surrounded by a bunch of people who shared my Puerto Rican blood, I felt very out of place, very American.

Chapter 27

I was on my second soda. At least three guys had approached me in a span of thirty minutes, offering a hand to lead me onto the dance floor. Each time, I stared at my glass and shook my head "no," with a polite smile. Eventually they skulked away. Though part of me wanted to take them up on their offers, I just couldn't pry myself from the bar stool I now occupied.

I tried to study the choreography of the women twirling on the floor. I knew flip-flops weren't exactly the correct foot-wear for spinning, kicking and swaying, but I still thought I might be able to pick up the moves. After a decade of pirou-ettes, allegros and *fouettés,* I figured I should be able to morph enough of that training to mimic the dance of salsa. Plus, I was incredibly flexible and I had always been noted for my supe-rior elevation, though I doubted jumps would come into play much in a scene like this.

But it wasn't really the dancing that was causing my trepi-dation. It was the men.

I had thought guys from Philly were supposed to be arro-gant and aggressive, but from what I'd seen of Puerto Rican guys so far, they definitely took the prize in those categories. Back home, if I caught the eye of a guy my age, he'd probably send a friend to scope me out and see if I were interested. He'd dance several feet away and slowly move in. Here, the guys approached with unwavering confidence. They whispered in my ear before even catching my name. And from what I could see on the floor, most felt free to place their hands on your butt and their mouths on your neck. I couldn't picture myself welcoming all of that uninvited touching.

"Hey! You're still here!" Lilly called, surfacing from the dense crowd with about a dozen guys tailing her.

She might as well have been walking in slow motion to a Celine Dion song, the devotion was so obvious. I imagined little red hearts oozing from the tips of their heads as they gazed at her, touched her and called her name for attention.

"Hey," I muttered, tilting my head.

"Guys, this is Mariana. My cousin from the States. She's Vince's sister," Lilly explained, pointing to my brother who was grinding against a busty blonde on the dance floor.

"Don't worry. Everyone speaks English," she whispered to me.

I flipped my wrist slightly. "Um, hi."

"*¡Ay Dios mío!* Lilly, she looks just like you," cried a guy in black pants and a tight blue shirt.

The crowd around him looked at me from head to toe.

"She could be your sister," he added.

"*Sí,*" they chimed in unison, nodding.

All but one.

"Nah, I don't think so. She's definitely got her own look," whispered Lilly's escort as he came into view, his dimples flashing.

He delicately grabbed my hand and his straight black hair dripped onto his forehead as our eyes locked. He leaned down and pressed his mouth to the back of my hand. No one had ever kissed my hand before. I thought that gesture went out with the Victorian era, but ancient or not, it still made my stomach flutter.

"I'm Alex," he stated with a soft Spanish accent.

"I'm Mariana."

"I know." He smirked, not letting go of my hand. "Nice to finally meet you."

I smiled blankly, unable to think of anything to say.

"So, how long will you be visiting?" he asked, rupturing the silence.

"Um, uh, for another few weeks," I stuttered, swallowing hard.

"Well, good. We'll have to show you a good time."

He was looking at me with such unbroken intensity that I turned away. In all of two seconds, he had made me nervous. But when I glanced back, I was happy to see his eyes still fixed on me.

"Mariana!" Lilly cried, snatching my hand from his. "I see you've met Alex." She giggled. "He's my escort for the evening, as you know. And these are some of my *other* friends from Utuado. I'd tell you all of their names but you'll probably just forget them anyhow. They're all very cool and *very* excited to teach you how to salsa dance."

"What?" I gasped, my mouth swung open.

From the eager looks these guys were giving me, I feared they'd devour me whole just to impress my cousin.

"Oh, come on. It'll be fun!" Lilly pushed me toward a Latino giant, at least 6 foot 4, with a shaved head and orange shirt opened at the top three buttons.

"Wanna dance?" he asked, grabbing my waist.

"Um, Lilly?" I whimpered, but she was already basking in the attention of another "friend."

"I'm Ricky," he stated, pulling my hips.

"Um, look, I don't know about this . . ."

Ricky fastened an arm around my lower back and half-pushed, half-dragged me onto the dance floor. I looked back desperately and caught a glimpse of Alex staring at me. I grinned and mouthed "help" with my most pathetic expression. He burst into laughter.

Through no effort on my part, Ricky and I inserted ourselves onto the congested floor. He quickly clasped my right hand, his palm spreading a clammy film. I wanted to pull away, but before I could, he yanked me close and guided my hips with his clenched grip. I strained my neck to look up at him—he was almost a foot taller than I was—as he poorly attempted to lead. Though I had never danced salsa before, I had danced with partners. And Ricky wasn't very good. His rhythm felt off and he couldn't turn me and bring me back to the flow of the music. I tripped on my flip-flops as he flung me around and then stomped on my bare toe with his hard black dress shoe.

The couples around us were nudging us out of their way. They were all clearly more skilled and thus felt entitled to more dance space. I was more than happy to give it. Thankfully, the flashy, seven-piece brass band concluded its number and I smiled at Ricky, assuming our uncomfortable moment was over. It wasn't. And the minute I heard the lead singer's voice croon out in a soft melody, I nearly gagged on my saliva. Ricky tugged me toward him and slid his moist hands onto my lower back. He reeked of beer, and I instinctively flinched back.

"Ah, don't be shy, *chica*," he whispered, his breath assaulting my nostrils. "So, do you like it here? In *Puerrrto Rrrico*?" He slowly rolled his "Rs" to mimic some sort of Latin lover.

"You know, it was really nice of you to dance with me, but—"

"You don't have to thank me," he purred, as he thrust his hips toward mine to close the space between us.

I placed my hand on his chest to gently shove him away, but he wasn't getting the hint. He tightened his lock on my waist, which made me struggle like a dog against a leash. I could have stopped in my tracks and refused to dance, but I didn't want Lilly's friends to think I was a snob. However, I didn't want to be mauled against my will, either.

I had just about decided to storm off when a man spoke up from behind me.

"May I cut in?"

Ricky peered up and frowned at the source of the voice. He paused, then abruptly unhooked his grasp on my waist, sending me stumbling backward and smack into the stranger's chest. I looked up awkwardly and saw Alex gazing down, his hands holding my biceps from where he caught my fall.

"Hey." I smiled weakly.

"Hey." He grinned back. "Wanna dance?"

I hobbled to my feet, careful not to break eye contact, and nodded.

"But—" Ricky cried, reaching out a hand.

"Later, Ricky," Alex stated as he led me further into the pulsing crowd.

His fingers laced with mine, and this time it was *my* hand sweating.

Chapter 28

Countless songs later and I was still entwined with Alex. He was an excellent partner. And though I was stumbling in my flip-flops, we managed to pull off at least one clean dance. He even complimented my turns—the one skill that translated seamlessly from ballet to salsa. I'd always had excellent speed on my rotations.

"For someone who's never done this before, you're picking it up rather quickly," he said, his accent simmering through.

"Thanks. I take a little ballet back home." I didn't want to draw attention to my experience. I kind of liked that he thought I was a natural.

"Ballet, huh? Well, that explains your figure." His fingers lightly squeezed my waist.

Hot blood rushed to my cheeks and I quickly turned my head.

In my fifteen years, I had danced with a lot of guys—most of them wearing tights, and without the slightest hint of masculinity. But still, I had never before felt this self-conscious while dancing. Usually dance was one of the few things I could do on autopilot, which was one of the reasons my instructors complained. *"You have beautiful technique, but no appre-*

ciation for the movement. Where's the magic?" they'd drone end-lessly. I had never understood what they meant. Only now, as my body moved in time with Alex, inhaling his soapy lemony scent and feeling his energy mixed with mine, I couldn't check my emotions enough to focus on the steps. I could barely hold my frame.

I gazed at him, his dark eyes only a few inches above mine, and I became keenly aware of the tiny bit of space that sepa-rated us. I felt the pressure of his hand on my back, the way his thumb rubbed the index finger on my right hand, the way his hips lightly brushed mine when I swayed to the left. I won-dered if he'd noticed too.

"You're really pretty," he whispered.

"Why? Because I look like Lilly?" I asked, downplaying the compliment.

"I never said that."

"No, but you thought it."

"So, you read minds?"

"Yup, it's one of my special gifts."

"Oh, really? Then you must know every guy here finds you attractive and it has nothing to do with your cousin."

"Oh, please." I sighed, rolling my eyes.

"Now *that* is American. . . ."

"What?" I huffed, slightly offended.

"It's just, a Puerto Rican woman would never question a compliment or roll her eyes at it."

"Oh, yeah. Well, these Puerto Rican women are just as American as I am."

"You know what I mean."

"I'm just saying—"

"You're dodging my point."

"Which is?"

"Which is Puerto Rican women already know how beautiful they are. But you don't."

I bit my lip. I never was very good at accepting compliments, especially those that couldn't be accurately documented with hard evidence. It was easy to say thank you when an adult applauded my intelligence—I had the grades to back it up. It was entirely different to have the same reaction to flattery on my appearance, or my smile, or my figure. And when those comments came from men, I almost always assumed that they were insincere, that they "wanted" something, though I had never really been pressured into giving "something" up. But that's probably because for a guy to try, I'd have to talk to him for more than five minutes outside of an academic facility.

"So, how come your English is so good?" I blurted.

"Changing the subject?" he asked, as he spun me around.

"No. It was just a question. You always this suspicious?"

"Of beautiful women, yes."

"Oh, weak! You're just dropping the cheesy lines now."

Alex laughed. "Fine, fine. I'll stop. I go to an English-language school with Lilly."

Just then, the band's trumpet player broke into a rousing solo and Alex twirled me in rapid succession. I looped under his arm, my hair whipping like an umbrella. After a long, loud note, the music suddenly stopped and Alex pulled me back, halting my momentum an inch from his face. My pulse spiked as I felt his breath.

"This was fun," he whispered.

"Uh-huh." I nodded, my mind numb.

We stood there, still embraced, only no music filled the air. I felt like one of those hokey couples who bantered back and forth on the phone, "No, you hang up first. No, you hang up first!" Neither Alex nor I wanted to be the first to break the moment.

"Well, guys! You seem to be having a good time!" yelled Lilly as she strutted up to us, put one hand on each of our shoulders, and pushed us apart. "Great night, huh?"

Alex looked away first.

"Hola, Lilly," he said, shifting toward her.

I realized it was the polite thing to do. Lilly was standing right next to us, her hands on our shoulders, engaging us in conversation. It would have been rude to ignore her. But when Alex turned away, my heart was swallowed by the pit of my stomach. It felt like rejection.

"Hey, there," I stated flatly, glancing at my cousin.

Several auburn locks framed her face, falling from her ponytail, and her forehead was damp as if she had been dancing hard. I looked down and for the first time realized my hair was also soaked to the tips, and my navy dress was so saturated you could see the outline of my white bra peeking through. The whole time I was dancing with Alex I must have looked like a drowning victim. I felt my ears burn.

"It's time for dinner," she said. "Alex, you're at the head table, with me."

"Oh, yeah," he muttered, looking me up and down one more time. I folded my arms across my chest to cover my now see-through top.

Lilly shot him a look and grabbed his arm.

"Enjoy dinner!" She smiled as she led Alex off toward her table.

Chapter 29

I plopped down next to my brother. Alonzo and José had already been to the buffet and were both enjoying the yellow soup I had almost destroyed earlier this morning.

"You look like you were having a good time," I said to Vince, nodding at his drenched dark hair.

"Did you see the chick I was dancing with? Hello, *Baywatch*!"

"Vince, I swear, you bring tacky to a whole new level." I shook my head as we both stood up to make our way to the buffet.

"Did you see Alonzo eating the soup?" I whispered, smirking.

"I know," Vince murmured. "I hope Aunt Carmen didn't scrape it off the floor."

We both chuckled as we grabbed plates and flatware and moved toward the spread of food.

"Holy crap," I mumbled, as I gawked at the dozens of brimming dishes filling at least three banquet tables.

"That's a lot of food to have been made by one person."

"Seriously."

Chicken, pork, fish, soup, beans, *mofungo* (shrimp and plantains), steak, vegetables and a bottomless pit of rice simmered in aluminum serving trays above small warming candles. It was enough to feed a small country.

"Mariana, if you even attempt to get picky and not eat the food, I'll hurt you myself," my brother warned.

He was right. I had to suck it up for my aunt's sake. I scooped small bits of almost every dish presented, along with a hefty serving of plantains, and exited the buffet line. We made our way across the tent and as soon as our table came into view, we both stopped in our tracks.

"Whoa." Vince stared, openmouthed.

"Um, is that the woman from the church? Sitting at our table?"

"You mean the mother of the devil-child. Yes, I believe that's her," Vince said.

"Well, what are we gonna do? We can't sit there."

"We already put our drinks there."

"So, we'll get new drinks," I suggested.

"Too late."

The woman swiveled her head, spotted us and waved. Alonzo and José smiled awkwardly beside her, which made me think she had already relayed the story about our rude behavior during the ceremony.

"Well, this is gonna suck," I mumbled as we trudged over to our seats.

I pulled out my chair and plastered a fake grin on my face.

The woman beamed back and said, *"Hola,"* as she adjusted her son's position in the seat next to her. I refused to make eye contact with the child. My only defense was to pretend as if nothing had happened. Maybe she'd eat her dinner, we'd eat our dinner, and then all go our separate ways—in silence.

"I'm Teresa," the woman said in perfect English, extending her hand.

No such luck.

"Um." I coughed. "I'm Mariana. This is my brother, Vince."

"Nice to meet you," she said politely.

I turned my gaze to my food and shoved forkful after forkful into my mouth. I didn't even like half of what I was consuming (there were onions in everything), but I figured if my mouth was occupied with food then it couldn't be occupied with conversation.

"So, Mariana," she began.

Crap, I thought.

"Where are you from?" Teresa gracefully sipped her water.

"I'm from the States," I answered briefly, hoping to discourage further inquiry.

"I figured that. Where exactly?" She brushed her long hair over her shoulder and for the first time I noticed it had flecks of red similar to my own.

"Philadelphia, the suburbs."

I shot Vince a wide-eyed look. He quickly turned his head in the opposite direction and pretended to speak to José.

"Oh, really. I lived in New York for a while." She cut her son's chicken as he sat silently beside her like a perfect angel. "This is my son, Manuel."

I nodded in the direction of the child, refusing to look at him. My cheeks flushed.

"How do you know Lilly?" she asked.

I saw Alonzo and José exchange a wary glance. This conversation was like Chinese water torture—endlessly painful in tiny, maddening increments.

"She's my cousin, my third cousin."

"Ah, she's my second cousin," Teresa responded.

It suddenly struck me the number of relatives Lilly had filling the tent. If my parents threw me a birthday party and invited every relative we had in the country, we'd be lucky to fill a small bathroom. Yet, Lilly was surrounded by hordes of family every day. I didn't think Madison invited one relative to her Sweet Sixteen, other than her parents, and that's only because they were paying for it. If she had had her way, they would have been bounced at the door with the rest of the adults.

"So, I guess that must mean we're related." Teresa elegantly batted her eyes in a look that for a split second seemed almost sinister.

There was something about her I didn't trust. If she wanted to complain about my poor behavior toward her son, she should just come out and say it. She was a grown woman, in her mid-thirties at least. She should have enough gumption to stand up for her child, especially to some obnoxious teenager.

"Now, are you related on your mom's side or your dad's side?" she continued, with a crooked grin.

"Look, I'm sorry about what we said about your son. At the church," I stated plainly, nudging my brother with my elbow to drag him back into the conversation. "It was rude. And I'm sorry."

If she wasn't going to be woman enough to acknowledge the obvious, then I was.

"Thank you. But it's no bother. He hadn't napped all morning and he *was* rather cranky."

"Well, still, it was wrong. Wasn't it, Vince?"

"Uh, yeah, sorry," he mumbled, looking the opposite direction.

"Let's forget it," she offered. "But I would like to hear more about your family in Philadel—"

Just then Lilly's father Juan tapped the microphone on stage. *"Hola, hola,"* he repeated as his voice boomed through the tent, interrupting our conversation (thank God). Lilly's grandparents and godparents stood beside him, holding hands and smiling with pride.

Juan held up a long champagne flute and offered a toast to his daughter, of which I understood almost half (quite an accomplishment on my part). Lilly smiled adoringly as the crowd held their drinks in the air. After a few moments, Juan winked, lifted his flute and bellowed, *"¡Salud!"*

"¡Salud!" we responded in unison.

I took a sip of my soda, stood up and walked out of the tent, leaving Teresa behind—hopefully for the last time.

When the alcohol supply began to dwindle, the party finally wound down. I was exhausted. It was almost two in the morning and with the countless guests traipsing in and out of the bathroom, I doubted I would get much sleep until they left. I slumped into my folding chair and yawned.

"¿Estas cansada?" Alonzo asked, as he took a final chug of his beer.

I nodded as I yawned again, showing just how tired I was.

My brother was still on the dance floor groping the blonde in the red dress. He felt no shame in sucking her face in front of a crowd of strange relatives, and apparently neither did she. Lilly was swaying in the midst of a pack of admirers when she finally rolled her head in my direction and caught my eyes half closed.

She stumbled over, her loyal subjects clamoring behind her. Alex was nowhere in sight.

"Hey. Ya look *purdy* wrecked," she slurred; clearly she had more than sipped the champagne.

"Lilly, I haven't had any alcohol to drink all night." I chuckled.

"Ya serious?" she asked, her eyes confused.

"Yup. It's just late. I think I'm gonna call it a night."

"No! Why? The night's *ssnot* over!" she protested as she wrapped her arms around two bleary-eyed guys.

I glanced around the tent. There were only about two dozen guests left, mostly immediate family members, and the band had packed up more than an hour ago.

I grunted and stood up.

"It's over for me," I muttered. "Enjoy the rest of your night. And happy birthday."

I swiveled toward the house and before I made it to the tent's exit, Lilly called out: "Sweet dreams! *Of Alex! Ooooo!*"

I stopped in my tracks as the guys around her "Oooed" and "Aahhhed" to worsen my embarrassment.

It was her birthday, I told myself. Just smile and nod, smile and nod.

Chapter 30

I was the only one who didn't struggle waking up the next morning. Uncle Miguel was in the kitchen by sunrise, as usual. Our crack-of-dawn breakfasts had become a ritual, and I could now hold entire conversations with him in Spanish. It's not like we talked politics or anything, but my linguistic skills had finally expanded beyond standard greetings and weather reports.

I sank into a chair at the table. The kitchen was overflowing with dirty dishes, the floor was stained with muddy footprints and the air was thick with the stench of alcohol. I couldn't imagine what the scene looked like outside. There was no cleanup crew coming to erase the mess and I was praying I wouldn't be recruited for the task.

"*Hola,* Mariana," my uncle said as he sifted through the filthy dishes.

He handed me a cup of coffee and asked for my reaction to the party. We spent the next half hour discussing the *Quinceañera* and my attempts to salsa dance, which he found rather funny. I told him how impressed I was that the family had arranged everything themselves and how welcomed I felt by my relatives. Truthfully, I had never felt that comfortable with my relatives from home. Most of my aunts and uncles lived only a couple hours away and still we rarely saw them. Family get-togethers just weren't important, and for the first time I felt like I was missing out on something.

Uncle Miguel patted my hand sympathetically and softly asked me to tell him about my grandparents. His eyes turned sad, but I didn't question him despite how odd it felt sharing stories about his brother like they were strangers.

I told him about going pumpkin picking with my grandparents every year the week before Halloween. How we'd trek out to a pumpkin patch in Jersey and my grandfather would insist we walk down every row before we made our selections. Vince always picked the largest orange heap he could find, and I always picked the one that was most symmetrical. Afterward we hauled them home and carved ghostly faces with my grandfather's pocketknives. He was always so proud of our creations, no matter how simplistic.

In return, my Uncle Miguel told me about my father. How he used to call him "Manny" when he lived here, short for his middle name, "Manuel," which I found bizarre. I had never heard anyone refer to him as anything other than Lorenzo, not even my grandparents. He also said my dad used to run around the house screaming and jumping until my grandmother lost her patience and chased him with a broom. The most physical activity I ever saw my dad engaged in was hoisting his laptop bag to his shoulder.

Finally, after my uncle and I had eaten and he was about to leave for work, Lilly and Vince staggered out of bed.

"Dude, Mariana, you're up." Vince trudged into the kitchen and straight to the refrigerator.

"Have fun last night?"

"Totally," he grumbled.

"Really? 'Cause you seemed kinda busy whispering in that blonde's ear," I joked.

"We did a lot more than whisper."

"Ew, gross!"

"You talking about Antonia?" Lilly asked as she tottered into the kitchen.

"Is that her name?" Vince grinned with a wink.

"Vince!" I shrieked, tossing a crumpled napkin at him.

"I'm just kidding. I know her name . . . and her cup size."

"Seriously, please shut up." I groaned, plugging my ears with my index fingers.

"All right, all right." He laughed. "So, where were you?"

I looked down at my tiny coffee cup. "I was dancing."

"With *Alex*," Lilly mocked.

"No way! Who's Alex?"

"No one," I muttered, shooting Lilly a look.

"Oh, be careful. I'll tell him you said that," she teased.

I couldn't wipe the smile from my face.

"You like a boy!" Vince shouted, choking on his orange juice.

"Shut up!" I said, the grin still plastered on my face.

"Oh, my God! You do! I swear, the world is gonna end. Someone check the news."

"Stop it! Why do you have to make such a big deal out of it? We just danced."

"Sure you did," Lilly said with a smirk.

"We did!"

"Uh-huh," she added.

"First of all, Mariana, you don't dance with guys unless they're assigned to you by some ballet teacher. And second of all, in the fifteen years that I've known you, you haven't shown interest in a single guy. Ever."

"That's not true," I said, kind of lying.

I did get crushes on guys, but they were usually seniors, or football jocks, or artist types, who I thought were way out of my league and not worth mentioning to anyone. Besides, none of them ever liked me back, at least not that I knew of. Unlike other girls, I was incapable of altering my personality for guys I found attractive. I couldn't bat my lashes on cue, or soften my voice, or laugh at unfunny jokes. I was myself, whether I was speaking to my brother, my best friend, my lab partner or a stranger. And to date, guys didn't seem to find my down-to-earth realism nearly as attractive as girls who pouted their lips and twirled their hair.

"Mariana, it's true and you know it. *This* is a big deal. And I think I need to meet this young man," Vince stated in his most responsible tone.

"Uh, you already did, loser. He's one of Lilly's friends."

"He was my escort, on the court," Lilly explained.

"Oh, I remember that guy," Vince said. "I didn't really talk to him much, but he seemed cool."

"He is," I added, rising from my kitchen chair in the hopes of ending the conversation. "Besides, we just danced. It was nothing major. I'll probably never see him again."

"I doubt that," Lilly muttered. "We're all meeting him and his friends at the beach later today."

"What?" I screamed.

Lilly immediately ducked out of the kitchen and dashed down the hall to avoid my reaction. I chased after her, almost slipping in my bare feet. She darted into her bedroom and tried to slam the door shut. I threw myself at it just in time.

"It's nothing," she explained. "Just after you went to bed last night, I kinda made plans with his friends to get together today."

"Well, how do you know Alex is gonna be there?" I asked.

The fact that I was being set up was horrifying, but not nearly as much as Alex seeing me in a bathing suit.

"Of course he'll be there." She sighed as she pulled out a beach bag and a red string bikini. "Considering you guys were all flirty last night I didn't think you'd mind."

"I was not flirty!"

Even I couldn't keep a straight face as I said it; my mouth spread from ear to ear.

"Look at you! You know you were!" she shouted. "Plus, I wanted to thank you for everything you did for my party. I mean, you didn't even like me half the time, and you still helped my mom."

"I like you!"

"Yeah, *now* you do. But, whatever, you know what I mean. If it weren't for you I probably would have been walking down the aisle wearing a pink fairy costume and eighties hair."

I laughed. "You don't know how close you came to that exact ensemble."

"I believe it." She laughed. "Anyway, the beach is gonna be fun. And it's not a date. It's a group thing. I'll be there, Vince'll be there, Alex's friends will be there. So don't freak out."

I paused and considered the situation. I wanted to see him again. I hadn't stopped thinking about him since last night. But what if we saw each other in daylight and the magic was gone? What if he saw my pasty skin in a bathing suit and was totally repulsed?

My mind was spinning.

"How many bathing suits did you bring?" Lilly asked, as if reading my thoughts.

"Three."

"Are any of them bikinis?"

"One. It's black."

"Okay, you're bringing that one."

I suddenly regretted drinking so much coffee. My hands were jittery and my stomach was swishing. I blamed it on the caffeine.

Chapter 31

The beach was deserted. It was the closest coastline to Utuado, which, being at the top of a mountain, still meant it was about forty-five minutes away. Lilly said it was a local hangout. Not too many tourists strayed this far from San Juan, which was their loss.

The beige sand flowed for miles, disturbed only by lush green trees and a few jagged rock jetties reminiscent of New England. The turquoise water rolled in low, lazy waves filling the air with a clean salty breeze. It was a strong contrast to the Jersey shores I frequented back home. Depending on the shore point, the beach was either two feet from the boardwalk or two miles. The water was a murky, unnatural shade of brownish green, and the scene was far from abandoned.

So far, I liked the Puerto Rican coast better.

I snuck a peek at Lilly's freakishly developed fifteen-year-old figure. She looked like a swimsuit model in her red string bikini with unlined triangle cups filled to perfection. My suit, however, came with the boobs already included. There was enough padding on my chest to act as a flotation device in case of an emergency.

"You can't tell that they're not real." Lilly sighed, after catching me staring at her again.

"Okay, let's not talk about my boobs while you look like Pamela Anderson."

"Oh, please. You look fine. Of course, he may notice that you've grown a few sizes since last night," Lilly stated cautiously. "But guys are stupid."

"Gee, thanks. I feel so much better." I crossed my arms over my chest.

We had been plopped on the beach for almost an hour. Lilly was peacefully basking in the sun while Vince swam in the ocean and I adjusted my swimsuit again and again. My foot was bouncing uncontrollably and I could almost hear the second hand on my watch ticking.

"He'll be here. Will you relax?" Lilly said, as she held her hand to her forehead to block the rays.

"I wasn't thinking about him."

I had already considered the idea that he might stand me up. His friends might not have told him about the plans or he could have decided not to meet us. He might have forgotten all about me, or he might have woken up this morning and decided he just didn't want to see me again.

"No, you're just posing on your towel and fixing your top for the benefit of Vince and me."

"I'm not posing! I'm just uncomfortable. At home we usually bring chairs to the beach."

"Oh, yeah. *Back in Spring Mills* . . ." Lilly droned.

"What? I don't talk about home that much!" I screeched, kicking sand on her feet,

"Oh, really? Then how come I know that Madison wore a silver dress to her party and that some girl showed up in the same color, and that her cake looked like designer purses and that some movie star showed up and stole the show, and . . ."

"All right, all right! At least I don't talk about it *as much* . . .
anymore," I defended, pushing my sunglasses up on the bridge
of my nose.

"Fine, I'll give you that. Plus, we now have *my* party to talk
about! So, how awesome was last night?"

Surprisingly, I did think her party was awesome, even with
the homemade food and plastic cups, and folding chairs and
sweltering heat. It was probably the most fun I'd ever had and
I barely knew a single person. No Emily, no Madison, just a
bunch of relatives and complete strangers salsa dancing to
Spanish music and enjoying each other without pretenses. As
much as I loved my best friend, I doubted her Sweet Sixteen
could have matched Lilly's *Quinceañera* in atmosphere—
Orlando Bloom or not.

"Ya know, it really was great." I smiled.

"See, and you thought you were missing out back home,"
Lilly said as she rolled over on her towel. "I can top a ritzy
Sweet Sixteen any day."

I chuckled and reached into Lilly's beach bag. All she had
was SPF 4 sun oil. It seemed that skin cancer hadn't yet hit
Puerto Rico and Lilly swore she didn't burn (must have been
some recessive gene I didn't inherit). She packed the oil on my
behalf, thinking it qualified as sun protection. Given that my
freckled skin glowed a ghostly shade of white, I had no choice
but to smear myself repeatedly in the only liquid available. My
hope was that if I continuously reapplied, it would up its potency
(like, could an SPF 4 become an 8 if I reapply it twice in thirty
minutes; how about a 12 if I reapply once more after that?).

Thankfully it was cloudy, and the sun wasn't blasting with
nearly as much heat as usual. But it was still high noon and
temperatures were probably in the upper eighties. If Alex didn't
get here soon, I feared I'd be a puddle of boiling water by the
time he saw me.

"Here I come!" screamed Vince as he suddenly ran towards us dripping wet and shaking water like a grungy dog. "Dah-hhh!"

His hair whizzed back and forth, spraying us with a mist that actually felt kind of refreshing though I was kicking my legs and swinging my arms at him with full force. I wasn't big on swimming in the ocean. The thought that I could drift out into a vast body of water and be unable to swim back was terrifying—and so was the seaweed. I hated not knowing what I was stepping on: shells, crabs, seaweed, jellyfish, hypodermic needles. Sure, the oceans here were crystal clear on a bad day, but it was still hard to wipe away fifteen years of Jersey shore experiences. I preferred to lie on the sand in peace just staring at the sea.

"Hey, it looks like your friends are here," Vince said as he grabbed a pink-and-yellow towel from Lilly's bag and wiped his face.

I spun around and saw two cars pulling up next to Aunt Carmen's beat-up brown sedan. I bit my lip and looked away, trying to pretend it didn't matter. When I glanced back, Alex and his friends were strutting towards us. He looked taller than I remembered, and his calves were skinny and hairy as they poked out of his black-and-gray board shorts. I immediately adjusted the wide band that ran along the bottom of my halter bikini top and glanced down to make sure nothing was peeking out that shouldn't be.

"Hola, chicas," Alex said as he approached, staring straight at me.

I watched his eyes scan me up and down.

"Hey," I said.

"Hola, mi amor." Lilly batted her mascara-caked eyelashes as she called Alex "her love." I hoped she was kidding.

The guys immediately took turns kissing Lilly on the cheek before fighting for towel space as close to her as possible.

"Mind if I sit here?" Alex asked, as he unfolded his green towel beside me.

I shook my head.

"So this is your first day at the beach," he stated matter-of-factly as he sat down.

"How'd you know?"

"Your tan needs a little work."

"Uh!" I grunted. "Maybe I just like the pale look? I'm going for the whole 'Nicole Kidman' thing."

"Sure you are."

"Hey, I could be. Anyway, I think tanning is on its way out."

"For who?" he asked, raising an eyebrow.

"For everyone. I'm calling for a comeback of the Renaissance era when fat women with pasty skin were all the rage."

Alex rolled his eyes. "I like your body the way it is."

"Oh, *please*. Did you practice that line?"

He looked at me with a crooked grin. There weren't too many people who I could banter with so easily and I was glad that he was one of them.

"You have fun last night?" he asked, ignoring my dig.

"Of course. I had a blast."

"You're a great dancer."

"Not at salsa," I groaned, flicking my hand at him. "You're just a great partner."

"There you go again not accepting compliments."

"Fine. Then let me *thank you* for complimenting my phenomenal dance skills. I believe you will see me popping up in salsa videos sometime very soon," I teased.

"No, not videos. But I could see you on TV. Maybe on a soap opera."

"A Spanish soap opera? Because I've been working on my dramatic pauses and you should see me slap someone across the face. Now *there's* a talent I need to share with the world."

Alex reached over and let his arm fall next to mine. He slowly inched his fingers toward me, and lightly brushed the sand off the back of my hand. My arms flooded with goose bumps. I looked at him, his dark eyes sparkling.

"You're funny," he said.

"Oh, wait. Let me be sure to accept the compliment. I don't want to seem too *American*."

Chapter 32

I never thought Spring Mills was so interesting, but a few hours after Lilly's friends arrived they gathered around Vince and me dying to hear the details of our lives back in the States. They wanted to know what our house looked like, what classes we took, what music we liked and even what we did on weekends.

Vince had a ball telling them all about his friends' mishaps while wasted, including his "monstrous kegger" (a story he now found funny, despite the fact that it kept him from going to Europe this summer). He even talked about his expectations for Cornell. They loved hearing about the climate in Ithaca, New York, and that it sometimes snowed in May. Most of Lilly's friends had never seen snow (Lilly included), and had never felt the temperature drop below sixty degrees.

I, however, was staying out of it. I sensed stories of ballet camps and science projects would not interest this crowd much. Only, I was wrong.

"So, Mariana, what would you be doing right now if you were back home?" asked Lilly's friend Javier, as he scooted toward my towel.

Alex was seated as a buffer between me and his friends. We

had been softly holding our own conversation while Vince babbled. I still couldn't get over how easily our conversation flowed given how little we knew each other. Alex hung on my every word, he teased and wasn't worried about causing offense. I was disappointed that I had to share him with the rest of the group.

"Well, I'd probably be hanging out with my friends," I explained, letting my eyes slip from guy to guy.

There were four other boys present, aside from Alex, and they were all very good-looking. I sensed that Lilly was the Puerto Rican equivalent of a homecoming queen. "My best friend just had her Sweet Sixteen the other night."

"Sweet Sixteen? That's like a *Quinceañera,* right?" Javier asked.

"Yeah, but without the religious and cultural significance."

"Well, my party had tons of significance, and dancing," Lilly joked, but no one seemed to hear.

"Yeah, Sweet Sixteens are for a bunch of spoiled brats," Vince huffed.

"Hey! Your friends had them too," I defended.

"So, your friends are rich?" Javier asked.

I thought about that for a second. I had never considered my friends as rich, but compared to most people they probably were. They had huge suburban houses, four-bedroom shore homes, trips to Europe and the Caribbean, and enough cars to fill a few garages. But for some reason, none of these things ever consciously stood out to me as part of a social class. Categorizing someone as rich almost felt disrespectful, like you were betraying their privacy.

"Um, I guess so," I explained. "Their parents work a lot—doctors, lawyers, whatnot."

They all nodded like they understood, which amazed me. If they were speaking Spanish I probably wouldn't understand half of what they were saying, but all of them seemed perfectly bilingual.

"I gotta say, my Spanish sucks and you all speak English like we do. You even use the same slang."

"Well, Lilly and I go to school with kids from the States. And we do have TVs," Alex pointed out. "But don't let these guys fool you. They only understand about every third word you say."

"Really?" I asked, looking at the group with my eyebrows raised.

"What?" Javier asked. "Are you talking about me?"

"See, I told you," Alex teased, nudging me with his elbow.

"Wow, they're pretty good at faking it because I totally thought they were bilingual geniuses," I whispered.

"Me too," Vince added.

Alex laughed. "I'm definitely not telling them you said that. Their egos are big enough."

"Do you play sports?" asked Javier, unaware of the conversation we were having under our breath. Vince, Alex and I burst into giggles.

"What?" Javier asked innocently, unaware that Alex had blown his cover.

"Nothing," I stated, shaking my head. "I dance ballet."

"You're a dancer?" confirmed another friend.

I nodded.

"That explains a lot," Javier stated, tossing his hands in the air. "Usually tourists are terrible dancers, but you were good last night."

"I'm not sure if I should be flattered or offended."

"It was a compliment. You're a good dancer," Javier repeated.

All of the guys nodded their heads and beamed in my direction.

"Did you hear that, Lil? They think I can salsa dance. Talk about crazy, right?" I joked, glancing at my cousin.

She was seated upright, her thin legs stretched before her and her stare focused on the ocean. She didn't respond, which felt very uncomfortable because I thought I had spoken loud enough for her to hear.

"Mariana does not like to accept compliments," Alex mocked, as he butted his shoulder against mine.

"Not that again," I groaned.

"So what's ballet like?" Javier asked.

"Have you ever seen it?"

"They wear skirts, *verdad*?"

"Yes, we wear skirts and tights. But there's a little more to it than that. It's the hardest type of dance there is."

"Says who?" Lilly snapped, glaring at me through narrowed eyes.

"Um, I, uh, didn't mean to offend anyone," I stuttered.

I wasn't sure what I had done to annoy Lilly, but I clearly wasn't her favorite person at the moment. Whenever Madison or Emily used that tone with me, it meant they were angry. Only with them, I never really had to guess why. We weren't that hard to figure out.

"I just meant that the technique required for ballet is more extensive than other dance styles. Most prima ballerinas have been training since they were, like, three years old. If you start at ten, you're considered a late bloomer with no real future," I explained.

I smiled at Lilly only she didn't smile back. She silently returned her gaze to the ocean.

"So do you want to be a professional dancer?" Alex asked, his face a few inches from mine.

"Um, no, I doubt it. I'll probably just go to college and get a normal job."

When Alex and I gazed at each other from such a small distance, I found it hard to look him in the eye. I got the impression that Puerto Ricans didn't have as many issues with personal space as Americans did. I preferred a buffer zone.

"Hey, Mariana?" Vince called as he rolled over. "You look kinda red. Do you have sunblock on?"

"The stuff Lilly brought," I said.

Lilly's head jerked toward me and her mouth fell open.

"*¡Ay, mierda!* You're fried!" she hollered, clamoring to her feet.

I dropped my gaze toward my torso. Through my brown-tinted lenses it was hard to tell what color I was. I pressed my index finger onto my stomach and when I pulled it away, it left a pale halo that starkly contrasted with the surrounding flesh. I pulled at the edge of my bathing suit near my hip and saw a remarkably straight tan line that hadn't been there a few hours ago and that should not have developed so quickly if it were just a "healthy glow."

"Damn it," I whispered, closing my eyes.

"Get up!" Lilly ordered as she extended her hand to help me to my feet. I quickly stood and shoved my toes into my flip-flops.

"We gotta get you outta here. Sorry guys," Lilly said, as she gathered our towels and shoved them into her beach bag.

"Do you *have* to go?" Alex asked.

"*Chico,* she's toast. The day is over," Lilly replied.

By this point my face was as red as the rest of me out of sheer embarrassment. Here I was, trying to pass myself off as a somewhat cool person, and I end up proving just how much of a tourist I really was. I knew I would burn. I should have stayed in the shade or at least kept my T shirt on, but I was too worried about looking cute. If I saw a girl on the Jersey beaches surrounded by guys and burnt like a lobster, I would go out of my way to identify her to my friends so we could ridicule her together. I was such an idiot.

"I'm sorry, Alex. But I really should go." I shrugged with defeat.

"It's okay, I understand. I don't want you to die on us," he joked, as he stood up to face me. "It was fun hanging out with you today."

He took a step, closing the gap between us.

It wasn't exactly the most romantic moment, but I didn't want him to move away. Part of me wanted to reach up and touch his face, but I didn't have time to act. Lilly swiftly grabbed my hand and yanked me toward the car.

Chapter 33

Two days, countless aspirin, four cold showers, a dozen iced milk compresses, a bottle of refrigerated aloe vera, a few ice packs and some vitamin E cream later, I was still red. But the swelling had at least gone down and I hadn't developed blisters, which I saw as a major positive. Two summers ago, my shoulders bubbled like melted cheese after I spent twelve hours at an outdoor concert, running through a mist tent with nothing but a tank top and one application of SPF 8. It took almost a week for the pain and oozing to subside. You would think I had learned my lesson.

"I have honestly never seen anyone burnt so badly as you are right now," Lilly commented as she stared at my ruby legs.

"Really? This isn't that strange to me," I noted, as I smoothed another cool layer of green gel on my skin. It was sticky, smelly and a pure slice of heaven.

"Does it hurt?"

"Not as bad. It should start peeling soon."

"That's disgusting."

"No, it's fun. I like to see how big of a piece I can rip in one single peel. And it makes this cool sound as it comes off, kinda like cellophane." I smirked at her.

"You realize that's your skin you're talking about? Eck!" Lilly stuck out her tongue and squeezed her eyes.

"But Lilly, you're pale. You have freckles. Don't you burn?"

"I did when I was little. I went to the beach with my parents when I was, like, eight and totally fried. But that was the last bad burn I remember. I guess my skin just got used to it," she explained as she opened the refrigerator. "Want some leftovers?"

"Do I have a choice?"

"Not really."

Due to my debilitating burn, I got a reprieve from my hotel duties and Lilly was appointed as my personal babysitter-slash-entertainer. In the past two days we had dissected every minute of her show-stopping *Quinceañera,* opened all of her birthday presents (mostly cash and gold jewelry), and written nearly fifty thank-you notes (I addressed the envelopes). The house had virtually returned to normal. Her father Juan dismantled the tent, her mom Angelica scrubbed the house, and Uncle Miguel tossed the garbage. Aunt Carmen did nothing but rest; she'd earned it. But we still had a refrigerator full of scraps—everything from ham to rice to the infamous soup.

My brother, however, was stuck at work. Vince checked in guests, carried their bags and stripped the beds. I was so on his bad side at the moment, despite the fact that he still found time to hit the bars with Juan and Alonzo—who were dying to see my now infamous sunburn—every night. At this point, the only person who hadn't expressed interest in my flaming skin was Alex. I was now convinced I had blown our "attraction" out of proportion. If he liked me, he would have called. That's what guys do.

"Are you still thinking about Alex?" Lilly huffed as she plopped a sandwich in front of me.

Ham and cheese with mustard served on a paper towel. It

was a staple in the Ruíz-Sanchez household, and yesterday I finally broke down and ate it. I also explored some other left-over options, like chick pea soup and yucca (which kind of tasted like potatoes, but not exactly).

"No. I mean, whatever. If I see him, I see him," I said, staring at my sandwich.

"It's not like you guys are boyfriend and girlfriend. He probably just feels weird calling you," she said, as she chomped her food.

"You're right. It's no big deal. And I'll see him again. He's your friend."

"Exactly. Plus, I know he's a good guy. He's not playing you."

"I know. It's just, I guess, I don't know if he likes me," I mumbled.

"Oh, well he hasn't said anything to me. But I'm sure you guys will hook up."

"Oh, so you think that's what he wants? A hook-up?"

"Probably. Why, do you want something more? You're only gonna be here for, like, another five weeks." Lilly swallowed a bite of her sandwich.

I stared at my water. I had drunk more tap water in Puerto Rico than I had in my entire life in Spring Mills. My family always had bottled water or at least a filtered pitcher in the fridge. I had been taught that tap water was dirty and undrinkable, but here, it was the norm.

"I don't want a 'relationship,' " I said, wiggling my fingers like the word was taboo. "But I also don't want to hook up and never see him again."

Lilly nodded and continued to eat her lunch. I wanted her to open the vault and dish all the details she knew about Alex; that's what Madison and Emily would have done. But Lilly wasn't volunteering much.

"So the girls he's hooked up with before, what were they like?" I asked, casually taking a bite of my sandwich, as if it weren't a loaded question.

"Well, none of them were American, that's for sure. We all pretty much date locals . . . or each other," she explained, not looking me in the eye.

Then it struck me; it was so obvious. All of Lilly's friends were guys. She had probably hooked up with half of them, if not all of them. She may have hooked up with Alex. I would never, ever, date someone Emily or Madison had dated first. That was just wrong. It went against the cardinal rule of Girl Code.

"Wait, um, have you and *Alex* . . ." I asked, hoping I wouldn't actually have to say "made out," or worse, "had sex."

"No, no," Lilly said with a deep, booming tone, shaking her head. "Never. We've know each other too long. He's totally asexual to me."

"Oh, good." I sighed. " 'Cause I would never—"

"No, I know. It's cool."

We ate the rest of our lunch in silence. There didn't seem to be anything else to say.

Chapter 34

That night, Alonzo and his friend José stopped by to see the sunburn everyone was talking about. Somehow this crowd of relatives, most of whom appeared as pasty as I, had very limited exposure to serious burns. Though I didn't really think it was that bad, they were staring at my skin like it was green with orange polka dots.

José was a nurse, or at least that's what I gathered. They called him an *"enfermero,"* and were quick to state he was not *"un doctor."* Amazing that the word for doctor translated so flawlessly, you just needed to throw in a bit of a Spanish accent. Same with "hospital" and "hotel." I wondered if those were legitimate Spanish words or whether they were just accepted forms of Spanglish that had morphed over the years.

José and Alonzo, both wearing oddly similar outfits consisting of white pants and pastel shirts with loafers and no socks, brewed a tub of tea with several boxes of teabags. Once it boiled, they added a bucket of ice and let it cool before covering my body with half the bags (saving the rest for a later application). It felt fabulous. I even sat with the bags on my eyes like I was a diva at a day spa. After the second application, they must have felt confident I would do anything they said, because they handed me a tube of hemorrhoid cream and insisted that I slather my face. José swore the cream would reduce swelling and prevent scarring on my *"cara bonita,"* or beautiful face. I squinted my eyes suspiciously but the two sincerely swore that the remedy worked. At this point, the hard cracked skin on my nose had me desperate.

I slowly smeared the cream on my skin and with every stroke tried to block out how it was a product intended for a disgusting growth on the butt that I wasn't even sure I understood. I had never had a hemorrhoid (at least I didn't think so and I figured it was something you'd know if you had). The cream didn't smell, thank God, but it was incredibly greasy and added to the sensation that I was morphing into a gruesome leper. Alonzo insisted that beauty queens all over the world used the stuff to rid redness and puffiness around the eyes, though I had no idea how or why he'd know that.

Their final remedy was a full to the brim bottle from Puerto Rico's Bacardi Rum Distillery, the largest in the world. It was guaranteed to be the cure for what ailed me.

"Seriously, it's not a bad idea," Lilly suggested. "I'm sure if you drink enough of that, you won't care about the sunburn."

I swayed back on the wooden rocker as Lilly, Alonzo and José sat around me on white plastic chairs. The sun was beginning to set behind the tropical hills and I could hear the coquis gearing to sing. I had a few more hours before my normal bedtime, and last night my sunburn was so painful I could hardly sleep. For the first time, a glass of rum was looking pretty good. At the very least, it would help me get some rest.

"Seriously, relax. You're not going to get in trouble if you try it," Lilly said.

She continued to speak to me in English, and then translated everything we said into Spanish for the benefit of Alonzo and José. I tried my best to squeak out enough responses in their language, and they often politely nodded as if they understood. I didn't know if they truly did.

"It's just, I've never really drunk before," I explained. "I'm only fifteen."

While the drinking age in Puerto Rico was officially eighteen, it was rarely enforced—or even mentioned.

Alonzo asked if I didn't like the taste of alcohol and I explained that I wasn't a huge fan of beer, but I hadn't really tried much else aside from champagne at family weddings. As soon as Lilly finished translating my words, José and Alonzo shot up, looked at each other and disappeared into the kitchen.

"What? What did I say? Did I offend them?"

They were already clanging around in the cabinets.

"Uh, no. You pretty much offered them a challenge," she explained. "They're in there trying to make a drink that you'll think tastes good."

"What? I didn't mean that!"

"Uh, too late."

When I heard the blender going, my pulse raced. I stood to protest but Lilly blocked my way.

"Sit down and relax. Or I'll pour it down your throat by force."

They emerged moments later with four tall drinks, one in each hand, presented with the skill of an upscale waiter (they placed white folded towels on their arms and everything). I was informed that there was a piña colada, a planter's punch, a rum and coke, and an orange juice with rum and tonic. Apparently, in addition to the scraps in the fridge, the *Quinceañera* had left an alarming number of drink mixers.

"Awesome," Lilly said, as she checked out the spread.

"I'm not drinking all of that!"

"They don't want you to drink them *all*, they want you to *taste* them all and pick the one you want. We'll drink the rest."

"Which one do you like?"

"I'm not telling you, it might unfairly sway your decision."

I stared at the cocktails. Clearly I was being peer pressured, which instinctively made me want to refuse to participate. But given the amount of effort José and Alonzo had put into them, and how helpful they were being with my sunburn, I didn't want to be rude. Plus, I was on vacation; in Puerto Rico; surrounded by family; with no one driving; and I was burnt to a crisp. If there was ever a good time to drink, now was it.

I sighed and grabbed the rum and Coke. The liquid burned a trail down my throat as I swallowed and winced in pain. I handed it back, and both guys laughed. Next, I sipped the orange juice, which might not have been as strong as the first but the acidic aftertaste made my stomach slosh. I handed it back and faked a grin. Third was the red planter's punch in which I actually couldn't decipher the juice (or juices) mixed but of the three I had tried, this one was at least tolerable. I nodded weakly.

Then Alonzo held out the piña colada. I knew I would hate it. Both pineapples and coconuts had been on my hit list for quite some time. I had tried them only once before, when I was at a second grade "Hawaiian Day" party at school. A kid's mom brought in whole coconuts, the furry skin still attached, with the tops sliced off and a straw inserted. She said it was "coconut milk." I slurped down the drink and followed it with several slices of fresh pineapple. I was blissfully happy until about an hour later when I ran to the toilet with only seconds to spare. The coconut juice was coming straight out of me in a way that I didn't very much appreciate. From that day on, I associated both coconuts and pineapple with a horrific bathroom experience I'd prefer to block from my memory.

I stared down the drink as if it were a sworn enemy. If anyone else had handed it to me, I would have refused it without a single taste. But Alonzo and José were looking at me with such hope that I felt compelled to take at least a tiny sip. I slowly tilted the glass, a droplet squeaking through my lips. It hit my tongue and tasted sweet and creamy, not nearly as bad as I expected. I paused, slightly stunned, and decided to try another nip. It was cool, frothy with barely an alcoholic flavor. It was good—really, really good, almost like a sugary dessert or light milkshake. I swallowed the mouthful and smiled.

Alonzo and José erupted in cheers and hugged each other like I was *The New York Times* food critic offering a rave review. Lilly immediately grabbed the fruit punch.

"Sweet, I was hoping you wouldn't pick this," she stated as she took a giant gulp.

Alonzo handed José the rum and coke as he sat down and sipped the orange juice.

"They thought you'd pick that one," Lilly explained, translating for Alonzo. "It's a chick drink."

"What's that supposed to mean?" I asked, mildly offended.

"It means it's sweet and it goes down easy." She smiled. "Drink up."

Two hours and two and a half piña coladas later and Lilly was right, my sunburn was no longer throbbing. I also couldn't feel my tongue, my fingertips or keep my body from slipping off my chair. Apparently I was the only one having these problems.

"Ya can feel ya tongue, really?" I asked, swaying slightly and knocking my elbow off the arm of the rocker. My body jerked to the right and swung forward. I quickly straightened up thinking I was capable of covering for my lack of balance. "'Cus min feel swollen. Es swollen?"

I stuck out my tongue as I spoke, thinking I was proving my point. Lilly, Alonzo and José erupted in laughter. I was getting the impression that I was becoming a source of amusement, because everything I said was suddenly hilarious. Only I didn't think I was being funny.

"Your tongue's fine," Lilly said, as she wiped tears from her eyes.

"I mus say, ma sunburn feels sooooo much bitter. Look, I can tosh it," I explained as I pushed on my fiery legs. Not a single pang of pain emanated from my skin.

"*Bueno,*" said Alonzo.

"*Es magnifico,*" chimed José, as he sat up straighter and adjusted the hemline of his pink shirt.

I stared at the millions of swirling lights in the sky. I couldn't tell if they were all shooting stars or if I was the only one who could see them moving. Even in my haze, I doubted the entire solar system could be turning this rapidly. I flung my head back on the chair, awkwardly swinging it backward. Lilly quickly reached out to prevent me from toppling over.

"Em all right! Em all right!" I shouted, waving her off.

"Maybe we should switch seats. I don't think you can handle rocking right now," she said.

She grabbed my arm as I wobbled to my feet. The moment I stood upright, the entire world (the house, my cousins, the trees, the air) swirled like the teacups at a carnival.

"Whoa," I mumbled, stumbling back. Lilly caught me by my shoulders and the two of us tumbled backward. Alonzo quickly leapt forward, grabbing our arms.

"Em fine!" I shouted as I tried to stabilize.

José silently stood and discreetly took the still half-full piña colada from my hand.

"Wha? Em not finisshhed," I protested.

"I think you are," said Lilly.

"Noo!" I yelled, swatting at her.

"Hey, what's going on here?" My brother's voice cut through the darkness.

Before I knew it, Vince stepped into the glow of the bare bulb hanging from the porch roof.

Then, so did Alex.

"Omigod," I muttered, covering my hemorrhoid-creamed face with my hands.

"Hola," said Alex.

I flopped onto a chair and curled into a ball, tucking my head into my lap. The stink of tea was radiating from my skin. My forehead felt slimed with greasy ointment. I could feel him staring at me. Even with my head buried in my hands, even after too many piña coladas, I could sense Alex's gaze. A ripple of nausea broke in my stomach.

Lilly immediately darted in front of me, and I lifted my head to peek through my hands. She was standing before me with her arms and legs spread wide to block Vince and Alex's view. She was protecting me. I didn't even have to ask.

"Nothing! Everything's cool," Lilly stated.

"What's up with Mariana?" asked Vince in a suspicious voice.

My brother and I were never the types of siblings who could sense when the other was in danger. But I swear we could sniff out each other's utmost humiliations from miles away, and we weren't the types to let them go. My brother was going to escalate this horrific moment just for the sheer joy of watching me, "responsible Mariana," squirm.

"Is she drunk?" he asked, his voice high.

Alonzo and José rattled off in Spanish to which Lilly yelled at them in Spanish, then Alex chimed in with something I couldn't understand and they all laughed. None of this was encouraging. Vince bounded toward me. Lilly kept her ground, pushing him away.

"Back off!" she shouted, thrusting Vince with all her might. "Vince, it's not a big deal. She had a few drinks to ease her sunburn."

"She's wasted! I *have* to see this." He charged at Lilly again. "You don't understand. Mariana never does anything wrong. I absolutely *have* to see this!"

"No, don't!" she yelled. "Look, we convinced her to try all these sunburn treatments and they helped. But she's all goopy and—"

"Oh! Wait! This is for *his* benefit!" Vince cried. "Alex is here. *Oh, my God! Whoo hoo hoo!*"

My lungs froze. For a second, I felt dead sober—enough to wish I had a large object to pummel my brother into a coma. No girl would ever do this to another girl. Acknowledging a person's crush *in front* of the crush was pure evil. My brother was Satan; he was an evil boy-shaped Satan. I would never be able to face Alex again. Nothing would happen between us now. I was pathetic. I'd have to catch the next flight back to Pennsylvania just to maintain some small fragments of my dignity.

I lifted my finger to my temples and rubbed.

"Okay, Vince, I know you're not my brother, but I think it's safe for me to tell you to *shut up* right now," Lilly spat.

At that moment I wanted to jump up and kiss her.

"Dude, come on! This is classic!"

"Uh, look, I'm getting the impression that I came at a bad time," Alex mumbled.

I refused to look in his direction, but I knew he hadn't stepped foot onto the porch and for that I was grateful. I didn't think my rank tea stench could drift that far.

"Yeah, you know, why don't you call us tomorrow?" Lilly suggested.

"*Sí, bueno.* Mariana, I hope you feel better," he called.

"Uh-huh," I squeaked, still hiding my butt-cream-covered face with my hands.

I heard his footsteps fade as he crossed the lawn. A few seconds later his car's engine started and he drove away.

I yanked my hands from my face, pushed Lilly aside and jumped to my feet.

"I'm gonna kill you!" I shouted, diving toward Vince, my arms swinging wildly.

Lilly grabbed my hands and dove in front of me. I wasn't hard to stop considering I could barely stand up straight. Vince burst into laughter, and I wasn't sure if it was from my greasy face, my drunken display or my death threat.

"Dude, whatever." He laughed. He looked around at our glasses of alcohol. "You got any more?"

Lilly placed me back in my plastic chair.

"Girl, you need some water," she stated, then she turned toward the house and headed for the kitchen.

I rested my head on my hand and closed my eyes.

Chapter 35

I woke up in bed not knowing how I got there or when I left the porch. I was consumed with a pulsing pain that felt like a musician had played the bongo cha-cha on my head and afterward made me swallow his musical instrument—wood, leather, metal and all. It was early morning, and I tossed in the sticky heat for more than an hour, painfully aggravated that Vince was sleeping peacefully in the bed across the room.

My mind slowly searched for details from the night before with one vivid memory repeating on a loop—my brother's mortifying remarks. After days without contact, Alex had shown up (unannounced by the way; seriously, who does that?) while I was covered in butt cream and drunk like a sailor on Fleet Week. Couldn't I, just once, run into the guy I was crushing on while I was standing in my prom dress with Brad Pitt on my arm? Alex must think I'm a total loser and the more I stared at the sleepy expression on Vince's face, the more I wanted to smother him with my pillow. I decided to get up.

Judging from my watch (I was still wearing my red T shirt and white capris from the night before, along with all my jewelry), Uncle Miguel would still be in the kitchen eating breakfast, probably unaware that I was slowly dying from a piña colada overdose.

I slumped off the side of my bed, landing on my hands and knees. The cement floor was blissfully cold. I lazily sprawled out, lifting my shirt to expose my stomach to the cool, hard surface and allowing the feeling to melt into my still burning flesh. Once I had warmed the cement and it had stopped cooling me, I peeled myself off. My head throbbed as I stood, and I stroked it with my palms hoping to ease the pain inside. With the balance of a one-year-old taking her first steps, I inched down the hall in my bare feet. The kitchen was glaring with light at a level I didn't remember the sun ever shining before. I squinted my eyes and held my hands in front of my face as I stumbled in. A roar of laughter quickly greeted me.

"¡Ay, Mariana! ¡Ay, pobrecita!" yelled Uncle Miguel as he rushed to my side.

He wrapped a tan arm around my shoulders and guided me to a kitchen chair, chuckling the entire time. I groaned, fell into the vinyl seat, swung my elbows onto the table and rested my head in my hands. Uncle Miguel ran to the sink and filled a tall glass with water. He rushed to my side, shoved it in front of me and loomed above as I chugged. Then he darted off to the bathroom and returned moments later with two aspirins. I had been on a high-aspirin diet since my sunburn kicked in, so the pills were of no surprise. He filled another glass of water and I gulped down the medicine.

My mind was blank and unable to absorb any information until Uncle Miguel placed a heaping plate of ham and cheese scrambled eggs before me. Even with my nauseated belly, the grease on those eggs never looked so good. I grabbed my fork and ate while Uncle Miguel filled me in on the details I had blocked. (At this point, my great uncle had perfected speaking slowly in basic Spanish and I could almost understand everything he said—a fact that would have made my Spring Mills Spanish teacher very proud.)

Apparently, Vince had arrived about thirty minutes before my uncle returned home from the hotel (actually the bar, but he would never admit that). At that point, I was lying on the porch floor croaking "coqui" noises while my brother searched for frogs to put on my head so he could take a picture. Thankfully, my uncle stopped him. And while Uncle Miguel and Vince were arguing on the lawn, I passed out cold. Lilly and Alonzo nudged me a few times to make sure I was still breathing, and when I yelled and swatted at their hands, everyone figured I was fine. My uncle carried me, like an infant, to bed.

Now, I had experienced embarrassing moments before in my life, but tripping up the steps or dropping a tray at lunch paled in comparison to becoming a belligerent drunk in front of distant relatives who were going out of their way to host me. Even worse, all of these relatives would now see me as "that girl" who drinks too much and makes a scene. I was not that girl. Really, I wasn't. At least I hoped not.

I pressed my hand to my forehead, looked at my uncle with complete desperation and pleaded that I was sorry. He immediately rushed to my side and laughed while hugging me close to his chest. He mumbled something about how rum can be "el enemigo," and swore that what had happened last night was not important. If anything, he said, it showed that I was part of "la familia."

"¿Bien?" he asked, looking down at me in a way that reminded me of my grandfather.

"Sí," I responded, wiping at my damp eyes.

After that, the subject was dropped. He dove into stories about my father, telling me about the house he grew up in and how smart he was in school. Uncle Miguel also complimented my improved Spanish and said that when my grandparents left for New Jersey neither one spoke any English. It amazed me that they were able to make a life for themselves when they couldn't speak the language. It must have been grueling for them, and I wondered what my grandparents disliked about their lives here so much that they would uproot their entire family for a world so foreign. My grandfather spent twenty years in Camden working as a short-order cook for a mediocre restaurant; he could have done that here. And my great aunt and great uncle's house might seem like bare-bones roughing it compared to Spring Mills, but compared to low-income housing projects, it was practically a five-star resort. I couldn't picture myself ever being so selfless as to give up my entire life for the prospect that my kids might someday, possibly, have something better.

A few hours later, my hangover subsided, or at least was more manageable, and Lilly and Vince finally awoke with their own aching heads and puky stomachs.

"I can't believe I drank so much," Lilly moaned.

"Me neither," Vince added as he flopped into a kitchen chair.

"How you feelin'?" Lilly asked, peering at me through glazed eyes.

At this point the color had returned to my cheeks and the buzzing in my head had quieted. "I'm a little better now. Thought I was dying this morning, though."

"How long have you been up?" she asked, as she filled a glass of water.

"Since around six o'clock. I couldn't fall back to sleep. It was torture."

"Oh, that's happened to me before," Lilly groaned.

"Your sunburn better?" Vince asked.

I had already decided that I was still angry with him, so at the sound of his voice I swiftly turned my head in the opposite direction.

"The silent treatment, really? I thought we were older than that," he snapped.

I wasn't. Actually, I thought the silent treatment was good for all ages and quite effective. After the party he threw last year, which ultimately landed us here, I didn't speak to him for a solid week. At first he said it didn't bother him. He pretended as if it were funny. But eventually he cracked when he realized he had no one to complain to about our parents.

"Fine, so I'll ask," Lilly said. "How's your sunburn?"

"It's better now," I stated, looking directly at Lilly as I spoke. "Alonzo's friend really knows what he's doing. All that stuff he brought worked—"

"Alonzo's 'friend'?" Lilly interjected, her eyebrows raised.

"Yeah, José."

Wasn't that obvious? We had been hanging out together all night.

"Um, he's not Alonzo's 'friend.'" Lilly formed air quotes around the word with her fingers.

"What do you mean?"

"Mariana, please . . ."

"What?"

"Are you serious? Have you not noticed that José eats dinner here all the time?"

"So?"

"And that they eat off each other's plates and that he lives in Alonzo's house . . ."

"They're roommates," I stated, matter-of-factly.

"For the love of God, woman. They're gay!" yelled Vince, joining the conversation despite the fact that he wasn't invited.

"What?" I shouted.

"Alonzo and José are gay," Lilly stated plainly, as if she were saying the sky was blue.

"No way."

"Mariana, they wear matching outfits. What types of guys do you know who wear matching outfits?"

I paused. They did wear a lot of pink, but everyone in Puerto Rico wore pastels. Of course, their shorts were rather tight and their hair was meticulously styled. And now that I thought about it, last night they were smiling at each other a lot, and I saw José touch Alonzo's face and drink out of his glass and pat his thigh.

"They're gay?"

"Yes, they are two gay men in a gay relationship," Lilly explained like I was a three-year-old.

"Huh. So I know a gay person?"

"Wait, these are the first gay people you've ever met?"

"Well, yeah. I think so—at least that I know of."

Of course I knew that gay people existed. I watched *Will & Grace* and I followed the "don't ask don't tell" struggles in the military. But I had never met a gay person. I thought they were kind of like celebrities: I knew they lived in the world, but I never expected to meet one in person.

"That makes me kinda cool, doesn't it? That I know a gay person?" I asked.

"¡Ay, Americana! You two live in a bubble," Lilly said.

"Hey! Don't lump me into this," Vince snapped.

"Oh, please! What gay people do *you* know?" I asked in my brattiest tone.

"So you're speaking to me now?" Vince smirked.

I grunted. It was a momentary lapse in judgment, but it blew my silent treatment out the window. Once you broke the vow of silence, even if accidentally, it was permanently shattered.

"Mariana, the tennis coach at our school is gay," Vince explained.

"Mr. Wolf! *Shut up!*"

I shook my head in amazement. Mr. Wolf was hot, like celebrity hot, with buzzed blond hair and a scruffy goatee and huge blue eyes you could spot from space. He was barely out of college and wildly popular with the student body, mostly because he had the sense of humor of a stand-up comic. Guys would walk around the halls quoting him all day: "Dude, your life is like Chinese. I don't understand it," or "Lose some weight, you're lookin' trans fat." Mr. Wolf was the coolest authority figure our school had ever seen.

"How do you know Mr. Wolf is gay?"

"How do you *not* know? It's not a secret. His boyfriend comes to all the team's matches. Everyone was trying to convince them to go to Massachusetts to get married. It was this big thing. Where the heck have you been?" Vince shook his head.

"I guess I don't pay attention to gossip."

"No, you just don't pay attention. Unless it has something to do with Madison or Emily." Vince whispered their names like forbidden words.

"Oh, my God! I never wrote Madison back!" I screeched. "I can't believe it! I have to go."

Before Lilly or Vince could protest, I was already halfway down the hall.

I hadn't e-mailed Madison or Emily since they dumped the Orlando Bloom photo spread in my inbox. They didn't know about the *Quinceañera* or my crush on Alex or my third degree sunburn or my friendship with Lilly.

I rushed into the Internet café and clicked on my laptop. It had been days. I wasn't consciously avoiding them . . . well, at first I was. How could I not be jealous of Orlando Bloom? But then I just got busy.

It was like the diary I received as a gift before entering middle school. At first everything was so scary and confusing that I wrote in it every day. I needed the outlet. But by the end of seventh grade, I hardly used it. I had grown accustomed to my new school and schedule and friends. Now I only wrote in it when something major happened, like when my grandparents died. My obsession with e-mail was very similar.

I logged on to my account.

I expected my box to be clogged with more tales from the legendary Sweet Sixteen, only it wasn't. There were only three new messages. The first asked if I had received their photos and whether I had listened to their radio interview. They were dying to know my reactions. The second asked if I was getting any of their messages and had the word "TEST" in the subject line. The third message expressed their confusion at my lack of communication and assumed that I had lost Internet access due to my "Bumblehump" location; they asked that I message them as soon as I got online.

My stomach tightened. If they knew the truth, that I had just forgotten to contact them, they would hate me. If they knew how much fun I had at Lilly's *Quinceañera,* they'd feel betrayed. Major things had happened to them, yet I had completely neglected their existence.

So I lied. I opened a new message, flew my fingers over the keys and told them the Internet café had suffered a power outage. I pretended to be angry about how long it took to fix, and then went on endlessly about how I wished I could have attended Madison's birthday party. I wrote about how amazing her photos were, how incredible the Orlando Bloom appearance was, and how happy I was for her party's success. I raved about their radio interview and included as many quotes from the broadcast as possible to prove that I had listened. Then I told them about Lilly, Alex, the *Quinceañera,* the beach, the drunken incident, everything.

The message was enthusiastic, but almost forced. I stressed over what to write so I would sound like the girl that they remembered. I needed to make sure that I included enough references to our inside jokes and silly slang words, and that I didn't sound too happy so they'd know that I still missed them.

But the whole time I couldn't stop thinking about Alex. It was as if Emily and Madison were wiped clean and all my memory space was being used for a new purpose, for a new life.

Chapter 36

My sunburn healed. It took a few days, but I finally looked like a normal-colored person, which was cause for celebration.

Early this morning, Lilly called Alex and Javier and we all headed for one of the island's main tourist attractions, El Yunque Rain Forest. It was an opportunity for redemption after my drunken spectacle, and I couldn't wait to be alone with Alex in an exotic tropical locale. But as soon as we pulled into the forest, water droplets tumbled from the sky (I don't know why this surprised me, the word "rain" is in the location's title). I was forced to buy a fluorescent orange poncho that looked like a cross between a trash bag and a crossing guard belt. It wasn't the most attractive look and the thick muggy air in no way helped the rapidly frizzing mop on the top of my head.

I closed my eyes and inhaled the scent of summer: fresh wet grass on a hot day. I thought of Vince playing baseball—and as I slowed my mind, I could almost hear the crack of his bat above the hum of tropical birds and swirling insects. It was odd that something so foreign could remind me of something so American.

"Hey, La Mina's this way." Lilly pointed as she led us down one of the forest paths.

"So, have you ever seen a waterfall?" Alex asked as he strolled beside me.

"Nope. I've actually never been in a rain forest before," I admitted. "We don't have too many of those in Philadelphia."

"Ah, right. You have the Liberty Bell and Paul Revere, *verdad*?"

"No, Paul Revere's from Bahston," I said in my best Massachusetts accent. "We've got Ben Franklin and Betsy Ross."

"Who's Betsy Ross?"

"Who's Betsy Ross! She sewed the first American flag. I'm surprised you don't know that. I figured she'd be an important figure in Puerto Rico; you guys obviously ripped her off." I curled my lips into a sly smile.

"What?" he shouted.

"Come on, your flag—red, white and blue with a star. That's gotta be some sort of copyright infringement."

"Hey, we're a part of the United States."

"Oh, yeah. A 'territory.' " I grinned. "Why don't you just commit? Put your star on our flag."

"You'd like that, wouldn't you?" he said, suggestively raising a brow.

"Are you trying to make a conversation about patriotic flags dirty?" I asked, sounding shocked and appalled.

"Why? Do you want me to?"

He smiled at me in a way no other guy ever had. I almost wanted to pull out my camera and take a picture of the moment so I'd remember it forever. But somehow I knew I wouldn't forget.

★   ★   ★

The waterfall was huge—at least two stories high—and gushing white water. Thick streams surged down a cliff of black, jagged rocks until it landed in a clear, cool pool at the bottom. All around it was a glow of green—leaves, trees, bushes, flowers, even an emerald parrot with a red-tipped head swooped above the falls. I had never seen anything like it outside of Hollywood movies. If I couldn't smell the water (it had a scent, not salty like the ocean, but fresh like laundry detergent mixed with earth) and feel the spray, I wouldn't have believed it was real. I stared silently. It amazed me that something so massive, beautiful and natural could exist, and that there were people who would go their whole lives not seeing it. I felt very small.

"Mariana, *chica*! Come on!" Lilly yelled as she ventured off the path.

"Where are you going?" I watched her, Vince and Javier head toward the water.

"Swimming," Alex explained.

He was holding my hand and had been for the past five minutes. It was an unfamiliar gesture. Once when I was a flower girl in my cousin's wedding, I had to hold the ring bearer's hand, but aside from that (and the occasional ballet partner) I had never held hands with a male romantically. In that moment, I felt like his girlfriend despite the fact that we hadn't kissed and we barely knew each other. His attention was focused solely on me, asking if I was happy, thirsty, tired, etcetera. And everyone else felt like spectators—they were present at what was happening between us but we didn't really need them.

"I don't have a bathing suit on."

I looked down at my olive shorts and yellow cotton tank top—I had borrowed the outfit from Lilly. I hadn't expected to go swimming. If I had, I would have worn my bikini or at least a shirt that wouldn't immediately become transparent at the slightest hint of water.

The rain had stopped midway through our hike and Alex was carrying my poncho. It was an act of consideration I usually only got from my father. It was nice to have a guy carry my stuff again, not that I was being anti-feminist (I considered myself a feminist because, being a female, I didn't see how I could possibly be against women's rights. I mean, weren't all women feminists?). It wasn't like I was incapable of holding my things; it was just nice not to have to.

"That's okay, we don't have to go in," Alex said, squeezing my hand.

"Well, no. If you want to, go ahead. It's cool."

"I want to hang out with you. I've been here before."

"Really, it's no big deal. I'd feel bad if you didn't swim just because of me. Seriously, swim."

"Really, I want to hang out with *you*."

I could sense that I was protesting too much and I didn't want to come across as "difficult." I looked at Alex, then at the water. I wanted to be that carefree girl who jumps in without a thought of her clothes, her hair or her bra showing through, who just swims around enjoying the moment and not worrying about what happens next or what other people thought. I knew I wasn't that girl, but part of me wished that I was.

"Why don't we just go down to the edge?" I suggested, walking forward and slightly tugging at Alex's hand.

I got the impression that swimming was probably not encouraged (there were no park rangers or official employees around to help should something terrible happen). I jumped from rock to rock to make my way to the edge. It wasn't easy, especially since I was trying not to step on the muddy grass and ruin my new flip-flops. I stopped on a large, black rock near the surface of the pool and Alex halted on the one behind me. I could feel his breath on the back of my neck.

"Mariana, come on! You *have* to come in!" Lilly shouted as she splashed in the water. It was only waist high where she was standing, but the spray off the falls had soaked her white tank top straight through. She was leaving very little to the imagination.

"*¡Ay, que pecho bonito!*" yelled Javier as he stared at Lilly's breasts.

It seemed to be the American equivalent of "Hey, nice rack!" but Lilly smiled in response. She was happy with the compliment, and I would have been too. No one had ever commented on my boobs. But I guess I had to grow them first.

"Mariana, get in here!" Vince yelled as he dipped his head back in the water and began to float with his toes pointed up.

It was one of Vince's true talents. He could float better than anyone I had ever seen, straight as a board. Whenever I attempted it, my arms flapped wildly under the water, my butt dropped, and my toes barely broke the surface. It took every ounce of strength in my abdomen not to sink, and I thought floating was supposed to be easy.

"Really, I don't want to," I replied, shaking my head.

I wasn't staying out of the water for attention, though it probably looked that way. I really didn't want to get wet. I was the type of girl who sat on the beach all day without venturing into the ocean. I just wasn't a big swimmer, unless the water was chlorinated.

"We're on vacation!" Vince yelled, splashing water from where he stood. Thankfully, the distance prevented the drops from hitting me. "Live a little!"

"Seriously, I just don't want to. I like it here. It's pretty." I waved my hands at the scenery around me.

Just then, Javier lost his balance on an algae-covered rock and his leg jutted out from under him. His arms flapped as he caught himself, and I could see the rocks were slimy and green. Lilly, however, was maneuvering well. She slowly inched her way toward me with the look of a football player about to toss the cheerleader into the pool.

"Lilly, don't!" I ordered when she got within a few feet. "I really don't want to get wet."

"It's fun! Trust me!" she shouted, inching closer.

Alex tightened his grip on my hand as if to reassure me that he'd protect me from the attack. I turned my head and smiled.

"Lilly, I believe you. I just don't feel like being wet and cold the rest of the day," I said as I swiveled back to face her.

"It's Puerto Rico! It's, like, ninety degrees. You can't possibly be cold!"

She shot out her hand and I instinctively lifted my foot to move away. As I tried to shift my weight, I felt my other leg give. My flip-flop slipped on the edge of the rock and my entire body jerked hard toward the surface of the water. I felt a sharp ache as muscles I didn't know I had clenched to try to stabilize me. I knew I was going to fall—like a driver suddenly realizing it was too late to stop the accident about to happen. I closed my eyes, preparing myself for what was about to hit: water, rocks, algae.

And then, unexpectedly, I felt a strong pull on my arm, my waist, and my shoulders.

I opened my eyes and saw Alex bent over me—one arm wrapped tightly around my back and the other cradling my head in a dip that was almost elegant. Before I could react, he lowered his mouth and kissed me. I didn't see it coming—my first kiss.

I wrapped my arms around his neck and let the weight of

my body fall into his arms. I wasn't sure what I was supposed to do. Did I keep my lips closed so I wouldn't look easy? Or was I supposed to make goldfish lips like actors in the movies? Could he tell I hadn't done this before?

My mind raced until I felt a flick of his tongue. I could taste him, but not in a way I could describe. Not like pizza or toothpaste or coffee. It was just his natural taste. Prior to this I thought sharing someone's drink was gross, but now I had someone else's saliva dripping in my mouth. And I wondered if I was supposed to be thinking about this, or about anything at all, and whether it was making my kissing worse.

I felt his fingers dig into my hair. He tugged gently at the locks above my neck, and of everything I was feeling, that gesture felt the best. His hand in my hair. It made me feel pretty.

Slowly, we pulled apart and he looked at me from inches away. We had been this close before, on the dance floor, but it had been dark. He couldn't *really* see me. Now the air was full of sunshine and every freckle, every imperfection, was visible. I felt a desire to pull away, but I didn't have to. He gradually stood up, his arm guiding me out of the dip. When we were standing upright on the rock again, face-to-face, no longer kissing and with no imminent threat of falling, that's when I remembered we weren't alone. That's when I heard them screaming.

"Woo hoo!" yelled Javier.

"Dude, that's my sister! That's disgusting! Stop, please! Ugh!" groaned Vince as he pretended to gag.

Lilly didn't say anything. When I looked at her, she smiled. She was happy for me. *I* was happy for me.

Chapter 37

He wasn't my boyfriend. How could he be? I'd be leaving for Spring Mills in a few weeks. But at the same time, I didn't think it was a fling, either. Our attraction wasn't fleeting, or momentary, or a mistake, or superficial. I didn't know what we were. But I saw him almost every day for ten days straight.

The day after El Yunque, he stopped by the hotel. Lilly was still stripping beds and I didn't have any guests to check in, so Alex and I took a walk. We held hands as we strolled through the campus of UPR. It still amazed me that this was a university. The buildings were pink, canary yellow, and tangerine, and the grounds were lush, green and trimmed with exotic flowers. All the college campuses I'd seen back home were dark, historic stone facades lined with oak trees—and they in no way resembled a vacation resort.

We stopped at a bench and before Alex even settled onto the wooden slats, he reached over and touched my face. Maybe it was because I was more prepared—or maybe because I had a kiss's-worth of experience under my belt—but when his lips touched mine, I felt chills tickle my skin. He was warm and familiar. It was perfect.

I opened my eyes and realized we were still in the center of campus. Any number of people passing might have known him or his family. I would have been mortified to kiss anyone in such a public arena in Spring Mills, and the fact that he wasn't embarrassed made me feel special. He wasn't hiding me from anyone.

We walked back to the hotel. Lilly and Vince had already left for lunch without me. I didn't expect them to wait, but their absence still made me feel unwanted. It was like finding out all your friends went to a movie without you because they thought you were sick. Even if you were, you still wanted the invitation. And when Alex left for work (he was a cashier at a local bookstore), I ate lunch in the hotel bar, alone.

After that, Alex stopped by the house to see me almost every evening. He, Lilly, Vince and I would lounge on the porch, listening to the frogs. We'd talk about everything—from what we wanted to be when we grew up to why women's clothing designers sold pants in "long" but not shirts.

The one night Alex couldn't make it, because he had to work late, he actually called to apologize. Since I'd been in Utuado, the only other person I'd spoken to on the phone was my mother. She called every other day, mostly to make sure I didn't hate her for shipping me off. I briefly told her about a boy named "Alex," but didn't hint that he was more than an *"amigo,"* even though he was. My new extended family had taken to calling him *"mi novio,"* despite my protest.

Alex was coming to dinner. My Uncle Miguel had extended the invitation despite my panicked attempts to explain the delicate complexities of "talking" versus "seeing each other" versus "going out." Either I didn't possess the sufficient Spanish language skills or he didn't possess the sufficient pop culture know-how to comprehend the situation.

The dinner was going to happen.

I convinced myself that it wasn't a big deal. Vince, Lilly, her parents, my aunt and uncle, Alonzo, José and I would all share some food with Alex. Big whoop.

But when Lilly and I pulled up in front of the house, after two hours of work at the hotel, a raging party was in full swing.

"What's with all the people?" I whispered to Lilly, assuming that there was a holiday, birthday, or some celebration no one remembered to tell me about.

"They're here for you," she grunted, as we walked across the lawn.

"For me? Didn't I already meet everyone?" I muttered as I saw the dozens of figures inside moving to the booming salsa beats.

"They're here to meet you and *your boyfriend*." She snorted.

"What? He's not my boyfriend!"

"Whatever. It's an excuse to throw a party, not that they really need one," she said, shaking her head.

We stepped inside the house and Lilly immediately disappeared into the crowd. I hadn't seen any of these relatives since Lilly's *Quinceañera*. I hated that feeling of being surrounded by strangers in a place you shouldn't feel strange—like when the only person you know at a party is the birthday girl. I didn't even have Vince to keep me company. He was still back at the hotel downing beers with Uncle Miguel, which seemed rather inappropriate given that my Aunt Carmen had clearly spent the day slaving in the kitchen.

I had stepped two feet into the house when a crowd of women engrossed me. Distant aunts and cousins, whose names I couldn't remember, rattled off a million questions in Spanish—of which I could comprehend about every other word. I tried to explain that the boy coming was Alex, Lilly's friend, and that he was *not my boyfriend* but that I liked him more than a friend. They burst into laughter at my explanation like I was some cutesy girl playing hard to get. I continued professing, in a voice like a concertgoer shouting over the crowd, that he was a nice guy and I really liked him but we weren't technically boyfriend and girlfriend, until the room suddenly fell silent. Everyone stopped speaking simultaneously and my lungs clenched.

"*Buenas tardes,*" Alex said, from somewhere behind me.

I didn't turn around. I considered slowly slithering into my bedroom so I could pretend like what he'd overheard was a figment of his imagination. But my relatives parted like a well-rehearsed marching band and I heard Alex's footsteps halt at my back.

"*Hola,* Mariana."

"Hey," I said sheepishly as I turned around.

Chapter 38

Just like when we'd first arrived, the seats at the dining table were reserved for the guests of honor. I was seated in my usual high-back wooden chair with the yellow cushion, with Alex on one side and Vince on the other (he and my uncle got back from the bar about five minutes before dinner, with alcohol radiating from their pores). Lilly was seated across from me, flanked with her parents on one side and her grandparents on the other.

Everyone else ate either with their plate poised on their lap or seated at the kitchen table. From the way people kept approaching Alex and me, one could have thought we were the bride and groom at our wedding reception. The whole soirée seemed like a lot of trouble for nothing. My aunt had cooked enough food to feed half the island and before dinner had started, a group of relatives pushed back the furniture in the living room, turning the area into an impromptu dance floor. Now, with drinks in hand, they swiveled their hips and shuffled their feet like they were in the *Quinceañera* tent. That was something I would never, ever, see in my parents' house; my mom would be too worried about damaging her hardwood floors.

"Mariana, this is the most I've ever seen you eat," Vince whispered.

My plate was filled with Spanish rice, chicken and sweet plantains, and I had a bowl of *asopao*. There was an entire pig on the table that I refused to look at, which my aunt and uncle found hysterical. I had nothing against eating meat, but seeing the "meat" in its animal form was a bit much. It was like picking a lobster out of a tank. It was one thing to have a lobster tail placed before you—it was dead already, you couldn't stop that—but it was quite another to be responsible for ordering the murder of that specific lobster.

"Does this mean that Mom won't have to force you to eat roast beef when we get home?" Vince teased, raising his eyebrows.

"I wouldn't go that far."

"You're not a big eater?" Alex asked.

"I eat enough."

"Oh, please! My grandmother's been making you a plain chicken breast almost every night since you got here!" Lilly mocked from across the table.

"That's not entirely true," I mumbled. I had begun to expand my taste buds in recent days. "I ate at your *Quinceañera*."

"Yeah, one night," Lilly huffed. "Other than that, you complain about how the food's so different here. *Because back in Spring Mills* . . ." Lilly mimicked in a high-pitched tone, mocking my voice.

"I don't sound like that."

"Sure you do," said Vince, joining the fun.

"Whatever, *Vi-cen-tay*," I snipped.

"Yup, that's my name."

"Please, you're such a poser."

"I am not! Just because I like it here—"

"*I* like it here!" I interjected.

It was the first time I had said it out loud. Sometime during the past few weeks, my mood had changed. Sure, I wasn't about to give up my cell phone, my queen-size bed or my unlimited spending cash any time soon, but even without all that stuff, this life had begun to fit. I now could see myself here, with these people, in this culture—in *my* culture.

"Sure you like it here *now*." Vince stared directly at Alex as he said that.

"Don't start, Vince," I spat under my breath.

Vince and I fought all the time. It wasn't something I was ashamed of, but it also wasn't something I wanted to share with a guy I was still trying to impress. If I threw verbal jabs at my brother, Alex could think I was mean or immature.

"Sorry about that," I whispered to Alex.

"It's okay, I fight with my sisters, too," he replied, as he lifted a plantain to his mouth.

"You have sisters?"

"Three of them, all younger."

"Wow, that's gotta make the bathroom situation interesting."

Alex chuckled. "Well, my dad and I are outnumbered. We're lucky if we can pee in the morning." His dimples flashed as he took another bite of his food. "*So* how much longer are you gonna be here?"

"Three and a half weeks."

"You must miss home," he said plainly.

"I do, but I'm getting used to it here," I answered, my eyes smiling.

"Yeah right!" Lilly shouted. "I seem to remember you being a mess not that long ago because you missed your friend's party."

"She has a point," Vince added.

I was getting the distinct impression that Lilly was angry with me. It's not like she was shooting me snotty looks or cursing me out. It was more like up until dinner she was utterly avoiding me. Even after Alex arrived, she didn't talk to either of us. And since we'd started eating, she had done nothing but subtly attack the tiniest comments I made. She was undermining me in a way that only a girl could, in a way Emily or Madison would, only I couldn't figure out what I'd done to upset her.

"Lilly, of course I'm homesick. I've never been this far from home before."

"That's understandable." Alex reached his hand under the table and squeezed my thigh. Blood rushed to my cheeks and I saw Lilly's gaze instantly follow to where Alex's hand was concealed. She rolled her eyes.

I shrugged my shoulders as if to ask, "*What?*" But she ignored me.

"If I moved to the East Coast, I'm sure I'd miss home too," Alex said.

"Do you wanna move?" I asked, slightly shocked

I couldn't comprehend how people had the strength to move so far away. If my parents moved from Philly to Jersey, I'd throw a fit. But my dad had done it and so did a lot of Alex's relatives, so I guess the idea didn't seem that foreign to him.

"I've thought about going to college there after I graduate next year. My goal is to be the first in my family to get a degree."

"My dad was the first in our family to go to college. Well, actually his brothers went to college first, but he was still the first generation."

"It's weird that your dad grew up here, and now here *you* are. You're so different. Not in a bad way, but for being only one generation removed, you're very . . . American." He looked at his plate as he said that.

He was right. And I had thought about it a lot since I'd

come to Puerto Rico. This is where my dad was from—this exotic, tropical, Spanish-speaking mountain town. And now he's a suit-wearing corporate executive in a major U.S. city living in a fancy suburb and speaking without a hint of an accent. I wondered if he missed home, or if he'd stopped considering this his home a long time ago. If I left Spring Mills, would I eventually stop feeling connected to it? That was hard to imagine, but so was spending the rest of my life speaking a different language. My dad did it. And because he did, I am who I am. My grandparents' decision to take that leap across the ocean to seek a better life radically changed the future for the rest of us. If they had made a different choice, a safer choice, I wouldn't be here or, at the very least, I wouldn't be who I am. I could be Lilly, or some variation of her, in some alternate reality where I called Utuado my home.

"It's strange," I answered, trying to figure out a way to voice what I was thinking. "To think that my dad lived here. He's changed so much. Like you said, not in a bad way, but in a way that's very different from this place."

"Does he talk about Utuado a lot?" Alex had completely stopped eating and from the level of his intensity, I sensed he was serious about traveling to the States. He wasn't asking me for information about my father, he was asking to get a picture of what his life could be like if he followed my dad's example.

"No, never," I answered honestly.

"Does he speak Spanish?"

"Not since my grandparents died. But he listens to Spanish music."

"I'm sorry about your grandparents."

"It's okay."

"I didn't know your grandparents died," Lilly stated softly. Apparently she had been listening to our conversation.

She turned her head toward my Uncle Miguel, who from

the looks of it had cleared his plate long ago. He was leaning back on the hind legs of his chair drinking a dark brown liquid from a short glass. Lilly rattled off in Spanish to her grandfather, and I could make out that she was inquiring about my *"abuelos,"* or grandparents. Uncle Miguel looked at me before he responded and then uttered something I didn't understand.

"What did he say?" I asked after she finished her conversation.

"Nothing, just that he knew your grandfather had died. Your dad wrote them after the funeral."

"After the funeral? Wait. Uncle Miguel wasn't invited to his own brother's funeral?" I asked, my jaw falling. Vince dropped his fork.

"No, it doesn't sound like it," Lilly said, shaking her head.

My parents, my mother especially, thrived on etiquette. She stressed over which name came first when addressing a married couple on the outer envelope of an invitation. She would never forget to invite my grandfather's brother to his funeral. That had to be a mistake.

I turned to Vince, my eyebrows crumpled as if to ask, *"Did you know anything about this?"* Vince shook his head, *"no."*

"I'm sure it was nothing," Alex stated. "Probably just a mix-up."

"Yeah, I guess." I shook my head in wonderment.

"So, colleges. Where do you want to go?" Alex asked, changing the subject. "Because I hear all the good schools are in the Northeast. That's where you're from, *verdad?"*

"Sí," I stated, my Spanish squeaking through as my mind still grappled with the previous conversation.

"The University of Pennsylvania—that's in Philadelphia?"

"Yeah, but I doubt I'll go there. It's too close to home."

"Why, Alex? You thinking of moving closer to Mariana?" Lilly butted in, her tone biting.

"No, I was just trying to get a sense of what things are like there," he mumbled.

"Sure you are."

"Do you want to go to school in the States?" I asked Lilly.

"Maybe. But I won't just be following some *guy*," she choked, staring at Alex.

I let the innuendo drop. I didn't want to fight with Lilly over nothing. And for some reason, I was no longer in a very good mood.

Chapter 39

Alex went MIA after the family dinner. Not in an official call-the-police sense, but it had been four days since I'd heard from him. He hadn't stopped by and he hadn't called, and I had spent every minute of his absence trying to pin down exactly what I had done wrong.

"Mariana, seriously, you're reading too much into this," Lilly said as we strolled down Calle del Cristo in Old San Juan.

The cobblestone street reminded me of Old City in Philadelphia, only all of the buildings were either whitewashed or slathered in bright pastel paints, from pale peach to mint green, with second-story balconies reminiscent of New Orleans. I was surprised to find a Coach store and Ralph Lauren Outlet, but in true Puerto Rican style the Ralph Lauren facade was painted baby blue with white trim. It was a stark contrast from the brand's stodgy building in Philadelphia, which I frequented so often I had the layout memorized.

"I just don't get it," I said, as I stared down the street to the old chapel below. "Everything was going so well. It was, wasn't it? You thought so?"

"It's only been a few days. Why get so wrapped up in a guy you'll never see again? Just enjoy Puerto Rico," Lilly said, as

she flopped behind me in white platform sandals, a pink flowing skirt and a white tube top.

Back home, I never got dressed up to go shopping; at most
I wore a T-shirt and jeans. But Lilly had convinced me to wear
a blue skirt and tube top. (*"We're going into town. Look hot,"*
she'd said.) It was the first strapless top I had ever worn and I
felt certain it was going to slide down my torso at any moment. I didn't have the boobs my cousin did, but I still felt
oddly sexy. I was being noticed in these clothes in a way I had
never been before, but considering most of the guys leering at
us were probably over forty and closet pedophiles, I guessed it
wasn't exactly the kind of attention I wanted to encourage.

"I *am* enjoying Puerto Rico," I said, not wanting to sound
ungrateful.

Lilly had devoted most of her summer to me and she was
becoming a close friend. Since her *Quinceañera,* we had grown
so tight that I hardly felt the need to contact Emily or Madison. I felt guilty for ignoring them, but I had a lot going on to
distract me. I also had Alex. But now, given his sudden disap-
pearance, I was itching to get in touch with my girls from
home. They'd know what to do, or at least they'd offer advice
pretending to know.

"I just, I *like* him," I admitted as we continued walking toward the chapel.

Lilly had promised that the plaza alongside the chapel was
a must-see. It was filled with hundreds of pigeons and their
"pigeon tamer." I didn't want to disappoint her by pointing
out that I'd seen plenty of pigeons before: pooping on cars,
begging for soft pretzels, filling park benches. So I smiled and
followed my tour guide.

"Look, Alex is a cool guy. But I wouldn't obsess over him,"
Lilly said.

I wasn't obsessed, but I thought about him a lot. I thought

about the way he made me feel when we kissed, the way my stomach trembled when he touched me; I wanted to feel that way all the time. It's not like we had these long make-out sessions; mostly we just kissed in front of his beat-up car before he left my aunt and uncle's house for the night. But I loved the anticipation of knowing that we would kiss, that before I went to bed that night I would be kissed by a boy who liked me. And when he pulled me close, I wanted to melt right into him to fully consume the moment.

"I'm not obsessed."

"Then why do you keep talking about him?"

"I didn't realize I wasn't supposed to talk about him. If I'm getting on your nerves, I'll stop."

I'd never brought up Lilly's snippy attitude toward me the night of the family dinner. When we woke up the next morning and the house was empty once more, things returned to normal. We went to work and goofed off until it was time to skip out and catch a movie. I didn't want to ruin things by bringing up a tone of voice that I might have been reading too much into.

Part of me realized that I was probably avoiding the inevitable, and that I should trust my instincts. Whenever I got mad at Madison or Emily, even when I tried to brush it off and let it go, it always found a way of resurfacing. It would lurk within me, bubbling quietly, until one day we'd be sitting at a lunch table wolfing down French fries and Madison would ask me to pass the ketchup. *"No! I will not pass the ketchup! God, what's wrong with you? Would it kill you to say 'please'?"* Ultimately it would lead to a long conversation about what was actually upsetting me.

Given the amount of time Lilly and I were spending together, there was a lot of potential for irritation. It was hard enough to live with the family you grew up with, look at how often Vince and I fought, let alone add strangers into your daily routine. We were suddenly in each other's faces every minute of every day: sharing a bathroom, eating the same meal, working in the same place. I didn't know how I would react to having a foreigner latch on to my life to this degree back home. I really couldn't blame her if she was fed up.

Lilly took a deep breath.

"You're not getting on my nerves." She sighed. "I'm just sick of talking about Alex."

"Okay, that's fair. Let's talk about something else."

We walked down the street in silence and by the time we reached the chapel the moment had passed. Gray cooing birds covered the historic street, bursting into flight as an old man in a cap threw bread crumbs in the air. I didn't bring up Alex again that day—at least not aloud.

Chapter 40

Three days later, Alex still hadn't called or visited. At this point it had been a full week of no contact and I was assuming we had broken up—not that we were ever together. I had watched Vince cut off communication before as a way of ending a relationship rather than verbalizing the breakup aloud. It seemed like an awful thing to do, because there was no official end. Technically the other person could be out in the world thinking they're still part of a couple, forever.

Lilly, Vince and I were seated on stools in the hotel bar. The leather was sticking to the backs of my thighs. I tugged on my baggy khaki shorts. It was the first time I had ventured into the bar with my brother after dinner. Usually I just watched Spanish TV or, lately, waited for Alex. Lilly and I were the only girls there; my aunt had stayed back at the house to clean. Lilly and Vince had ordered beers while I, as usual, sipped a Coke.

"¿Otro?" asked the bartender, pointing toward my almost empty glass.

I nodded. "So, Vince, you're a guy. What do you think?"

"About what?"

"About Alex. Why do you think he's ditching me?"

"You don't know he's ditching you. Maybe he's just busy.

It's not like he has to check in with you. You're not his mother," Vince said, before releasing a long beer burp.

Lilly laughed.

"But he wasn't busy before. We saw each other all the time," I defended as I picked at the bar's raised, wooden splinters.

"Well, maybe that's the problem," Lilly snipped.

"I suffocated him? You think so?"

"I don't know," she conceded, as she drank her beer.

"Mariana, you're over-thinking this. Guys aren't that complicated. He's probably just busy," Vince said.

I couldn't imagine this was true. Even if I were busy I would still make time to see him, at worst I would call him to explain. Clearly he wasn't thinking about me as much as I was thinking about him, and the only logical explanation was that he was busy thinking about somebody else.

"Do you think he met someone?" I squeaked in a low voice, staring at my soda.

"Dude, it's possible," Vince muttered.

"Gee, thanks,"

"You asked."

"Well, you didn't have to be so quick to agree with me."

"Then why'd you ask?"

"*Forget it.* Do *you* think he's met someone else?" I asked Lilly, my eyes as sad as a basset hound's.

"I honestly don't know. It's not like he's some big stud—"

"So you don't think he has," I quickly interjected.

She looked at me, shook her head and smirked. "Fine, no. I think there is no way he could have ever met anyone to replace you, almighty Mariana. It's impossible," she teased.

"That's what I was thinking," I said, laughing at myself.

"Can we please talk about something else," Vince moaned, rolling his eyes.

"Thank you," Lilly added.

"Fine," I huffed. "Can you believe Mom and Dad are coming in a week?"

"I know," he said, his voice almost sad. "One week of quality family time and then we're all flying home together."

"That sucks," Lilly mumbled.

"I don't see why we can't fly home ourselves," Vince griped.

"Because our parents want to see us and Mom wants to meet everyone."

"They could see us when we got home," he huffed.

I rolled my eyes. "Did you know that when Dad lived here they used to call him 'Manny?' "

"Really? Who told you that?"

"Uncle Miguel. He also said that Dad used to want to be a pilot when he grew up. He used to run around everyone's yards with his arms out to the side, pretending he was a plane." I held my arms out to mimic the gesture.

"Wow, you and Uncle Miguel talk a lot, huh?" Vince asked, kind of surprised.

"In the mornings."

"Well, my grandfather's a big talker," Lilly added.

"Don't you think it's weird that we didn't even know we had an Uncle Miguel before we came here?" I asked, still picking at splinters on the bar.

"We didn't know we had *any* of these relatives before we came here," Vince pointed out, nodding toward Lilly.

"Well, I didn't know you or *Vicentay* existed, either," Lilly stated.

"But that's weird, right? Why wouldn't Dad have come back here sooner? He grew up here."

"I don't know. Maybe he didn't like it here. No offense," Vince said, lifting his chin at Lilly.

"But this was still his home. He knew he had family here, you'd think he'd want to see them. Or you'd think Grandmom

and Grandpop would have wanted to see them. I don't remember them ever visiting," I said, successfully pulling a small
strip of wood from the bar. I didn't know what I was going to
do with it, but the accomplishment felt oddly satisfying.

"No, they never visited," Lilly confirmed.

"Well, Grandmom and Grandpop were poor. They probably couldn't afford the trip," Vince stated plainly.

"True, but Dad's not, at least not anymore."

"He had *us*. Who would want to trek over here with little
kids?"

"Yeah, I guess."

Alonzo, José and our Uncle Miguel walked into the bar at
that moment. We all waved lazily and the guys sat down beside
us already deep in conversation. They seemed to be having an
argument about which country produced more major league
baseball players, Puerto Rico or the Dominican Republic. At
this point, both Vince and I could understand most of what
people said around us and we could hold entire conversations
in Spanish. Vince was even somewhat conversant in the language while drunk, which I found rather impressive.

"*¿Dónde está Alex?*" my uncle asked innocently, looking
around.

"Ahhhh!" I yelled, grabbing my red hair in my fists.

Lilly and Vince laughed. We all hung out at the bar for another hour and no one brought up Alex again.

Chapter 41

The next day, Lilly trudged up the stairs with her empty laundry basket in hand and a suspicious grin on her face. Vince was sitting on his usual stool watching Spanish soap operas and I was dusting the hotel's front desk, for the fifth time that morning.

"Hey, Mariana, I've been meaning to ask you something," Lilly said, as she opened a closet door and tossed her basket inside. "You know my friend Javier? Well, he's starting at UPR in a couple weeks and he doesn't know much about computers. He's all freaked out that he's gonna look like an idiot. I was wondering if you could show him some stuff."

"Why me?" I asked, my nose crinkled.

"Well, you have your own laptop and you're pretty good with the Internet . . ."

"Well, what does he need to know? I'm pretty good with computers," Vince offered from across the room.

"He just wants to learn some Internet and e-mail stuff. Pretty basic, that's why I thought Mariana could help him."

"I guess. When?"

"Today, at lunch," Lilly said quickly.

"Where, here?"

"No, I told him you'd meet him at the Internet café around one."

"Gee, thanks for asking me first," I mumbled.

"Well, it's not like I thought you'd say no."

"Is it because I'm that predictable? Or because I'm a loser with nothing else to do because the one guy who liked me dropped off the face of the earth?"

Vince groaned. "Not him again! How could you possibly have more to say on this topic?"

"Really, this Alex thing has gotten worse than your *back in Spring Mills* stories from the beginning of the summer," Lilly mocked.

"I know, sorry. I just thought he liked me." I tossed my hands in the air.

"I'm sure he did. But you're still having fun without him, right?"

"Oh, yeah. Definitely." I nodded.

But the truth was, it was kind of hard to have fun when I was spending every second thinking about what he could possibly be doing at that exact moment. Maybe he had gotten in some horrible accident and was unconscious in a hospital somewhere, unable to contact me. Or maybe he went on a sudden trip with his family and didn't have time to tell me before he left. Or maybe he was kissing some other tourist he met at a different *Quinceañera*.

"But don't you think it's weird he hasn't called *you*?" I suggested, peering at Lilly. "It's one thing for him to avoid me, but you're his friend. Wouldn't he still want to see you?"

"Alex and I never saw each other every day. We only hung out that much because of you guys," she said.

I sighed. I knew I had to accept that there would probably be no explanation for his sudden lack of interest and that I would probably leave for the States having no idea why he stopped wanting to see me. But knowing that didn't make it any easier.

Javier was rather computer illiterate. I sat in the Internet café teaching him how to change the settings on his e-mail messages. He wanted to use my laptop, because he had never used one before, despite the fact that it was in English and the desktops at the café were in Spanish. This only made my tutorial more difficult.

"You go to 'Edit,' then 'Preferences,' " I explained, showing him commands with my index finger. "Then click on the tab 'Messaging.' "

Javier followed my instructions. Every once in a while he'd look at me and smile, proud to have finally understood what I had been trying to explain to him for several minutes. He was a nice guy, but even with our limited communication skills, I got the impression that he wasn't very bright. And he smelled a little funny. I had never seen him smoke, but he reeked of cigarettes, and his breath had a weird kosher pickle aroma. I held my breath when he spoke directly facing me.

I glanced at my watch. It was almost two o'clock. We had been at this for an hour. I hadn't designated a time when we were going to wrap it up, but I was thinking that time was rapidly approaching. Any more of this and I would start counting the freckles on my arms.

"Ya know, you really shouldn't pick a cursive font for your e-mails," I explained when I saw the messy, bolded, swoopy text message he had composed. "It's kinda annoying to the people reading your messages. Why don't you change it to something standard, like Times or Arial? You remember how to change the font, right?"

He blinked at me like I had just suggested he solve a logarithmic equation off the top of his head.

I reached my hand out and rested it on top of his. I moved my finger slowly on the laptop's mouse pad to show him where the fonts were on the toolbar. But before I finished scrolling through the drop-down menu, something near the café's front window caught my eye. I swiveled my head and saw a glimpse of a guy standing outside on the sidewalk. As soon as he met my glance, he quickly turned and sped away. It was Alex.

"Holy crap!" I yelled, jumping to my feet.

I ran out of the café without saying another word to Javier, pushing open the heavy glass door and darting down the sidewalk. Unlike most cities I'd been to, Utuado didn't have a lot of foot traffic. I didn't have much trouble spotting Alex.

"Alex! Alex!" I yelled, charging after him.

He kept moving.

"Alex, stop! I want to talk to you!"

He paused but didn't turn around. It took only seconds for me to close the gap between us. I stopped in the shade of a palm tree.

"Alex, why'd you run away?" I puffed, catching my breath.

He turned around slowly.

"You were busy . . . with Javier," he stated curtly.

"I know, I'm helping him learn some computer stuff."

"Is that all?" he asked, his dark eyes squinted like tiny slits.

"Yeah, what'd you think?"

"I don't know," he mumbled.

"Alex, where have you been this past week? Why haven't you stopped by?"

I thought for a moment that I should be more subtle, beat around the bush until I quietly figured out why he was ignoring me—be more like a regular girl. But I didn't have much time left on this island and I had zero experience playing "games" with boys. I wanted to know the truth, and frankly, it just seemed silly not to ask.

"Where have *I* been? What are you talking about?"

"Alex, you came to this big family dinner then, *poof,* you disappear. What happened?"

"What happened was you not wanting to see me anymore!" He shook his head at me like I was an escaped mental patient still wearing the straightjacket.

"What? Why would you think that?"

He paused and examined my face for several moments. His head jolted back. "You really don't know, do you?"

"Know what?"

"That Lilly called me the morning after the dinner and told you you got freaked out by how the family reacted to us. That you thought we were going 'too fast.' " He sneered slightly. "She said you asked her to call me to tell me to back off. That you came to Puerto Rico to have fun, not to get wrapped up in some serious relationship."

My mouth fell toward the gray cement sidewalk about as quickly as my stomach did. I could hear the words he was saying, but my brain couldn't conjure up a single rational thought. How could I respond to that?

Alex stared at me.

"You never told her to say any of that stuff, did you?" he asked, raising his hand to his dark hair.

I shook my head *no,* slowly dusting the cobwebs off my brain.

"*¡Ay Dios mío!*"

"Oh. My. God," I stuttered in response.

We stared at each other for several seconds, not saying anything.

"Alex, I thought you lost interest in me. I couldn't figure

out why you stopped coming by. I thought it was something I did—"

He quickly leaned in and kissed me, cutting me off mid-sentence. I tried to kiss him back but my mind was still dizzy.

"I never lost interest. I thought I was pressuring you. I wanted to give you space," he whispered when he pulled away.

"Wait, then why did you come by the Internet café? Or was that just a coincidence?"

Alex took a deep breath and slowly sighed. I had never seen him angry before, but I was guessing from the heat of his breath and the look in his eyes that he was struggling to contain his emotions.

"I stopped by the hotel. I wanted to see you. It had been a while, so I thought it would be okay. But I ran into Lilly. She said you were at the café with Javier. And that I shouldn't go there, that I should just let you guys *be together*," he snipped through gritted teeth.

I sighed and shook my head. I couldn't look him in the eye. I felt like such an idiot. I'd trusted Lilly completely, and this wasn't a one-time lapse in judgment on her part. It was an ongoing deliberate plot. She had set me up as recently as this morning.

"I can't believe I listened to her," he mumbled.

"I can't believe she lied."

Chapter 42

I walked into the hotel alone. Alex wanted to join me, to confront her together, but I didn't want to create an ambush. Plus, I assumed the reasons Lilly did this (like she really had any) had more to do with me than him. I didn't want her to censor her comments because of his presence. And I didn't want to have to censor my own. Fighting with Lilly was intimidating enough without adding Alex into it.

The lobby was empty. Vince had already left, probably to go to the beach. He had been complaining recently that he couldn't return to Pennsylvania from a tropical island without a tan. The hotel was utterly silent, but I knew Lilly was still there. She had sent Alex to find me; whether she wanted to get caught or not I didn't know, but I was pretty sure she wouldn't skip out before hearing the result of her handiwork. My guess was that she was expecting me.

I heard a clang of glassware from the bar. Though she had never worked in the restaurant's kitchen before, I knew it was her. I could feel it.

I walked in and saw her unloading clean glasses onto the proper racks. She stopped immediately. And for a few moments we just glared at each other. I didn't say anything. She knew that I knew. Despite the fifteen feet separating us, I felt like we were staring at each other from across the Grand Canyon. The air locked in my lungs and I felt my fingernails dig into my palms.

"Look," she started, carefully putting down the tray of glasses and slowly moving to the other side of the bar. I wanted her to stay where she was. I liked having the buffer zone between us. "It's not as bad as you think."

"Really!" I snipped, my eyes wide and my tone instantly going on the offensive. "Oh, please, then explain it to me. Explain how you lied to me and how that's 'not that bad.' "

We were alone in the bar, which was a blessing. I hadn't intended to start off so harsh. I planned on hearing her out first. It wasn't as if she was Madison or Emily or Vince. I could yell at them recklessly and know that we'd live through it, that we'd still be friends afterward. Lilly didn't have that absolution.

"Oh, come on, Mariana. I did you both a favor!"

"And how is *that*?"

"You guys didn't even know each other and you were acting like you were ready to walk down the aisle. It was ridiculous."

"I'm sorry *you* felt that way, but how you felt wasn't really relevant to *us*, now, was it?" I asked, my head jerking from side to side.

"That's exactly my point! You didn't care how I felt. You both acted like I didn't exist." She threw her hands in the air in frustration.

"You didn't exist, really? Because I remember you introducing us at *your Quinceañera,* you sitting on the beach with us, you eating dinner with us, you hanging out on the porch with us. Exactly how did we ignore your existence?" I tugged at my fingers as I shouted the list of events.

"God, do you hear yourself? I shouldn't have to be the

third wheel in my own house. *You* were the guest here, Mariana, not me!"

"We never treated you like a third wheel. I thought we were friends."

"We are!"

"Well, friends don't lie and scheme and hurt each other! Not like this. What you did was mean. I don't see any way you can justify it!"

"I'm not trying to justify it. I just think you should at least *try* to see this from my side!"

"Then, what is your side? Why did you do this? Because you were jealous?"

"Jealous? Jealous of what?"

"Of me and Alex."

Lilly paused, caught her breath, and looked toward the doorway that led to the lobby. I wondered for a moment if she was going to walk out. But then she lifted her hand to her forehead and mumbled, "It's not that I *like* Alex."

My heart seized.

"Oh, my God," I rasped.

"What?"

"Lilly."

"What?"

She refused to look me in the eye.

"You can have any guy you want. You know that. Your friends, all guys by the way, swoon over you. All of them. They fight for your attention. And the *one guy* I like. The *one guy* who likes *me* back, you decide you have a crush on!" My mouth stayed open as I shook my head.

"I never said I had a crush on him!"

"Oh, please! You might as well have."

"Mariana, it's not like that," she defended, taking a few steps back.

"Then what is it like?"

"Forget it! It doesn't matter. You're not going to listen to anything I say anyway."

"Obviously that's not true because Alex and I fell for your crap pretty easily."

"*Alex and I. Alex and I.* That's all you care about!"

"And clearly all you care about is *yourself.*"

As soon as I said it, I wanted to take it back. Lilly's eyes instantly watered and her whole body wrenched backward. Only it was too late. I had said it. It was out there in the universe. And I would have to live with it. So would she.

Chapter 43

When you're in a strange place, it's hard to find a private place to cry. Especially when the person you're crying about lives in the same house. I couldn't go there. And I couldn't stay at the hotel. I stormed out of the bar moments after Lilly did, only she probably had a place to run off to and I didn't.

I walked around aimlessly for about an hour, wiping tears from my eyes. My head was swimming with everything we'd said. I went into the fight certain I was unequivocally right and she was undeniably wrong. But now I wasn't so sure. I had said some mean things. I knew I'd hurt her feelings. And though she'd hurt me first, that didn't erase my guilt.

The idea that she could have done all of this because she had a crush on Alex was too much. It didn't make any sense. She'd known him for years, if she liked him then something would have happened between them by now. I didn't get the impression that Lilly was ever refused what she wanted. It was amazing that someone who looked so much like me could have a completely opposite effect on guys. I'd gone my entire life barely being noticed by the opposite sex, while Lilly was instantly revered by them.

I ended up back at the Internet café. I needed someone to

talk to, even if it was only electronically. It's not like I had much of a choice. I couldn't call my mom, my aunt and uncle didn't have long-distance, so whenever I spoke to her, she called me. Not that my mom would be much help. She'd just tell me to apologize no matter what the circumstance, even if it wasn't my fault. *"Do you want to be right? Or do you want the fight to be over?"* she'd ask. Like it was ever that simple. And Vince was useless. If I attempted to confide in him, he'd zone out midway through.

Apparently, Javier had left my laptop with the cashier at the snack bar after I had run out. I grabbed it and logged on to my computer. There were only two people in the world who I knew would take my side. I smiled through my tears when I saw Madison connected to IM.

MARIRUIZ: Hey, Mad. Long time, no talk. Sorry I've been MIA.

I waited for several seconds, chewing my fingernails. No response.

MARIRUIZ: You there? I really need to talk.

MADISONAVE: Busy.

Great, clearly she was mad at me too. Granted, I hadn't written her in almost two weeks, but I had hoped she'd let that slide. It was an emergency; couldn't she hold her grudge later?

MARIRUIZ: Sorry I haven't written. But things here are really screwed up right now.

MADISONAVE: Gee, Spic, are they? I wouldn't know.

MARIRUIZ: Ya know, you really shouldn't call me Spic. It's kinda offensive.

MADISONAVE: What, you're all PC now? Please, if you come back thinking you're all Jennifer Lopez and speaking with some fake Spanish accent, I'm gonna puke.

MARIRUIZ: I didn't say that! But a lot of people consider it a curse word. You shouldn't call me that anymore.

MADISONAVE: Whatever. It didn't bother you before.

MARIRUIZ: Well, maybe it should have.

MADISONAVE: Yeah, 'cause you've been in Puerto Rico for two months so now you're all ethnic.

MARIRUIZ: Why do you need to be like that? It's my nickname, and I don't like it anymore.

MADISONAVE: Whatever.

MARIRUIZ: Look, I really need your advice. I'm fighting with Lilly, ya know the girl I've been staying with? She did this totally messed up thing. And because of her I didn't see Alex for almost a week.

MADISONAVE: I have no idea who Lilly and Alex are. Busy. G2G

MARIRUIZ: Come on, Mad! I really need to talk to you.

MADISONAVE has logged off, read the pop-up window.

She was obviously a lot angrier than I realized. Given that I was going home in less than two weeks, it was not the best time to alienate my best friend. We were starting sophomore year in the fall and I didn't want to go back to school with Madison and Emily hating me. Just the thought of it tightened the knots in my stomach.

I dropped my head in my hands and started to cry. I hadn't felt this alone since the day I arrived in Puerto Rico. Thinking about how bratty I acted then mortified me now. I couldn't believe I had refused my aunt's cooking. Could I have insulted her more? And to think my Uncle Miguel was still nice enough to cook me breakfast every morning. He even went out of his way to engage me in conversation. If it weren't for him, my Spanish probably would have never improved. I probably wouldn't have even tried.

And then Lilly, the one relative in the entire world who shares my likeness, I treated like some homeless person I'm embarrassed to be seen with. I didn't talk to her for two weeks. I turned down so many invitations to hang out with her friends, and why? Because I misinterpreted a comment she said while I was eavesdropping. If it weren't for her *Quinceañera,* I might never have opened myself up to this island or to this experience. She was the one person who went out of her way to make me feel at home, to make me feel like I fit in, like I belonged in Puerto Rico. And to thank her I go and hook up with her friend.

The tears continued to spill down my cheeks. I wouldn't blame her if she hated me.

I heard the door to the Internet café swing open. I spun around half hoping to find Lilly but instead I was face-to-face with my brother. His skin was covered in sand and his swim trunks reeked of ocean water.

"What's with you?" he asked, as he slid his hand through his sticky, knotted hair.

I swiped at the tears on my face and sniffed my runny nose.

"Nothing," I mumbled.

"Uh, yeah right. Why you bawlin'?"

My brother was as unsympathetic as usual. At least I could count on him to be consistent.

"I got into this fight with Lilly," I said, my voice cracking.

"What'd you do?"

He walked over to one of the computer terminals and logged on, barely looking at me. I could see he was checking the latest MLB stats.

"Why do you think *I* did something? She's the one who lied."

"Oh, God. About what?" he moaned. I could tell by his tone he was focused on his screen.

"She told Alex I didn't like him anymore. That's why he hasn't been coming around."

"So?"

"So!" I yelled, banging my hands on the table and shaking my laptop in the process.

"Well, it's his dumb fault for believing her. He could have asked you himself. It's not like he didn't know where to find you."

"Gee, thanks."

"It's true."

"He said he was giving me space because that's what he thought I wanted. Because Lilly lied."

"Oh, please. I'm so not going there with you." He sighed and opened his e-mail account.

"God, Vince! Would it kill you to be there for me just this once?"

"Stop being so melodramatic. It's a stupid chick fight," he mumbled as he typed.

"A chick fight? What's that supposed to mean?"

"It means you're being retarded and I'm not about to get involved in some stupid fight over nothing."

I gripped the sides of my laptop. If it didn't cost a thousand dollars, I would have flung it at his head like a Frisbee. I couldn't comprehend why guys felt it necessary to deem all arguments between girls as stupid or catty. Guys were allowed to fight. Two guys fighting was considered masculine, dangerous, even cool. But just because they solved their problems by beating the crap out of each other, didn't mean our way of handling things was any less painful. Not that I would expect my brother to understand this.

I stood up, shoved my laptop in my bag and stormed out without saying good-bye. Vince probably didn't even notice.

Chapter 44

The hotel bar was filled with its evening regulars. Two old men playing dominos were seated on the front porch; three tan, wrinkled men in white, brimmed hats sat in their usual seats in the far left booth; and at the bar, sat Tomás and Ricardo. The two men, about my father's age, sipped dark rum several evenings a week while arguing over the TV news. Once, Tomás grabbed my butt while I was leaving the hotel for the evening and my uncle screamed at him with such fury I thought flames were going to shoot from his nose like a blowtorch.

I glanced around the establishment hoping to find Lilly. She wasn't at home (I had already checked) and I had run out of places to look. I could already sense that she wasn't there. I spotted my Aunt Carmen and Uncle Miguel seated at a table near Tomás and Ricardo. I needed the company. Even if they couldn't help with my current problems, at least I was no longer alone.

"*Buenas noches,* Mariana!" yelled my Uncle Miguel from across the room. My aunt immediately waved.

I walked over and plopped down on a wooden chair.

"*¿Cerveza?*" my uncle asked, pointing to his beer.

I hated beer, but at this point, I figured nothing could make me feel any worse.

"*Sí.*" I nodded.

Ricardo, who was seated at the bar not far from me, awkwardly grabbed a can of Medalla Light from the bartender. His torso swayed slightly on his stool as he turned around to hand me the beer.

"*Gracias,*" I said.

He continued to hold the can after I took hold of it, touching my skin to savor the moment. His eyes were glassy and his nose red, and I could smell alcohol floating off him in waves. The perverted curve of his smile made my stomach lurch, and I scrunched my nose in disgust. Finally, he released the can.

It was damp and cold, and part of me wanted to rest it on my forehead to relax but I didn't want to concern my aunt and uncle with the gesture. I took a small sip and winced, the flavor rank and bitter.

My uncle looked at me, tilted his head and asked if I was tired. I thought of lying, of telling him that I was tired, but I realized that there really was no point. We all lived in the same house; he'd figure out Lilly and I were fighting, eventually. So out of a sheer desire to have an audience to listen to my problems, I unloaded everything that had happened the best I could, given the language barrier. They nodded their heads at the appropriate times, looked shocked and horrified at others, and then quite sad after I discussed the big blow-up I'd had with their granddaughter earlier that afternoon.

"*¡Ay Dios mío!*" cried my aunt, placing her hand over her heart.

"Mariana Ruíz," said my uncle sternly. "*Esto es un problema.*"

Hearing him state that I had a problem seemed like the

most obvious observation in the world, but it still made me sad, like I had disappointed him somehow. And all this was happening right before my parents were set to arrive, which was just perfect.

"Dad's gonna be pissed," I mumbled to myself. "The great Lorenzo Ruíz sends his kid off to get cultured and I cause a scene."

Ricardo suddenly swung his fat, drunken body around to face us, the leathery skin on his forehead wrinkled with confusion.

"¿Lorenzo Ruíz?" he asked in a raspy voice.

I glared at him from my chair a few feet away from his bar stool and cocked my head without saying a word.

"¿*Americana, verdad?*" he asked, hiccupping slightly as he stared down at me.

"Yes," I replied in English, hoping to deter further conversation.

"¿*Tu papa . . . es* Lorenzo?" he asked slowly. His head rocked above his shoulders like a palm tree in the wind.

"Yes, Lorenzo Ruíz," I stated again, continuing in English to discourage him. "He grew up here. Why? Did you know him?"

My great aunt and great uncle loudly adjusted their weight in their seats at the sound of my father's name, and I turned and saw them both staring in opposite directions. They weren't catching my gaze.

"Yup, yup. Ah knew ya papa," Ricardo slurred, but in English this time. "Ah went to sh-chool wit 'lil Lorenzo. Fun, fun we had! And, yah know whah? Ah still see his sidder from tim to tim."

"I'm sorry, what did you say?" I asked, shaking my head at him.

"Lorenzo's sidder," he repeated.

"Sidder? What the heck's a 'sidder?' "

"His sissster," he moaned slowly.

"Like, 'hermana?' "

"Yeah, sidder. Dat's wha Ah said." He glared at me like I was an idiot who couldn't understand my own language.

"I think you've got the wrong guy, mister. My dad doesn't have a sister. He's got two brothers who live in Jersey."

"Ah know!" he shouted. "Roberto and Diego Ruíz."

My breath caught in my throat. Those were my uncles' names.

"Your granfadder, Arturo, he had a dahter, Teresa."

I blinked at the man. *Teresa.*

A flash of the woman from the church flickered in my head. The woman with the small toddler, the woman who spoke English, the woman with red hair, the woman who sat next to me at the *Quinceañera* reception, the woman who wanted to know about my family in the States.

I swiveled my head to look at my aunt and uncle. Their faces were as white as clouds, even their lips. Realizing they couldn't have possibly understood our conversation in English, I knew that the mention of her name must have triggered this reaction.

"What's he talking about?" I yelled in English. My aunt and uncle stared back, saying nothing. "What the *hell* is this guy talking about?" I screamed again.

If I had been more rational, I would have attempted to communicate with my aunt and uncle in Spanish. But I could barely form a clear thought let alone translate those thoughts into Spanish.

"Who's Teresa? Teresa!" I shouted, all the blood rushing to my face. "*¿Quien es* Teresa?*"

"Teresa, Teresa," the old man sang to himself as he swayed. My uncle slowly put down his beer and stared directly into my brown eyes. I could feel the air thicken between us. I knew whatever was about to happen wasn't going to be good. I almost wanted to stop him from saying it.

"Teresa *es tu tía*," he stated softly.

She was my aunt.

Chapter 45

It took nearly thirty minutes, which included Ricardo standing in as a drunken English translator, for my aunt and uncle to explain to me exactly what was going on or, more accurately, exactly what had happened more than three decades ago.

Apparently my grandfather was no saint, no noble man who'd moved his family from Puerto Rico in search of better opportunities. He was an adulterer, a womanizer, a deadbeat dad. He cheated on my grandmother (they wouldn't say with how many women, but I got the impression that the list was rather lengthy) and one liaison had resulted in pregnancy. The woman, who my uncle referred to in several colorful Spanish curse words rather than by name, made sure the entire town knew who the father was. That's how my grandmother found out about her husband's infidelity—from neighborhood gossip. She was the last to know.

According to my Uncle Miguel, my grandparents may have survived the ordeal if the *"otra mujer,"* or "other woman," wasn't so *"loca."* He told stories of the woman screaming on their front lawn, stripping her clothes off until she was completely nude and demanding my grandfather take responsibility for the baby in her stomach; she ambushed my grandmother in the center of town and hollered that her husband didn't love her and that she wasn't enough to keep him. My uncle called it *"los días oscuros,"* the dark days.

Being human, my grandmother could only take so much; but being Catholic, she couldn't accept a divorce. She demanded the entire family leave not just Utuado, but Puerto Rico. She wanted no reminders of what her husband did and my grandfather, who was in no position to argue, complied with her demands. They left Utuado before the baby was born and never came back. My father was ten at the time.

According to Uncle Miguel, to the best of his knowledge, my father had no idea what was going on but his older brothers, my uncles Roberto and Diego, may have figured it out. Even if they had, my uncle was certain Roberto and Diego would not have told my father. He was the baby of the family, five years younger than Roberto and seven years younger than Diego. He said those boys spent their lives protecting my father from bullies, from teachers, from all things negative. Once, when my dad came home from school with a swollen black eye, my uncles tracked down the kid who slugged him and dangled him over a rushing river by his ankles. The kid was so petrified, he peed his pants. It was the last time anyone in Utuado messed with my father.

But, of course, Uncle Miguel couldn't be certain who knew what, because the entire family cut off contact with everyone from Puerto Rico the day they left. That's why my uncle didn't attend my grandfather's funeral, that's why none of them did.

He paused as he told that part of the story. His voice was low and sad, but not bitter, just defeated. He said he didn't think my parents chose not to invite him; he suspected my grandfather had asked them not to out of respect for my grandmother. They had spent their lifetimes hiding this secret from their children and their grandchildren, and my uncle knew that neither would have wanted the truth to come out during their funerals.

I don't know how long I had been crying. The tears dripped from my eyes like a leaky faucet, slow and steady but not fitfully. It all just didn't seem real. I was sitting in a dilapidated shack of a bar on a rural mountain in Puerto Rico with relatives I had known for less than two months, listening to a story that made my family sound like the cast of a bad movie. My grandfather, the villain; my grandmother, the victim; my uncles, the co-conspirators; and my father, the innocent. Things like this just didn't happen to my family. We didn't have dark secrets or skeletons in our closets; we were far too boring. I was certain of it. Or at least I had been, up until an hour ago.

But now everything was different. They were telling the truth. I could see it in their eyes.

My grandfather had another child, a girl, named Teresa. She was thirty-five years old and she had a child. I had already met her.

Chapter 46

There's not much a great aunt and great uncle can do to comfort a girl who's just found out her whole family is a lie. As soon as the story was finished and reality sank in, I bolted from the bar and ignored their calls. They didn't come after me and I wasn't surprised.

Standing on the road surrounded by palm leaves, banana trees, tropical flowers, exotic birds—the setting just added to the foreign feeling raging inside me. It seemed unnatural for a teenager to be disappointed in her grandparents, but I was. I doubted everything they had ever told me. All those stories about wanting to provide a better life for their children, about how proud they were of the accomplishments that stemmed from their "struggles"—they were all lies.

And that woman from the church. She knew who I was. She knew she was talking to her niece. Yet she didn't say anything. I felt like I had been played or manipulated, but I didn't know by whom. I didn't know who to blame.

I ran down the road, my thin white sneakers pounding the dirt, my lungs gulping thick, hot bursts of air. I saw visions of my grandparents seated around the dining room table on Christmas, smiling like a happy couple on the eve of their golden anniversary. I saw my uncles sitting silently in the family room watching football on Thanksgiving (one of the three times they visited their parents each year), drinking beers and ignoring their family. It was obvious they knew. I could always sense the tension in the air when my grandfather was around them, only I mistook it for disinterest or bad manners on my uncles' parts when it was actually resentment. I remembered thinking that my grandparents died so close together because they were so much in love, that my grandmother died of a broken heart. The thought seemed so ridiculous now, so naïve.

My strides lengthened as I continued to run down the dusty road. I was not a jogger; actually I hated it. I despised the mile run requirement for gym class—with every lap, I would silently curse my teacher more and by the end of it, my stomach would be cramped in knots and my lungs raw from panting. But today, I could have kept running forever. If I was tired, I couldn't feel it. I couldn't feel anything.

I saw my aunt and uncle's house in view before I even realized that's where I was headed. I knew my brother could be inside, quietly oblivious. I didn't know if I should tell him. Well, I knew I *should* tell him, but I didn't want to. I didn't want to be the person to break this story to my family.

I charged across the front lawn, staring at the blades of bright green grass the same way I did the day I had arrived. I wished I could go back to that day, or even better yet, I wished I could have found a way to convince my father not to send us here, so then I would never know the truth. I wished I could forget everything.

I swung open the front door and it crashed loudly on the wall from the weight of my throw. The house was dim, and it was hard for my eyes to adjust. I couldn't see if anyone was home.

"You're slamming doors now? Real mature. Why don't

you revert to a full-out temper tantrum, start pounding your fists on the floor," mocked Lilly as she stepped into the living room where I was standing.

She stopped in her tracks the moment she saw me. I could feel the beads of sweat pouring down my forehead and mixing with my tears. My breathing was staggered and my nose was running.

"Whoa," she mumbled, her head jerking back. "Mariana, really, I'm sorry. I didn't know you'd get this upset. I am so sorry. It was an awful thing for me to do."

I started sobbing harder. I wished that was what I was upset about. Actually, I would do just about anything to make Lilly's minor betrayal my biggest problem again.

"Is, is Vince here?" I stammered, gasping for air, my hand on my chest.

"No." She shook her head, slowly walking toward me.

I covered my face with my hands and tried to catch my breath.

"What happened?" she asked softly.

My head was pounding.

"I was at the bar, and there was this guy, and the woman from the *Quinceañera* . . . and Uncle Miguel had to tell me the truth, but I didn't believe him, but he was telling the truth and . . ."

"Mariana, you're not making any sense. Slow down. What happened?"

I pulled my hands from my face and looked at her through teary eyes.

"My grandfather, he slept with some woman and he got her pregnant," I mumbled, the air finally flowing back into my lungs at a manageable rate.

"Your grandfather? I thought he was dead."

"He is," I huffed. "Before he died. Before he left Puerto

Rico. He cheated on my grandmother with some *slut* and she got pregnant and my grandparents just left. They went to the States to avoid it all, like it never happened. Only it did, and the woman had the baby—"

"Holy shit," Lilly interjected, shaking her head.

"And now the baby's, like, thirty-five and you invited her to your *Quinceañera!*"

"What? I did! Who?"

"That woman, Teresa. She had that screaming toddler. . . ."

"Teresa! Holy shit!" Lilly yelled a second time, her jaw dropping.

"How do you know her?"

"I don't. My grandfather does. He said she used to work at the hotel."

"Yeah, well he lied. Figures."

"Hey, don't go there. This is a bad situation all around. I mean, do you think your dad knows?"

"I don't know. I don't think so. But who knows anymore? Can you believe it? My father's sister sat next to me at your *Quinceañera* asking questions about my family, which is also *her* family, and I had no idea. I'm such an idiot. My grandparents let everyone believe they moved to the States to 'find a better life,' " I mocked in a deep, newscaster tone. "It was all bullshit! And now *I* have to tell my whole family the truth! I don't want to, but I don't want to be a liar like the rest of them, either."

I exhaled quickly and stared at Lilly. We stood there silently for several moments with just empty space between us.

"Are you waiting for me to say something? Because I don't know what to say, but wow, this sucks. I'm sorry." Her tone was more shocked than sad.

I couldn't blame her for being at a loss for words. Even

Dr. Phil would have a hard time tackling this one. I rested my fingers on my forehead and breathed slowly for a while.

Finally, Lilly hissed out a puff of air, breaking the silence. "Well, I guess this makes our fight look kinda petty, huh? I got a free pass on that one. . . ." She chuckled slightly.

Despite everything, I laughed. I had to. There was nothing else to do.

Chapter 47

The house was packed with people. Once again, relatives drove in from all over the island to join the Ruíz-Sanchez festivities. Only instead of celebrating my arrival, they were celebrating that of my parents.

After three days of worry-induced stomachaches, I told Vince the truth. He didn't take it nearly as hard as I did. Hearing it from me took away some of the shock factor. Apparently, I was a better messenger than Ricardo, the drunken barfly. Plus, Vince said he had always noticed the way that our uncles treated our grandfather, and that he had assumed our father didn't grow up in a very happy home—happy children visit their parents more than three times a year, especially when they live less than an hour away. We agreed that our Uncles Diego and Roberto knew the truth, but neither of us were certain about the real question: did our father?

I looked at my watch. We'd find out soon. My *"tia"* would be here any minute.

While I realized Teresa was born into our family—just like I was—and that she had done nothing wrong, I still had a hard time calling her my aunt. It was too weird. I preferred *"tia,"* it was at least foreign and removed—just like her.

"So, what are you going to say to this chick?" Lilly asked, as she brushed her hair.

I rolled my head toward her and shrugged. I had been getting ready for more than thirty minutes and I hadn't gotten farther than putting the clothes on my back. My head was on overload and my body in slow-mo.

"What? Was I not supposed to ask? I mean, it's the obvious question," she noted, as she pulled her red hair into a high ponytail.

"I have no idea what I'm gonna say," I muttered, as I slipped my feet into a pair of flip-flops. "Technically, I've already spoken to her. The ice is broken. I insulted her child. But now, she knows that *I know*. And my father's going to be here and he has no idea . . ."

"So you're just gonna ambush your dad? Is that the plan?" The girl was blunt.

I sighed and tossed my head back.

"I don't know yet. I couldn't tell him over the phone. How do you have that conversation? 'Hi, Dad, it's Mariana. I met your long-lost bastard sister. Want to check her out while you're here?' I just didn't see that playing out well."

I rubbed my temples. My head had been pounding for days now. I was exhausted.

"Well, maybe you should just let him meet her. Maybe he'll figure it out for himself, like twins separated at birth. . . ."

"Yeah, I doubt it."

"You never know." Lilly sat on her bed and fastened the straps of her strappy heels. "Anyway, when's Alex getting here?"

"Any minute."

Alex had been glued to my hip for the past three days, trying to make up for lost time. He was already starting to talk about not wanting me to leave, even though I still had another week left (of course, I'd be with my parents, but still). I liked that he was going to miss me, because I knew I'd miss him, too. Part of me wanted to take him with me.

"Yeah, well you should have heard the riot act Alex read me the other day. He went all psycho over what I did."

"Can you blame him?"

"Nah, not really," she conceded, then took a long pause, staring at her feet. "You know, I never really like-liked him, right?"

I said nothing; in fact, I held my breath. Lilly and I had let our entire situation drop given the severity of my current family problems. I needed her more than I needed to deal with her issues surrounding Alex. I really didn't want to disturb that balance.

"I just saw my friends falling all over you and . . ."

"Over me? Are you kidding?" I asked, snapping my head toward her.

"Mariana, they didn't stop talking to you every moment you were around and—"

"You're nuts! You are certifiably insane. Lilly, they are all in love with *you!*" I shouted, looking at her with amazement.

"No, they're not!"

"Oh, my God! They practically trip over themselves to see who gets to stand closer to you or sit next to you."

"That's not true."

"It is! If you could have seen the way they looked at you at your *Quinceañera*. Some of them actually had drool coming out of their mouths."

"Oh, please." She shook her head and a lull fell over the conversation. I sat on the bed beside her. "Look," she said, "I never liked Alex in that way. But seeing how much he liked *you*, made me wonder why he never liked *me* that much. I mean, it's not like I *wanted* him to, I just, I just wanted *him* to want to. It's retarded. . . ."

"I know what you're saying." I nodded.

"It's just, I have all these guy 'friends,' " she said with a sarcastic tone. "And maybe they want to kiss me, or whatever, but that's it. None of them want to be my boyfriend, or at least not like Alex wanted to be with you. For God's sake, he was talking about moving to Philly after knowing you for, like, two weeks!"

"First off, he didn't mean it that way. If he goes to college in the States, I'm sure it'll have nothing to do with me. And second, *you're* the one pushing these guys away. Lilly, they're all about you, but you string them along and act too cool. How can any of these guys think that you *really* like him when there are fifty other guys waiting in the wings? You're the reason you don't have a boyfriend," I stated plainly.

Lilly twisted her head toward me. "Wow, that was deep. Are you always that deep?"

"I watch a lot of *Oprah*."

"I can tell, it's paying off. Now if you could only apply that to your family situation . . ."

"I know, seriously."

Just then, I heard a loud chatter of excitement erupt in the living room. The front door opened. Even on a tropical island, I could recognize the sound of my father's footsteps.

"They're here," Lilly said, patting my leg. "You ready for this?"

"No."

She laughed. "Well, you better get ready."

Only I knew that was impossible.

I knew when I walked out into that living room, my parents were expecting to see the same girl who'd left Philadelphia for the summer. Only, ever since the *Quinceañera,* I felt like I had changed—the clothes, the food, the language, the boyfriend. I stood now in Lilly's bedroom, in a tank top and denim skirt, depressed at the thought of leaving this world behind. My brother was right when he predicted on the plane that I'd be crying when I left. But now I had more tears to add to the mix. I had grown up more in this past week than I had the entire fifteen years preceding it. Yet, somehow I had to find a way to waltz into that living room and look at my parents the same way I had before all of this happened, before the truth came out.

How was I going to tell them?

My father had no idea he was about to learn that everything his parents ever told him, all the reasons they gave for leaving Puerto Rico, all the stories they told about wanting to give him and his brothers a better life, all of those were lies. He was going to learn that his father cheated on his mother, that he had an illegitimate sister to add to his conservative Catholic family. And he was going to hear all of this from me. I was so scared that he would resent me. I'd be ruining the perfect image of courage and sacrifice that he had of his family.

I didn't know if I could do it, if I could take all of that away from him.

Lilly babbled in the background as my mind raced. I stared at my reflection in her full-length mirror.

Wouldn't I want to know if I had another sibling out there? Wouldn't I want to know who that person was? Shouldn't that decision be mine to make?

My mind drifted to my grandparents, the way my grandfather looked while he was lying in the hospital with tubes coming out of his nose. He knew he was dying, we all did. And I cried by his bedside. So did my father. And here he had another child, a daughter (his only daughter), and she wasn't

Chapter 48

The party was buzzing with energy. Relatives were dancing in the living room, the porch was filled with guys downing beers, and women chattered around my mother, not noticing that she couldn't understand. Alonzo and José were setting the table while Lilly's mom helped my aunt cook in the kitchen. My parents were stunned at the spectacle and for the first time I realized what I must have looked like the day I arrived—shocked, scared and uptight. Now, all this activity seemed commonplace and these people felt like family. This was no longer strange.

Alex was in the kitchen getting me another soda. My parents thought it was nice I'd made a "friend," and they utterly ignored the fact that he held my hand. I had never dated before, and I think they were in denial that I might have started to while they weren't looking.

I hadn't broken the news yet. I was waiting for the right moment, when we could be alone. But there was always someone approaching my dad to talk about old times. He was busy remembering his Spanish and trying to translate on my mother's behalf. We barely had time to catch up. I fidgeted with my hands, an impassionate smile plastered on my face.

Just then, Uncle Miguel emerged from the kitchen and

yelled to me in Spanish that a car had pulled up, and that there was *"una mujer especial"* in front of the house.

My father turned to me to translate, only I was busy replying, in perfect Spanish, that I wasn't ready. *"Necesito un momento, por favor,"* I said.

"Whoa, I guess a lot changed while you were here," he said, smiling.

"Yeah, it did, Dad, which is what I've been meaning to talk to you about."

"You know, I'm really proud of you, Mariana. Both you and Vince." He nodded out to the porch, where my brother was chatting with Lilly's dad, Juan. "You both have grown up a lot."

"We have Dad, but I need to talk to you about something else."

"Mariana, I'm sorry we didn't listen to you before planning this trip," my mom said. "I know Madison's party was important to you—"

"Mom, I don't really want to talk about that right now," I stated quickly, my eyes focused on the porch door, praying it would stay shut just a little longer.

"It's just I saw the write-up about her party in the paper, about that actor who showed up, and I know you must be angry at us for having missed out on that. . . ."

"Really, Mom, it's no big deal. I had fun at Lilly's *Quinceañera*. Seriously, I did. Probably more than I would've had at Madison's party, even with Orlando Bloom. But that's not really the point right now. I need to tell you guys something important—"

Before I could finish, the porch door swung open and in walked a familiar face. She was tall and thin, with a pointed slender nose and small brown eyes. Her dark red hair waved in the breeze and fell to the top of her white summer dress. I could now clearly see the family resemblance. Teresa was my grandfather's daughter.

"Dad, I have to tell you something," I quickly said under my breath, only he wasn't listening.

He slowly walked to the porch door and stopped in front of Teresa. She extended her hand politely.

"Lorenzo. It's so nice to finally meet you."

"I'm so glad you came," he replied.

My jaw dropped toward the floor. I gawked, my breath held tight in my lungs as the blood rushed to my feet.

"Hello, again, Mariana," she said, turning to me with an easy grin.

I said nothing.

"I see you already met my daughter." My father then gestured to my mom. "And this is my wife, Irina."

"I've heard a lot about you," my mom said politely.

What? Since when? My brain felt moments from exploding.

"Dad, what's going on? I mean, um, do you know who this is?" I gasped, my face contorted in an uncomfortable shape.

"Uh, Mariana, there's something I need to tell you . . ." he started.

"About Teresa? 'Cause I already got the rundown from some drunk at a bar. Glad to see I panicked myself over how to tell you, for nothing. Have you known this whole time?"

Teresa coughed awkwardly and took a step back. I doubted she was offended. I had already called her child the spawn of Satan, so there wasn't really much worse I could dish out.

"Mariana, this is Teresa . . . your aunt. She and I spoke for the first time last week. It's a long story," he responded calmly.

Chapter 49

My father knew. Well, not his whole life, but at some point in his late teens my uncles told him the truth. They couldn't stand that my father didn't resent their parents the way they did. They remembered the crazy "other woman" on the front lawn, and the town gossip, and my grandmother's sobbing fits, and they hated my grandfather for it. They wanted my dad to feel the same way. Only he didn't.

Of course, he was angry at first, he said. How could he not be? But as he got older, he realized that all the sacrifices my grandparents made were real. Their reasons for coming to the States may have been tainted, but the realities they formed for themselves once they got there weren't. They did create a better life for their children, and they worked hard to get it. My dad felt like he owed all of his success to them and to the decision they made to leave Puerto Rico, no matter what the reason behind it may have been.

My Uncle Miguel was right. My grandfather didn't want any family from the island at his funeral. He didn't want to upset my grandmother. He thought he owed her that much. The last thing she needed added to her grief was a reminder of the crazy ex-mistress and her illegitimate child. So my father honored his wishes. It was out of respect for my grandmother that he kept his distance from Teresa, and his entire family in Puerto Rico, all these years.

So Teresa remained a dark secret. My dad knew her name. He knew she existed. But that was it. Until she called him a few days ago. She got his phone number from the funeral home that handled my grandfather's burial; she kept a copy of his obituary in her wallet. She didn't want to upset my father by showing up at this party unannounced; she felt like she'd already overstepped enough at the *Quinceañera* by speaking with me.

"This is so bizarre," Vince whispered, as he twisted his head to spy through the porch door at our father and our new *"tia"* chatting casually in the kitchen.

"I can't believe he knew this whole time. Do you know how many ulcers I've formed in my stomach over these past few days because of this?" I asked, sipping my soda as we sat on the porch.

"Ah, *pobrecita,*" Alex joked, patting my stomach.

"Well, at least you didn't have to tell him," Lilly added. "That's what you were really afraid of, wasn't it?"

"Yeah, I guess. But I'm also just kinda freaked out by the whole thing. My grandfather had another child, another family, I didn't know about."

"Mariana, there was a lot of family you didn't know about until a couple months ago," Lilly said, patting her chest. "Things change."

"I guess." I sighed.

"You realize I have to be at Cornell in three weeks?" Vince said, shaking his head as he gulped his beer (something else my parents chose to ignore).

"I'm gonna be *back at Spring Mills,*" I whined in the voice Lilly always used to mock me. "God, I hope Emily and Madison start talking to me again. I royally screwed things up. I think they hate me right now."

"No, they don't," Vince said. "They'll get over it. But hey, at least now you know you can make new friends."

I looked at Lilly.

"So you guys have to come back and visit sometime," Lilly said, with a nod of her chin.

"And you'll have to visit us. Both of you." I glanced at Lilly and Alex. "Maybe you can come for my birthday."

"Oh, God, the big Sweet Sixteen!" Lilly hooted. "What celebrity are you gonna try to get to attend? Brad Pitt?"

"Nah, I think I'm over that whole "Sweet Sixteen" thing." I rolled my eyes.

"Isn't it rather anti-American for a girl to skip her six-teenth birthday?" Alex asked.

"Who cares?" I shrugged.

"Hey, maybe you could have a party like Lilly's?" Vince suggested. "Hire a salsa band, wear a nice tiara, cook some Latin food, invite girls with boobs . . ."

"Very funny!" I chucked a balled napkin at him as we all giggled.

I glanced into the tropical fields, remembering that first morning I stood on the porch moments before my uncle ap-peared, hacking at weeds with a machete to make room for Lilly's party. I pictured the tent in the yard, and tried to imag-ine where on the grass I was standing when I first met Alex. I remembered the whole night vividly. It was when I changed.

"Excuse me, Lilly?" My dad had suddenly appeared at the porch door. "Your parents and I want to talk to you about something. What are your plans for next year?"

Lilly crinkled her eyebrows and flicked a glance at me, but I was too busy staring at my father. I had no idea what he was about to propose, how things were going to change next.

Keep an eye out for Diana's next book,
AMIGAS AND SCHOOL SCANDALS,
coming in November from Kensington.
Turn the page for a sneak peek!

"**A**re you sure you wanna do this?" I asked as I piled clothes into my super-sized suitcase.

It was officially my last night in Utuado, the tiny mountain village in Puerto Rico where I had spent the summer. I was going back to Spring Mills.

"Of course," Lilly answered as she scanned my 10th grade roster.

My mom snatched it from the mail before she hopped on the plane, and I was incredibly grateful that she did. Not that I didn't already know which classes I'd be taking, but it was nice to see the schedule in its official form. I now knew which teachers I had, which electives I got, and how my day was laid out. It was the predictable, comfortable order of home.

"Wow, that's a lot of classes," Lilly muttered.

"It's the normal course load. You get used to it."

I tossed my bathing suits into my luggage, tucking them into the sides. I wouldn't be breaking those out again for quite a while. There was something sad about packing up a swimsuit for the season, almost as if it signified the end of fun.

"So how are your parents dealing?" I asked.

"Eh, they've mellowed a bit. I know they want what's best

for me and to be honest, I've been thinking about it ever since you and Vince got here . . ."

"Switching schools is a big deal."

"I know." She nodded. "I just see your dad and . . . I want more than this."

She waved her hands around my bedroom. I guess it wasn't really my bedroom anymore. If it ever really was. I glanced one more time at my solid rock twin mattress, the powder blue walls, the cement floor and the stained window shade. I was going to miss it. I was going to miss all of this.

He kissed me when my parents weren't looking. They probably looked away on purpose so they could deny any evidence of my emerging love life. Though I doubted one semi-boyfriend really counted as a love life.

His lips pressed against mine. I wanted to lock the feeling into my brain, soak it in one last time, but before I could, my father subtly blew the car horn. Alex pulled away. His brown eyes looked dull and his eyelids drooped slightly. A lump pulsed in my throat.

"So you gonna meet some other American tourist tomorrow? Take her salsa dancing?" I asked with a nervous laugh.

"Absolutely. I've already got one lined up. Only she's Canadian," Alex replied with a grin.

"Canadian, eh?" I mocked, tossing in the one bit of slang I knew from our neighbors to the north. "Well, be careful; they might look like us Americans but they're a whole different breed. Bad weather, ice hockey, bacon . . ."

"I like bacon."

He grinned and hugged me tight. I let my head fall on his shoulder. His shampoo smelled like oranges.

"Mariana, it's time to go," my father said as he slammed the car door shut.

I paused and stared at my great-aunt and great-uncle's mountain house one last time. The blue concrete facade I had dreaded with a passion two months ago now seemed like home. Uncle Miguel, Aunt Carmen, my cousin Alonzo and his "friend" Jose—who were gathered on the crunchy green grass watching our family load up the car—felt like family. I could almost see my life fitting here in some odd parallel-universe. But now Vince and I were headed back to our normal lives.

Well, almost.

Lilly pushed the porch door open and propped it with her newly purchased travel bag, courtesy of my father. Her auburn hair was pulled in a high ponytail and two duffel bags hung from her shoulders—she looked a lot like I did when I first arrived. She paused to wipe the sweat from her freckled brow, and I could tell she was trying to mentally block out the Spanish mumblings of her parents. They were chasing after her, rambling with faces tightly twisted in worry. Lilly had spent the past few days reassuring them, in every way possible from conversation to pantomime, that this was *exactly* what she wanted.

She was moving to the States.

Once my dad realized how advanced Lilly's bilingual skills were and how dedicated she was to her education (she got straight A's in an English-speaking school), he couldn't help but offer her a chance to learn in the U.S. He wanted to give her the opportunity his parents gave him, and Lilly jumped at the offer. The girl had been riding on a bus for more than two hours each day just to get to and from school (meanwhile, Vince and I complained when there was no parking in our school's private lot and we had to walk an extra ten feet).

"Will somebody please tell my parents that I'm doing the

right thing, because I don't think they can actually hear the words coming out of my mouth. They're acting like the universe is going to explode if I step foot off this island!" Lilly shouted as she yanked her suitcase from her father and hauled it across the lawn.

My dad immediately jumped out of the rental car and headed toward Lilly's parents. They knew she was in good hands. She was going to be with family (even if we were distant cousins who were totally unaware of each other's existence until a few weeks ago). Plus, my dad had covered every detail with them numerous times. Within three days he managed to enroll Lilly in Spring Mills High School (the dean went to our church and played golf with my dad on weekends), have the housekeeping staff prepare one of our spacious guest bedrooms, and book all of my cousin's last-minute travel arrangements. He kindly traded in Vince and my first class tickets for three coach seats (he and my mom still planned to embrace the plane's high-class luxury accommodations without us).

Lilly's parents were thrilled at my father's generous offer and they knew it was a life-changing opportunity for her. They agreed to the move days ago, but Lilly was still their only child. She was fifteen and had never traveled farther than San Juan. Now she was moving to Pennsylvania where she would attend an American school, meet new friends and boyfriends, and live in a world completely separate from theirs. A world full of posh amenities they'd never even contemplated.

She was moving to Philadelphia's Main Line—a far stretch from the mountain town she was raised in. There would be no tropical rain forests, exotic birds, wild chickens in the backyard or laundry duty at her grandfather's rundown hotel. Soon her biggest worry would be which marble bathroom to shower in and which gourmet meal to order from take-out.

"So, you really ready for this?" Alex asked as my cousin trudged over.

"Are you kidding? A chance to be rescued from the island? I think I've been waiting for this since birth," she joked as she dragged her luggage to the back of the car.

Alex hurled it into the already packed, shiny rented SUV, which stood out drastically on the mountain road.

"Ya gonna miss me, Alex?" Lilly asked with a big grin.

"Funny, I was wondering the same thing," I smirked.

"Oh, really. Well, I'm sure he'll miss you more even though I've known him my entire life. Apparently years of friendship pale in comparison to a few weeks of smoochy, smoochy."

"Hey!'" I screeched, my cheeks burning.

"I will miss you both," he replied, squeezing my waist a few times.

I giggled and squirmed as he pulled me tighter.

"See! You two are disgusting! Vince, can you see this?" Lilly asked my brother.

He had been seated in the car and ready to hit the road for more than a half-hour. His exit to Cornell was merely days away, and he couldn't wait to detach himself from our parents.

"I prefer to believe my sister is asexual," he said flatly, leaning out the window of the car. "Mom, are we *ever* gonna get out of here?"

My mother was seated patiently in the passenger's side. I could tell the week-long trip was a whirlwind for her. Not only could she not speak Spanish (and thus not understand a word anyone was saying around her), she was forced to drink rum (I had never seen her sip any alcohol other than a crisp white wine), shower in moldy accommodations and succumb to the humidity-induced frizz in her blond hair. Her locks were currently tied in a sloppy ponytail similar to my own. It was the first time I realized how similar we were.

"We're gonna leave in a second. Let your father smooth things over with the Sanchezes. Lilly, why don't you go over there and help?" my mom suggested.

Lilly groaned.

"It *is* the last time you'll see them for a while," I reminded her.

"I know, I know. I guess I need to pretend that upsets me."

"Lilly, you are going to miss your parents," Alex stated plainly. "I don't think you realize how different Spring Mills is going to be."

"Are you kidding me? I know all about Spring Mills. She hasn't stopped talking about it since she got here. *Back in Spring Mills, back in Spring Mills.*" Lilly nudged my shoulder as she headed off toward her parents.

They were engrossed in conversation with my father. But I knew he'd have the final say, he always did.

A few hours later, we boarded the plane back home. I was squished between Vince and Lilly. Since Lilly was technically our "guest" (even though we were still on a plane and not yet on American soil), I felt compelled to offer her the window seat. Vince's extra inches of leg won him the aisle, and thus I was stuck in the middle for four straight hours.

I sipped my tiny bottle of water and fought my brother for the armrest. The elbow war was the only thing distracting me from my impending Madison and Emily drama. I knew they wouldn't let my MIA status this summer drop easily. They hadn't returned any of my e-mails from the past week and they still had no idea I was bringing a five-foot-four-inch redheaded souvenir back from the island. But they were my best friends, my only friends before Lilly. They couldn't hate me forever.

"Hey, you thinking about Alex?" Lilly asked, looking up from the gossip magazine she'd purchased at the San Juan airport. She wanted to brush up on her celebrities before she landed, which I agreed was a virtual necessity. If she didn't know Tom and Katie's latest relationship woes, there was no way she'd fit into Madison's world.

"Nah. We'll keep in touch. Or at least I know you guys will, so he can't exactly drop off the face of the earth . . ."

"Are you kidding?" Lilly interrupted. "Trust me, you have a better chance of hearing from him than I do. I wouldn't be suprised if he goes to college in the States next year just to be near you."

"Oh, please! Like that would ever happen! I wish I had that much influence over boys."

"You do . . ."

"Whatever," I scoffed, readjusting the headband holding back my stringy red mop. I flicked my eyes toward her. "You scared about moving?"

"A little," she said with a sad smile. "I'm excited, scared, sad and happy all at the same time."

"I still can't believe you're really doing it. There's no way I'd be able to up and move. I mean, you've got your whole life back in Utuado . . ."

"Yeah, and if I didn't do something now my life would always *be* Utuado. My parents have never left the island. Ever. I don't wanna be like that."

"Still, it's a pretty big leap from traveling to moving." I pumped my eyebrows.

"I figure I'll give it a year and if it doesn't work out, then I'll just come home. What's the worse that could happen?"

I stared at my hands. "You could be away for so long that your whole life evaporates. You could come back to a world that's completely different . . ." I said softly.

"I have a feeling you're not talking about me," Lilly said with heavy emphasis. "Lemme guess, the infamous Madison and Emily?"

I shrugged with a knowing nod.

"You think they'll hate me?" she asked.

"Well, right now they hate *me,*" I mumbled.

"If they're half as good of friends as you say they are, they'll get over it. And if not, you've got me, *chica.*"

Just then Vince turned toward us and unplugged his earphones. We had only been on the plane for an hour, but already his dark brown locks were shooting up from the headrest.

"Hey, I just remembered that when we were on the plane to Puerto Rico, and you were sulking like a baby, I bet you that you'd be crying when we left. And that you'd have fun this summer. I *so* won that bet."

"Too bad we didn't put money on it," I snipped. "Besides, I'm not crying."

"I think I saw you shed a tear. 'Oh, Alex I'm gonna miss you *so* much.' Maw, maw, maw," he teased, planting exaggerated kissy noises on the back of his hand.

"I don't sound like that!"

"Sure you do," he said with a crooked grin.

"I wasn't talking to you anyway."

"No, but I heard you. You're acting like Madison and Emily will never speak to you again. I thought they were your *best friends,*" he whined, wiggling his fingers.

Then he plugged his ear buds in and turned his attention back to his iPod.

"They'll speak to me again," I muttered under my breath.

At least I hoped they would.